Praise for
"GUARDIANS *of the* LATTE STONES"

"M.K. Aleja succeeds in crafting a complex narrative, rich in emotion and meaning, with well-defined characters and an authentic atmosphere."
- The Historical Fiction Company

"...an elaborate mix of suspense, romance, and mystery. Historical fiction lovers will enjoy reading this novel."
- Readers' Favorite

"*Guardians of the Latte Stones* is a story that transcends its historical setting, weaving together elements of a ghost story and a poignant commentary on the futility of war."
- April Pulliam, Literary Titan

"*Guardians of the Latte Stones* is a consistently engaging and frequently intense war drama."
- The BookLife Prize Review

"Aleja cleverly tells the story of Japanese-occupied Guam in an unexpected way that captures the tragic destruction of militarism."
- Kirkus Reviews

Published by Taotao-ta Press LLC

ISBN: 979-8-9900390-6-3 (Paperback)
ISBN: 979-8-9900390-0-1 (Paperback)
ISBN: 979-8-9900390-1-8 (eBook)
ISBN: 979-8-9900390-2-5 (Hardcover)

GUARDIANS *of the* LATTE STONES

M. K. ALEJA

Table of Contents

TRIGGER WARNING

This novel contains scenes of violence that may be upsetting to some readers. This violence includes depiction of physical, emotional, and sexual abuse as well as graphic war imagery, execution, and death.

The book portrays fictional characters in scenes that are partly based on the personal accounts of survivors and actual historical events connected to the Japanese occupation of Guam during World War II.

These scenes have only been included as necessary to adequately depict the experiences of the main characters.

To my beautiful, loving wife whose support has brought this story to life.

Prologue
The Time Before

"Takeshi! Can you help your father? I can hear him coughing."

"Yes, I'll get his bowl."

Takeshi lifted a small basin from the kitchen and ran through to the room where his parents slept. His father was wheezing as he entered. Choking and unable to talk, he waved his son forward.

Takeshi timed his move perfectly to collect the infected mucus that his father spat out.

"There's blood again, *Otosan.* Should we get the doctor again?"

"No, no. Don't say a word. They fuss so much. The more you tell them, the more they worry."

They were Takeshi's mother and sister. His father, Kenji, belonged to an even older generation than the one he was part of. He didn't believe that you should lie down to illness, but in recent weeks, there had been no choice. His condition had worsened. He had lost his job at the shipyards and times were hard.

He cleared his throat a little more and struggled to sit up. Takeshi placed a blanket around his shoulders.

"No, I'm too hot," his father complained. "I prefer the cold these days, and the doctors say it's better for me, though I'm sure it was working in the cold that gave me this. Tell me, how is your school?"

"It's alright. My counting is good, and I enjoy my sports. We had a soldier come and give us an army drill yesterday. It was exhausting, but I had fun."

"Oh, that sounds good. I think you would make a good soldier. You are very good at helping people."

"I thought you had to be good at shooting people."

Kenji laughed and began choking again. Takeshi helped him cough up more phlegm and patted his back to help. His father settled once more.

"No, you shoot no one as a soldier. They find other things for you to do." He paused, "I would like to talk to you about school. I think it would be better if you could maybe leave and start working. I know plenty of people down by the docks and the harbor; someone will give you a start."

"I know we need some money. Yes, I'll do it. School can be boring."

"Thank you, Takeshi. You have always been a good boy, and now you are becoming a fine young man."

Yuki appeared at the opening to the room, "I have tea for you, Otosan."

"Oh, Yuki. Now my daughter looks after me as well."

He passed the bowl of mucus to Takeshi so that his sister wouldn't see the contents. Yuki placed a small table to his side with a small pot of tea and a cup for drinking.

"Can you pour it for me, Yuki? I don't want to make a mess?"

"Yes, Otosan."

Yuki knelt and poured the tea, "The serving of the tea is just as important as making it."

Kenji laughed at his daughter, but it caused him to choke again. Takeshi rushed forward with the bowl, and Kenji gripped it. It embarrassed him to show the contents in front of his daughter, but he was too weak. Yuki plucked it from his hands.

"This needs to be cleaned, I'll take it to *Okasan*."

"No, Yuki!" Kenji complained, as she disappeared out of the room.

"Sorry, Otosan. Yuki's too quick."

"Yes, too quick for all of us. You'll need to keep an eye on her."

"Oh, when?"

"Oh," he paused, "anytime. You know your sister."

"Kenji!" a frustrated call confirmed that Yuki had run directly to her mother.

"Oh, now everyone knows!"

Naoko arrived at the bedside in a moment, frustrated by her husband's attempts to conceal his worsening health.

"Kenji. There's blood in this bowl again."

"I maybe cut my throat with coughing. It's nothing."

"I want to get a doctor."

"Stop fussing, Naoko. Change the subject. Takeshi, tell Okasan about you getting a job."

"Yes. I'm going to get work with the ships or the fishing boats."

"Don't you know which?"

"I know ships are the big ones and fishing boats are the little ones," Takeshi laughed.

"You see," said Kenji, "he has had an excellent education. He's more than ready to start a new job."

They all laughed. Kenji began choking again and Naoko ran to get another bowl.

***

"You're rushing me to school today," complained Yuki.

"I'm tired. I've been working at the fish market. I need a wash, and you can't even walk to school on your own."

"I can. I just like company. I just don't want to be rushed, that's all."

"Just today, Yuki. I have lots to do."

"Alright, go home. I can run from here."

She took off across the park, leaving Takeshi standing. He watched her until she had run out of sight and then he turned for home. The streets were already busy, but he knew other routes that took a whole five minutes out of the walk, even if it meant the odd shortcut through a neighbor's garden or two.

As he entered the house, he could see his mother was upset. The doctor was just leaving.

"*Sayonara*, Yoshida-san."

"Okasan, what is it?"

"Takeshi?" said the doctor, "I have given your mother some medicine to help her sleep. Will you make sure that she takes it?"

"Yes, of course."

"Good. Sayonara."

As the doctor left, Naoko wiped tears from her eyes.

"Your father won't last much longer, Takeshi. His breathing is very poor."

"Should I get Yuki from school?"

"No, she is too young. Leave her there. He will want to see you."

"Should I change? I smell of the market."

"No, you must go now. Your father always liked the smells of the sea."

Takeshi slid the divider over. Kenji was very weak. His breathing was struggling. He could only take quick breaths that were inadequate to fill his lungs. He spoke just above a whisper—faint and thin. Not the father that Takeshi had grown up with.

Kenji had been a tough shipyard worker at the docks in Sasebo. Working long hours to build the ships for the navy, he had always been fit and had never had a day of illness. Then an accident happened at work which left him with a chest injury, and the onset of Tuberculosis. His rapid deterioration had shocked everyone.

Takeshi approached his father as he lay propped up. He gripped his father's hand to let him know that he was there. Kenji turned his face toward him.

"Ah, Takeshi. I'm glad you made it home from work on time. I've not got much air left in me according to the doctor. At least I'm not full of hot air like him."

Kenji laughed and choked as one.

"Otosan, don't joke. It's bad for you."

Kenji smiled. "Alright, I will be serious now. I haven't looked after this family for months, but I have seen how you and Yuki help your mother. Just keep doing that, just help her every day, and she will be fine. At the docks, tell them you are the man of the house, and you need a better job with more pay. Tell them Kenji Yoshida says this. None of them would have challenged me a year ago."

"I will look after everyone, don't worry."

"Then you have made me happy."

Kenji smiled affectionately at his son, before the brief moment of peace was disturbed again. He closed his eyes and sighed as more voices could be heard arriving into the house. A distinctive wailing sound rose above the noise.

"Oh, now it's your Uncle Taro and Aunt Keiko; please let me die before she pays me a visit."

"You can't say that!"

They laughed together again. They had always shared the same dark sense of humor. They had a lot in common, while Yuki was more like her mother. Their family life had been so important to all of them, and now it was being torn apart. Takeshi couldn't hide his sadness. He had always found it hard to shut his feelings away.

Kenji could see it, and he worried that it marked Takeshi out for bullying or trouble. It was a flaw that others might use to mistreat him.

"How is your Kendo improving?"

"Good, I enjoy it."

"I suppose it's handy if you're attacked while you're carrying a sword. You should learn Judo as well. That is more useful. Will you promise me?"

"Yes, alright, I promise. Why?"

"It will be good for you. That's all you need to know."

Kenji began choking again. Wheezing as he tried to breathe. His voice crackled and fractured.

"I'm proud of you, Takeshi, you have always been my pride and joy. Live a good life, and find a good wife, and a good family will follow."

He was starting to drift away. Takeshi wanted to call for his mother, but Kenji had gripped his hand with his last ounce of strength.

"And don't let Aunt Keiko bully your mother. I will tell you something about Keiko-san..."

He slipped away. Takeshi gripped his hand one last time and said a prayer over him.

He left the room, slid the door shut, and looked over at his mother. No words needed to be spoken.

***

"Only a year since Kenji died, and now his wife is dying of the same thing. What will happen to the children, Taro?"

"I have already said. They are my brother's children. They will not go to someone they don't know. Kenichi and Ryo both like them. The entire street knows when they're playing together."

"Yes, that's what I mean. Oh, but how will we feed them and clothe them. I will need more money to spend."

"I'm sure Takeshi will contribute. He has a steady job."

"He pushes fish from the boat to the market. It won't pay for much."

"Some of the fish can fall off into his pocket. It happens all the time down there, and Yuki will grow into her mother's clothes. She can keep what she likes and we can sell the rest."

"She's not dead yet and you're selling her clothes!"

"Do you want to feel the back of my hand? I get enough of a hard time at work without coming home to a wife that gives me trouble."

Taro grabbed Keiko's *yukata*. It was how he always pulled her onto his fist.

"She will be dead soon. We will sell what we can. You will take Takeshi's money and make sure that we live as a happy family."

"We don't live as a happy family now!"

Taro connected his slap to her face and pushed her down at his feet.

"Maybe I should have a dead wife, too! Or at least one that doesn't talk back."

Taro stormed out of the house. As he left, their two sons came through to help pick their mother up.

"It's alright *okaachan*," said her younger son, Ryo, "we'll help you."

"Will you help me when there are more mouths to feed? We go hungry as it is. Your father isn't right about this situation. It will cause us too many problems."

"When I'm a navy pilot, I'll pay for everything," said the older son, Kenichi.

"When you're a navy pilot? I'll expect your cousins to have already gone. Takeshi can join the army. They can feed him and he can still send me his money."

Keiko stood up, a little happier that maybe a larger family could work.

"What about Yuki? She is only the same age as me?"

"It's different for girls. You and Ryo will have to find work, but Yuki only needs to learn how to be a good wife. If she has refinement and an excellent education, there are many older husbands in Tokyo or Osaka who would pay well for a beautiful young girl from Sasebo.

"I don't think Yuki will want to marry an old man," said Ryo.

"Of course she will. If he has wealth, why wouldn't she want to marry him? You are both too young to understand. All she needs is the firm training I can provide. She will be the better for it. Her mother is a pleasant woman, but she hasn't been a wonderful mother. She hasn't set them the right goals in life. It will all change when I take over."

***

Takeshi remembered visiting his aunt and uncle's house many times before. It had always been a place that had happy memories from when they were younger. All the Yoshida family had a good sense of humor and their father's brother, Uncle Taro, was no exception, especially when he had too much sake. He would sing funny songs and dance when he was happy, and that would make everybody laugh.

As Takeshi became older, he realized that Uncle Taro was *only* happy when he had too much sake. At other times, he could be stern, strict, and bad tempered.

Now that Takeshi and Yuki were living in the same house and not just coming round with their parents for a visit or celebration, they got to see what he was like most of the time. He would shout for a lot of reasons; his bath was too cold, his tea was too hot, he had a stomachache or a headache. It seemed that he didn't like children very much either.

Their cousin Kenichi was always getting into trouble, and after a few weeks of staying in the same house, Takeshi and Yuki received their share of the shouting, and worse.

"What do you think about living here, Yuki?"

"I thought it would be alright. I remember when we used to go shopping with Aunt Keiko, she was always happy to spend Uncle Taro's money, and she would tell everybody about her new clothes. She would always buy bright colored patterns. I wouldn't always say nice, but they were bright."

They giggled together.

"I thought things would be better when we came here," Takeshi replied, "I thought everyone would spend more time together, but it's different when you live with people. I suppose you get to see what they are really like. I always thought Uncle Taro and Aunt Keiko would have been more like our parents."

"They're definitely not like our parents!" Yuki exclaimed. "Our parents didn't hit us, for one thing. It only took Aunt Keiko two days before she slapped me the first time."

"I think it was a week," said Takeshi, "and I can't even remember why."

"Just make a really loud scream, she'll not hit you so hard."

"Is that what you do?"

Yuki nodded and smiled in response.

"I'm glad I have a sister like you. I would hate to be here on my own. I can manage because I know that every so often we get some time to sit together and talk. It makes me feel as if we're back in our own home. Where everything was better?" Takeshi paused, "I don't mean to be ungrateful, but I just don't feel this is home."

"You can make it better, Takeshi. Tell Aunt Keiko she's your favorite aunt."

"She's my only aunt," he laughed.

"I don't think she would mind about that."

"Yes, but she would probably scold me for lying."

"It won't be forever, big brother. One day we'll have our own houses, and they can come to ours and sweep up."

Takeshi began to cheer up. Since he had moved house with his sister, he'd had trouble adapting to his new life. He had taken the job that his father had wanted him to. He worked very early hours at the fish market, and just wanted to sleep when he came home, but instead there would be a list of chores to work through.

Aunt Keiko was quick to call him lazy, and even quicker to take all the money he earned for the house. She insisted that Uncle Taro handed over all his money too, but somehow he spent most of his on the way home. It took Uncle Taro ten minutes to walk to work in the morning, but two hours to get home at night. He would sing and dance through the door. It wasn't the family life that Takeshi and Yuki had known.

"What would make you happy, Takeshi?"

"I'd like to get a house just for you and me. We would have a bedroom each."

"Each? You're going to have lots of money then? How do you do that?"

"I'm still trying to work that out. I'd quite like to go to sea. Maybe I'll become a fisherman."

"If you're going to work at sea and we're to have a bedroom each, then you'll need to be a pirate!"

"Oh, alright. I think I could do that," he laughed.

"Are you still going to join the army?"

"We all have to, but it will be good. You get to go different places. They pay you better money than I get at the market."

"I would worry about you, though. I think you should just stay where you are right now. I don't really want my big brother to go away just yet. It's a terrible house to live in."

"See, I told you."

The pair giggled too loud; that wasn't what you did in Aunt Keiko's house. It only took seconds for the room divider to open.

Aunt Keiko stood with her arms folded. "What are you two laughing about?"

"Nothing," said Takeshi as he looked down at the floor.

"Oh well, if you have time to laugh, you have time to work."

"I do my work while all the rest of you are asleep, six mornings out of seven."

"Huh, that's not a job. Pushing boxes of fish about. I can see I'm going to be stuck with you in this house forever."

"I'll get something better."

"I'll believe that when I see it. Now your sister, she maybe has a slight chance of success. I am turning her into a perfect wife."

"Yuki doesn't want to be a wife."

"Takeshi, don't," interrupted Yuki.

"I've never heard of such a thing. Yuki will do well with a nice husband. She'll have so much money she won't know what to do with it all."

"Well, I hope she gets to keep *her* money."

Keiko responded with a harsh slap across Takeshi's jaw. The crack of her hand stopped the disagreement in an instant as she overflowed with rage. An anger that she would never display in public, but within the confines of her home it was a different matter. Her withering stare left Takeshi in no doubt about her contempt for him.

"Your Uncle Taro will hear of your ungratefulness. Be thankful if he doesn't kick you out the house, when I tell him about your shameful behavior."

"He won't kick me out. My money means he can keep more of his own to spend on sake."

"How dare you!"

Keiko was quick to raise her hand again, but this time Takeshi was prepared as he pushed past her.

"I'm going outside!" he yelled as he stormed from the house to the relative safety of the city streets.

"Well, go and get a better job so I can afford to have you here!"

Neighbors passing by the open door, gazed in at the source of the commotion. It forced Keiko to quickly adjust her demeanor, as if nothing was wrong. The pause gave Takeshi's sister her own opportunity for escape.

"I'll just see if he's alright," said Yuki.

"No, I have jobs for you to..."

It was too late. Yuki was very good at getting out of the house at speed, and she knew exactly where Takeshi would go. He liked to watch the ships down at the naval yard. It was a place he could spend hours. He would look out at sea and imagine a better world for himself. It calmed him down.

Yuki caught him before he'd even arrived at his favorite spot.

"You need to stop doing that with Aunt Keiko. She can always keep being mad until you get home, and then she'll tell Uncle Taro, and give him a headache, and then he'll get mad, and they'll all start shouting, and then it will probably end up being my fault. Yes, thank you very much."

"I'm sorry, Yuki, but she interrupted *our* conversation."

"About how bad it is to live at our uncle and aunt's house."

"Yes," he giggled.

"She made you mad, not me. Don't worry, it's a boy thing."

Yuki's smile was infectious. It didn't matter how terrible life got, she could always cope. Takeshi relied on her a lot. She knew how to make him smile when he felt down, which was quite a lot since they had moved into Uncle Taro's house.

"When we get that big house—with a bedroom each—I don't want to live in Sasebo. I feel as if I belong somewhere else. Not a city like here. Somewhere I can feel that I really want to stay for the rest of my life, and it's not here, I promise you."

"Just promise to take me with you."

"Do you really think I would leave you? What kind of brother would that make me? I just want to dream. Losing our parents has been really hard. I just want to do something or meet someone that makes life feel worthwhile. Is that so bad?"

"I'd be more annoyed if you didn't have a dream, and if I marry a very rich husband like Aunt Keiko wants me to. I'll pay for the cost of your dream, how about that?"

"And what if *your* rich husband doesn't want you to pay for *my* dream."

"Oh, it's okay, I have to kill him."

"What?"

"That's what Aunt Keiko says I should do. So that I'm still young enough to get another husband!"

"That's terrible!"

"That's why she's your favorite aunt."

The two carried on walking, dreaming, and laughing for another hour, until they were sure that Aunt Keiko would have calmed down.

Takeshi loved his sister dearly. She was his best friend, and she never liked him to be unhappy. Her good sense of humor proved she was a genuine member of the Yoshida clan. Wherever Takeshi's dreams took him, he could never imagine a life without his sister.

PART ONE

Hakko ichiu
"Eight crown cords, one roof"

Chapter 1
Dew Glistens White On Grass

Takeshi gazed up through the branches arching over the path. Patches of red, yellow, and gold brushed over the canvas of a cool blue sky. There were many people around him, yet all were seeking their moments of reflection and quiet contemplation—a mutual and unspoken pact between friends and strangers, a communal agreement to enjoy nature's colorful display in relative silence.

All maybe, except for Yuki, who walked beside him, her right hand pulling her school satchel over her shoulder and her left spinning a small twig with three bright leaves still attached.

"The trees are beautiful at this time of year, but I still prefer the blossom."

"Both are good," replied Takeshi, "I thought winter was your favorite season?"

"I just hate summer. It's too hot, but spring is my second favorite."

She smiled with a mischievous glint in her eye before breaking into song, "*Sakura, sakura, yayoi no sora wa.*"

"Yuki, don't draw attention."

"We sing in our class about the blossom. Is it wrong to let the trees listen to the words?"

"No," Takeshi considered, "but they can still hear you even when you sing in a quiet voice."

"Tanaka *sensei* says that I have a pleasant singing voice. I just need training to make it better."

She giggled and returned to humming the melody, but in such a hushed manner that even Takeshi felt that he couldn't complain. He couldn't help returning a smile. Nothing seemed to trouble Yuki. After all the misfortune they had suffered in recent times, she hadn't changed from those happier days of their own family life.

They walked on until they reached the edge of the park. The tranquility lessened with each step they took into the busy winding streets of shops and houses. They made up a network of curves and small hills that seemed to flow with the river down to the coast and the imposing presence of the shipyards and docks that formed the Sasebo Naval Arsenal.

The shipyards employed many of the local population. It was hard and heavy engineering work, which was rewarded with pride more than money. The triumphant march of war began in this town, providing the Emperor with a fleet of ships to carry his power and authority overseas. It was the transport for men and military might that would lead the charge for a better world.

Takeshi's father had worked there before his death. His uncle, Taro, worked there now—not that Takeshi saw much of him. He would hear an angry groan as his uncle stumbled home after a long day of work and a few brief hours of drinking. A cup or a bowl might break as he fumbled around to search for the meager serving of food that Aunt Keiko had cooked for him.

The rice that Yuki had cooked for him.

Looking down at his sister, Takeshi noticed that the bruising on the top of her cheek was starting to disappear.

"Is your eye still hurting?"

"No," said Yuki, "only when you remind me about it. Keiko-san is getting older, she's not as strong as she thinks she is. I discovered if I yell loud enough, then she's content with causing me pain. She doesn't mean to break me. She loves me. She loves both of us."

"Maybe once, but not now," said Takeshi, "I see her look at me and count each grain of rice I swallow and every sip of tea."

"You think you are a thief for taking your share? You work for it, too. She takes all the money you earn from the fish market. Can't our uncle get you a job at the shipyards? I'm sure it's better paid."

"I would like that, but I know what they want and expect of me. They expect every boy of my age to do his duty and serve the Emperor like a samurai. That is the only thing that will make Aunt Keiko happy."

Yuki gave her brother a knowing look from the side of her eye—just enough to stop the conversation which others might overhear. Talking about the Emperor in such a way might attract the anger of the people walking past them.

Takeshi felt as if they *had* heard his small protest, but chose to confine their reaction to muted looks of disdain. Sasebo had a large population, but they walked the same streets most days and many of the locals knew who they were and who they lived with. If any passerby felt that Takeshi had been disrespectful, then word of his offensive behavior would find its way to Uncle Taro. The lash of the cane would punish the crime; the cane was a family heirloom that had punished many in the Yoshida family over the years, including Uncle Taro, when he was young.

The road narrowed as brother and sister headed for home. Groups of small houses clung to the rise and fall of streets that followed the meandering route. A stranger might find themselves lost amongst the maze, but Takeshi and Yuki could weave past the wooden buildings and small gardens with ease, while always under the constant watchful attention of their older neighbors.

As they arrived at the front steps, their cousin, Kenichi, almost bowled them over as he leaped forward, with arms outstretched as wings. His voice recreated the dive of a Mitsubishi Zero, descending on its victims with guns blazing, and bombs screaming towards the target.

"Look at me, Yuki," shouted Kenichi, "I am the best pilot in Japan. Look at what I can do!"

He continued to spin and run around in circles. He knew just how fast his imaginary fighter plane could perform its aerial acrobatics. He knew how many bullets he had in each machine gun and cannon, and he imagined every single one killing an enemy soldier.

The others cheered at his performance, and it wasn't long before Takeshi launched himself into the game, flying his own invisible plane and joining in on the fun.

"You be the American pilot, Takeshi. You're flying a Hellcat!"

"No, I don't want to be American. I'm fighting for Japan. Yuki, you be the Hellcat."

"That's fine. I like cats," she laughed, before dropping her satchel on the ground and steering her way into the combat.

The noise level increased as the swooping and shooting gathered force. It seemed that they had an unlimited supply of ammunition as they acted out their dogfight and battle for air supremacy. In the end, the boys triumphed as Kenichi nudged Yuki just enough to send her flying onto the dirty ground. He celebrated his success, hands in the air, and giggling as he proclaimed his victory.

The door of the house slid open just as Yuki was standing and dusting herself off. Aunt Keiko looked angry as she dished out the blame in unequal amounts that fitted the relative crimes.

Yuki received the worst treatment. Cleaning her clothes would keep her busy for the rest of the day, along with her other chores. A slap on the back of her head encouraged her in through the doorway. Takeshi was next to feel the force of Aunt Keiko's hand as she glanced off the side of his head. He would also receive the criticism of acting like a child when he should have been setting an example. Takeshi's cheeks flushed with embarrassment. The thought that the neighbors would look on at his part in the commotion was worse than the physical pain. Kenichi seemed to survive with a softer chastisement. Japan's top pilot would live to fight another day as his mother dragged him inside by the ear, along with the others.

Sliding the door behind her, a threatening silence filled the air. Yuki had already gone through to the bedroom to change out of her school clothes, while Kenichi joined his younger brother, Ryo. The ten-year-old sibling was quieter than the rest, fond of reading about battles rather than re-enacting them. His mother would take great pride in assuring people that he was the intelligent one.

"Why did you take so long to get home today?" asked Keiko.

"We decided to go to the park. The leaves are changing color."

"Oh well, that's alright then," another slap connected with Takeshi's head, "You take all the time you need to enjoy the wonderful trees, while I need you here to help me. You know that I struggle with my health, and there's so much to do, with so many mouths to feed, and yet not even the smallest sardine can slip into your pocket."

"And what would happen then? If they caught me stealing, they would put me in prison."

"One less mouth to feed in the house. That is what would happen."

"If Takeshi admires the trees in the park, maybe he will become a great poet," laughed Kenichi.

"We'll have less of your opinions," Keiko responded, while striking Takeshi another time and thrusting a broom in his direction, "Sweep the floors and then organize the stove with wood. Maybe my dear husband will make it home before the sake fills his head and empties his pockets."

***

Takeshi sat back on his knees, taking time to maneuver the firewood at the base of the small *kamado* stove. Looking into the flames allowed him a brief escape from the rest of the household. It was a task that the others were happy for him to take care of, as it involved cleaning the ashes out first.

Yuki was already making herself busy preparing the small serving of rice for the meal of the day. Seaweed and pickled radish would add variety and a little extra flavor. Now and again, Uncle Taro would bring home salmon or sweet potato from the black market, but in recent months, it had become more expensive to buy.

Keiko stood in the doorway, observing her nephew and niece at work. Her anger was ever-present, with lips downturned and a frown perched on her brow. Her dark and bitter presence filled the room. Both Takeshi and Yuki had their backs to her, but they had taught themselves to sense even the smallest rush of air—a split-second of warning to tense themselves in readiness for a strike from a hand, or whatever the hand was holding at the time.

The violence happened every day. It wasn't a case of if, but when. Then the frustration that Keiko bore from remembering happier days would pour out in a well-practiced tirade of insults. Takeshi was lazy; Yuki was stupid. They were both weights around her neck, making her family poorer and hungrier, taking away their aunt's dreams of a happy home. Everything was their fault, including it seemed, driving their uncle into drinking too much.

All that brother and sister could do was keep their heads bowed, waiting for Keiko to tire of her daily ritual. They peered out of the side of their eyes to one another, offering snatches of sympathy between small glances.

"How can you put us through this, Takeshi?" asked Aunt Keiko, "My poor husband punished for staying loyal to his brother's memory. For taking you into our house, along with your ungrateful sister. Yuki, what were you doing crawling about on the ground? Are you an insect or a rat? The clothes that we bought for you out of our own heartfelt kindness, washed in the dirt with no respect for our efforts to bring you up as a presentable lady. What kind of husband can we find for someone like you? It will need to be one that can show you some discipline."

Keiko punctuated her statement with another slap to the back of Yuki's head. The smack delivered with enough force for Keiko to feel she had made her point, at least for the moment.

Satisfied that the stove was lit, she ordered Takeshi through to the adjoining room. Reluctant to leave his tearful sister, he hesitated just long enough for her to nod that she was alright being left alone with her aunt.

Kenichi and Ryo offered silent expressions of comfort as he joined them at the low table.

"What are you reading, Ryo?" asked Takeshi.

"*Shonen Kurabu*," his younger cousin replied.

"I haven't read that for years. My mum and dad used to get it for me. What's in it today?"

Ryo spun the magazine around to let Takeshi have a look. The front cover was a striking image of a young boy, dressed in traditional clothes with a Katana sword held high above his head.

"Who do you think he is going to fight?" asked Takeshi.

"The savages," said Ryo.

"No, the Americans," said Kenichi.

Takeshi smiled and shook his head. "The Americans will have guns. Do you think we can beat them with swords?"

"Of course!" his cousins replied together.

"Americans are soft," added Kenichi, "compared to Japanese."

"Yes, you're right. I think the Japanese spirit is stronger," Takeshi acknowledged.

Takeshi continued leafing through the magazine. The war and heroism of the Imperial Japanese Army dominated the content. Maps of parts of the world that now fell under

Japan's authority, fictional stories of glorious victories in battle, and details of the latest Akizuki-class destroyer.

"My dad worked on the Akizuki-class ships," said Takeshi, "He took me to see one being built when I was younger."

"That would be great," said Ryo, "Our dad works on submarines, you know that don't you?"

"That must be exciting, too. I would like to help build the ships."

"Ah, but you have to work on one first," reminded Kenichi, "You will sail across the seas to get the Americans."

"With my Katana?"

"Yes, with your Katana," laughed the cousins, prompting Ryo to stand up and demonstrate his favorite Kendo move.

The commotion attracted Keiko. What would have been a scowling rebuke for Takeshi or Kenichi, transformed into a smiling look of pride for Ryo.

"Look at him, look at him; he has skills. What a talented boy you are, Ryo. You will make a fine soldier. I pray the war doesn't end too soon, so that you may have your chance of glory."

"Japan is to rule for a thousand years, okaachan."

"A thousand years? Maybe that will even give your cousin enough time to join up."

The boys laughed, but Aunt Keiko wasn't joking. Takeshi sighed and closed the magazine as she returned to the kitchen to offer more criticism of Yuki's cooking.

"When do you think you will go?" asked Kenichi.

"It will be soon. Years ago, you had to be twenty years old. Then they brought it down to seventeen. But they'll ignore the rules and let you join younger now. We're winning so many battles and the Emperor needs us to help expand Japan's influence across the world. You know, *eight crown cords, one roof*, isn't that what they say? I heard that Koji Watanabe joined last week, and he's only fifteen," the cousins nodded to show they were considering the thought, "I'm sure it will be exciting, but I hate to leave my sister. I worry what might happen to her."

"We will look after her for you," said Ryo, "Our mother is a good person, but the war has made our family poorer. You understand that she feels she is failing everyone by not having enough food to put on the table."

"Yes, you're right. I just wish she wouldn't strike Yuki; that would be something at least."

"Tell my mother that you want to join. She will be different with you then—both of you—I'm sure."

Takeshi contemplated announcing his intention after dinner. He wouldn't leave right away. He would need to await the arrival of the *Akagami*, a red notification card that would tell him where and when to report for duty. If Ryo was right, then he would still have a short time to know that Yuki was going to be treated better. He couldn't avoid deciding, he could only delay it, and what would that mean for his sister in the meantime? Aunt Keiko had broken none of her bones yet, but maybe that was only a matter of time.

Maybe my aunt will be kinder when I'm gone.

Yuki entered to set the table and broke his train of thought. Having changed out of her school clothes, she wore her yukata. Still a little too big for her, she had inherited it from her mother. It was one of the few physical memories she had remaining. A pink rose print on black that would have suited someone older, but to Yuki it was just perfect. Her imperial-styled hair, *geta* sandals, and *tabi* socks completed the traditional look.

For all she had to endure, Yuki possessed the ability to rise out of the despair and harsh treatment. She had a good fighting spirit of her own. She was popular with the students and teachers at her school. The lesson she loved most was the training she received with the *naginata*. The pole-arm had a tradition of use by the *Onna-musha*, the female warriors who trained to protect the homesteads. The government encouraged schoolgirls to learn the ancient art as part of their physical education, and as a last line of defense if the enemy ever invaded. Yuki enjoyed learning the moves; it was better than sitting in the classroom and it made young girls feel strong and empowered, bonding them to the service of the divine leader—the Emperor.

Keiko observed the proceedings as the boys took their places, more than ready to eat the largest meal of the day. Yuki knew that her aunt would total up the mistakes ranging from the presenting of the simple rice bowls to the excellence of the cooking. Keiko had trained her to cook—any failure in the task would cause more punishment. Aunt Keiko would take it as a personal slight if the meal wasn't perfect.

Keiko took her place at one end of the table. At the other end was a space where Uncle Taro should be. His absence meant nothing. The shipyard workers were being asked to work longer hours to increase their contribution to the war effort. That was what Keiko told her neighbors to save herself from the shame. She knew it was far more likely that he was sharing a drink with his fellow workers.

Yuki served all one by one. Each of the boys offered their thanks. When Yuki returned with her own bowl, Keiko sneered at her.

"You know that those who prepare and cook the meal seldom dine with the party guests."

"I'm sorry," said Yuki, "I didn't realize we were having a party. I will eat in the kitchen."

She went to rise, but Keiko raised a hand to signal that she should remain. The boys, who had all paused, shared relief when the threat had passed.

"It was just a joke, Yuki. I know you like jokes."

All took time with their meal. It was important to not appear greedy even though they were starving. They celebrated the seaweed garnish as something special, but when they all discovered the small single slice of pickle hidden within the rice, it caused a delighted response from Yuki's brother and cousins. Kenichi was the first to taste the extra flavor in his mouth, while Takeshi and Ryo raced to uncover the surprise once they knew it was there.

It seemed to impress Aunt Keiko as well. For a brief few seconds, Yuki had provided her with a happy memory.

"Your Uncle Taro likes *Tsukemono*, especially pickled ginger. He will appreciate your thought."

"Thank you, Aunt Keiko."

Takeshi wondered if the gods were sending him a message. *Ebisu* was always present in kitchens, maybe he watched over

Yuki and would bring abundance to her life. Whoever was responsible, it seemed that a brief opportunity had presented itself where Aunt Keiko was maybe in the right mood to receive his news.

He cleared his throat and stood up in front of everyone at the table.

"I have an announcement to make."

"An announcement?" Aunt Keiko seemed curious.

"I have decided that tomorrow I will register to enlist in the service of the Imperial Japanese Army. I will become a noble warrior in the Emperor's service."

The words tumbled into a few seconds of silence as the stunned family members awaited Keiko's response. Her face burst into the broadest of smiles, as she rose to her feet and hugged Takeshi with genuine happiness. The others followed with a rousing cheer, patting Takeshi on the back and showering him with congratulations.

As the commotion settled, they took their places, back at the table. Yuki cleared away the bowls and the chopsticks and the family settled together, happier than they had been in months."

"Your father and mother will be proud of you. Your Uncle Taro will be happy too. I will be relieved as well and will make sure that all our neighbors know of your wise decision. We should expect a gift or two that will help support us when we can no longer claim your ration."

"What will you do, Takeshi?" asked Yuki, "Do you want to go on to the navy once you have signed up?"

"Not the navy," said Kenichi, "the army is better. Maybe you will get a tank to drive."

"If you get a tank," Ryo said with excitement, "you could drive it here to let us get on board."

"Takeshi will not be driving a tank through our neighbors' gardens. What would Saito-san say if you ran over his vegetables?"

"He would chase Takeshi with his walking stick," Ryo replied.

"Yes, but I would have a tank!"

All of them laughed in response. Ryo had been right about his mother's reaction. It was like an enormous burden removed from her shoulders.

An hour passed of light-hearted conversation. Ryo produced his magazine again and looked for some earlier issues he had saved. They poured over the content, the chatter growing more excited as they discussed the older wars in China, Russia, and now the World War, extending further south into the Pacific.

Aunt Keiko had left the house—to no doubt gossip with the neighbors and impress on them it was *her* nephew who was volunteering early for service in the ranks.

Takeshi sat back on his knees and observed the others. There was a genuine feeling of pride coursing through his veins. Serving the Emperor in battle was the greatest moment in his life. A modern samurai, living by the code of Bushido.

For most of his life, Japan had been at war. In fact, he couldn't recount a part of his life that was early enough to have known only peace. From his first days at school to this very evening, the teachers had filled his thoughts with the glorious notion of one day serving the Emperor, not as a citizen, but as a soldier.

34

Chapter 2
The Honorable Decision

Only ten days had passed since Takeshi's proclamation. The war machine moved with more haste than he had expected. After he had registered himself at the local police station, a military clerk had appeared at the Yoshida home within a few days. It turned out that he was an old friend of Uncle Taro and wanted to make sure that Takeshi wasn't trying to run away by joining up too soon.

Uncle Taro had confirmed that the family were happy for him to enlist. He spoke of Takeshi's honesty and integrity, insisting that he would be a good and respectful recruit, ready to follow orders and fight with courage for Japan.

It reassured the clerk that the family only wanted to play their part in the war. The meeting concluded with polite exchanges about the importance of the ordinary Japanese living by the code of the samurai. Japan was a country rising to power amongst the great nations of the west. The selfless duty observed by families like the Yoshidas fueled it. Through them, Japan would triumph.

Out of grateful acceptance of the family's wishes and in respect of an old friendship, the military clerk suggested that he would choose a more favorable division to assign Takeshi to. The local regimental headquarters in Saga would send their recruits to Burma, but the soldiers of the neighboring 11th Division, based at Zentsuji, reinforced the Pacific islands. The military clerk smiled as he suggested it would be a more picturesque location for Takeshi to serve out his military career.

The clerk left after delivering his uplifting message, and in the days that followed, Takeshi could feel a change in the atmosphere of life at home. A small flag of the rising sun now hung above their door for all to see. Yuki and Aunt Keiko had worked together on Takeshi's *sen'ninbari*, a white cloth belt worn around his waist as part of his uniform. Aunt and niece seemed to grow closer as they went around to the neighbors, inviting them to add a stitch of black yarn for good fortune. Aunt Keiko even allowed Yuki to complete the gift by sewing on the five-sen coin. Tradition said it would allow Takeshi to escape death by making the enemy bullets miss.

Now the day was here. He had woken with the sun and dressed in his clean shirt and trousers. His day was to begin by sharing breakfast with Uncle Taro, an experience he had not had since moving to the house following his parent's deaths.

Taro was already waiting as Takeshi entered the room, bowing to his uncle.

"Good morning, Taro ojisan."

"Good morning, Takeshi-san. Are you ready for your special day?"

"Yes, I'm excited. Ready to start my training."

"I'm sorry that I have not been able to spend time with you. Your father and I both served in Manchukuo. Our experiences would have helped prepare you for what lies ahead. Your life will not be easy, but in the end it will be glorious. Let us eat."

His quiet command caused the door to slide open from the kitchen. Yuki and Aunt Keiko appeared with tea, miso soup, rice, natto, and pickled ginger. Once served, they left Taro and Takeshi alone.

Takeshi couldn't remember seeing so much food in one place for years. He wanted to eat very little and leave some for his sister and cousins, but that would have been disrespectful. This could be his last home-cooked meal. It was a fact that many didn't return from this adventure. The family had already placed small wooden panels offering him best wishes at the local Shinto shrine, dedicated to the memory of his life. The way of the warrior dictated that he would fight until the end. There was no fear in his heart. An honorable death brought you to the gates of heaven. Surrender only brought eternal shame.

The two ate in silence, savoring the meal, but Takeshi was full of questions; it created a tension in the air that even Uncle

Taro could read. He nodded acknowledgement. Takeshi had permission to speak.

"Will I die?"

"We all die. The blessed die in the name of our leader. The rest are less fortunate. Your father and your mother lost their lives to tuberculosis. Death wrapped its cloak around them over time, in all its pain and discomfort. Your father would have always chosen death on the battlefield if he could have made that choice, but the decision was not his in the end. The Emperor will never visit *him*, but for those warriors who have fallen for their country, he pays tribute twice a year at the Yasukuni shrine. 'Will I die?' is not the correct question. You should ask 'Will people forget me?' or 'Will I receive the solemn thanks from a living god, in the memory of my name?'"

"I understand, ojisan. I know that they teach us not to fear this death. It's just that I hoped that one day I would have a wife and children of my own."

"Be careful what you wish for," replied Uncle Taro with a wry smile.

The loud cough that followed from Aunt Keiko, in the kitchen, caused them both to smile at one another. Uncle Taro seemed to resemble Takeshi's father in that moment—a connection that had never revealed itself before.

His face soon returned to a more serious appearance. "I'm glad we have shared this meal. It might be some time before you return, but I think you will. I will be happy for us to share stories of war, over some sake, and I will be happy for you to build a life and a family, knowing that your efforts as a soldier will have secured a wonderful future for your sons."

"Thank you, ojisan."

"Now I must take my leave. Your Aunt will see you to the train later this morning. Maybe some of the neighbors will want to say goodbye and wish you well. I will raise a cup to your good fortune later. I admit I am jealous. The war will not last forever. I'm sure we will meet again."

Both stood and bowed toward one another. Takeshi had become a man as soon as he had made it known he was volunteering. He deserved the full display of mutual respect. With that, his uncle turned and left.

The kitchen door slid open once more. Keiko and Yuki worked together to remove the breakfast dishes. Perhaps there was enough left over to help fill out the evening meal. Takeshi thought about how there would only be four hungry mouths around the table, but tradition also insisted that they would set his place in anticipation of the day he would walk back into their lives.

Yuki asked her aunt if she could sit with Takeshi for a little while. Surprisingly, Keiko agreed. It seemed that for today at least, she had suspended the normal house rules.

Brother and sister extended a hug to one another. Life in the last year had been bleak and devoid of the love they would have received from their parents. They only had each other to rely on.

Takeshi began to have second thoughts. Butterflies flew around in his stomach. He had seen his sister enjoying a better relationship, but he felt he was deserting *her* rather than joining with the Emperor. Yuki appeared to read his thoughts.

"Don't worry," she said, releasing him from her grip, and taking a place opposite him at the table, "you have improved my life already. I think Aunt Keiko and I *can* live together. Soon I will join the workforce and will bring money into the house, though I think she wants me to perfect my domestic skills so that I can be a suitable wife, worthy of a middle-class husband with a well-paid job."

"I will need to approve of him," Takeshi spoke with an implied sense of authority.

"Do not worry. If he has a lot of money, then I can fall in love with that."

They giggled together before a silence fell again.

"Please write to me, Yuki. I don't know where I'll end up, but I will receive your letters. The army will know how to find me."

"Of course I'll write, but you have to write back. I want to be the first to know of all your noble achievements. Tell me about the places that you visit. Tell me about the words that the people use."

"Their language?"

"Yes, and the food they eat, or the clothes they wear. I know they won't allow you to write about battles or exact locations, and don't try to, because it will make trouble, but you can tell me certain things by also showing me how the Japanese are better. They will allow such views to be included."

"I'll try my best. I think you can write to me about life at home, and how you are taking care of Japan from right here in Sasebo. As long as your letter is happy and inspired by devotion to the Emperor, I'm sure it will reach me, too."

They set the code—a way of telling each other about their lives and keeping in touch, without upsetting the authorities. Even after all the training at school, and the constant reinforcement of the code of Bushido, there was still the weakness of a grain of truth within their understanding. War was wrong. There was no public mourning for the sons who didn't return home, but in private, families always felt their loss.

Yuki's composed appearance did not betray her sorrow of losing her brother, her guardian, and her friend. Keiko's shadow lurked close by behind the door to the kitchen. Yuki sensed that her old life would return once her protector was gone, but the last thing she would do was reveal that thought to Takeshi. Drawing in a deep breath, she returned to her normal smile.

"Remember why I sewed the coin into your belt' it is not for spending on sake. It's for your protection."

"To save me from the bullets? I've always wondered why people choose a coin with a hole already in it. That has to be the worst kind of coin to use."

The laughter filled the room.

***

Takeshi led his family through the train station. Yuki stayed close, followed by Aunt Keiko and cousins Kenichi and Ryo. It was common for families to see their young heroes leave for camp with a last wave and a smile. The addition of so many well-wishers on the platforms created a squashed and vibrant atmosphere as the engines let out steam and rumbled into action.

Stern-looking NCOs of the Imperial Japanese Army watched out for the fresh-faced young men arriving with their red cards in hand. They checked their names off from lists and directed them to the correct carriages. Most were heading for training at Saga, but some were going further afield. They would have a few more hours of freedom before enlisting, but the army still recorded the journey. Failure to turn up for army service would mean the army would come looking for you in the form of the *Kempeitai*. The notorious military police were to be avoided at all costs, so it was always advisable to reach your destination on time.

Takeshi had a longer journey; first to Fukuoka, then through Hiroshima—to Okayama and Uno Port. After staying overnight in a traditional *ryokan* guest house, he would catch the ferry to Shikoku Island. There he would meet up with the military-escorted transport that would take him to his camp. It was the furthest he had ever traveled in his life. Even the thought of just passing through so many unknown cities was making the young recruit nervous.

The family did their best to remain together as they moved through the crowds. Calls of *sumimasen* rose above the hundreds of conversations to help gaps appear in the busy throng of those awaiting the departure of their cherished sons and brothers.

As they neared the train that would cover the first leg of the journey, a cheerful-looking army corporal stood in Takeshi's path. He looked friendly, but two privates who maintained a sober and threatening air accompanied him. They all stood armed with rifles slung over their shoulders.

The corporal took Takeshi's red card and scanned the information.

"Yoshida Takeshi-san?" he confirmed.

"Yes, *Gocho-san*."

The corporal smiled back at his men before returning his gaze to Takeshi.

"I see you have one more day before you will need to salute me, but it's good that you develop the habit now. You are a volunteer?"

"Yes, Gocho-san."

"We welcome your eagerness to serve the Emperor, though I see you are not joining us at the 12th Division?"

"The military clerk selected the 11th Division for me, sir."

"I recommend you learn the local words of the Shikoku islanders as soon as you can. You will need to earn their trust. Please know I am only giving good advice."

The corporal nodded toward Keiko, as the senior member of the family.

"Listen to him," she agreed, "the corporal and your other superiors will look after you."

The comment caused the other two soldiers to break into smiles.

"What is this you have with you? Lunch?"

Takeshi held up a small *bento* box in his hand, wrapped in a *furoshiki* cloth."

"It is for the journey ahead," Takeshi confirmed.

The corporal bowed and handed the red card back to Takeshi. "Enjoy your day with your journey and a pleasant lunch. Make sure you arrive on time for your transport to the training center. Stand tall and the medical staff will accept you as Class A. *Tennoheika banzai.*"

"Tennoheika banzai," the Yoshida family replied as one.

The soldiers departed into the crowd to find their next recruit. Meanwhile, the family became a little more relaxed.

"The corporal seemed very nice," said Aunt Keiko, "I think they treat volunteers differently, because of their bravery."

"Maybe," replied Takeshi, "I'm not so worried now. I think if I am a good soldier and follow orders, then I'll be fine, and you don't need to worry about me."

"Will you come back and tell us all about the battles?" asked Ryo.

"Some things are secret, but yes, when it is all over, I will be able to tell you about our triumphs. We are making a new world, remember. When the other races of the world bow down before us, then all our lives will get better."

"I want to volunteer now," said Kenichi.

"Let me, your older cousin, walk the road before you. Study hard, Kenichi. Japan needs pilots as well as infantry. Follow your dream first; that is the path to aim for."

Takeshi turned to his aunt. "Aunt Keiko. I am sorry if I have caused you trouble while I have lived with you. I know that you took on a great responsibility after my parents died. I hope that good fortune follows you from now on."

"Thank you, Takeshi-san. We have made offerings to the gods for your safe return."

An awkward pause followed. Keiko had spoken as if Takeshi was just another person in her neighborhood heading off to war. A sudden coldness emerged, and a sneer suggesting that she had rid herself of a problem, rather than a nephew.

Yuki broke the silence. She bowed and gripped Takeshi's hand with her two hands. It was a subtle physical contact that most would miss.

"Do your duty to the Emperor. Obey all his commands and the code of Bushido. Then you will find the way of the warrior from inside your heart. You will have become a noble soldier, a modern-day samurai. All of our family will rejoice in your return," Yuki's eyes moved in Aunt Keiko's direction, "Come back soon, and make sure you write letters to me, just as we agreed."

"Just as we agreed," said Takeshi.

The train beside them shuddered to life. A final surge of passengers boarded as the guard announced it was about to leave. Takeshi became caught up in the rapid movement of all those heading for the doors. He waved above the heads of the crowd as his family became harder to see amongst the crush of bodies.

Stepping on the carriage, he made his way toward the last window seat. Staring out at the platform, he glimpsed Yuki, rushing forward on her own. He could see that tears were forming in her eyes, no matter how she tried to hide it. Meanwhile, Takeshi felt breathless and sick. The excitement of the day, and the thought of leaving his sister behind, twisted around inside him. The train began to move.

Takeshi raised his hand in a last wave, not wanting to draw too much attention from the passengers surrounding him. As Yuki started to disappear, Takeshi could see Aunt Keiko catching up with her, screaming at her, and striking her on her back. The hatred had returned before the train had even left the platform.

Takeshi panicked. He left his bento box and rose from his seat, rushing through the carriage. The train had already picked up speed, as he faced the train guard, standing between him and the train door.

"Please take your seat. The train is already underway," said the guard.

Takeshi looked beyond him, the view of the outside showing that they had left the station. He uttered quiet frustration under his breath. He knew there was nothing he could do. The red card in his pocket had sealed his direction of travel and the destiny of his life ahead.

He bowed his head and gazed at the floor as he walked back to his seat. He could feel the glances and hear the thoughts of the other passengers, some sympathetic, others mocking his display of fear.

When he went to sit down, he noticed that the bento box was gone.

"Excuse me," he said to the passengers nearby, "I had a lunch box and now it's gone. Did anyone see someone taking it?"

He was met with silence and distant looks in the eyes of those around him. Food was precious, however it was obtained. Leaving it unattended was the unforgivable error, not the act of theft that had removed it from him.

Takeshi sat back down at the window and watched the world go by in silence. He could deal with the hunger in his belly, but the wasted effort that his sister had made to give him a last parting gift was now contributing to an agonizing emptiness in his heart.

*****

As the hours and the miles passed, Takeshi's mood hadn't improved. Amongst the rice fields and the hills, the dotted farm buildings, and the more crowded streets of small towns and cities, his first experience of the outside world felt cold and unforgiving. He had never felt as alone as he did now, and the stories he had heard of what awaited him caused his imagination to wander in a worrying direction.

He had learned from others he worked with at the harbor about life in the army. Their talk often mentioned beatings that were handed out to new recruits on the explicit instruction of cruel officers. They said the only reason for being a good soldier and moving through the ranks was that you would then be able to take your turn at handing out beatings to the others who followed in your place.

He thought of one elderly co-worker who suffered from bad arthritis in his leg. He blamed his pain on the broken ankle he had suffered in China. An angry and offended lieutenant wielding a five-pound hammer had ordered his fellow soldiers to hold the man down as he handed the punishment out for lack of respect.

Takeshi shook himself, and his thoughts moved on. He decided that it was time to listen to his teachers. He had spent much of his school life preparing for service. Learning your letters and numbers was one thing, but they wove the history of Japan into every subject, including physical education.

Textbooks told stories and displayed pictures of samurai heroes, alongside images of triumphant victory in the Sino and Russo wars. They detailed the events of almost seventy-five years earlier—the Meiji Restoration that had returned the Emperors to power. All students learned about the unbroken line of the Emperor, descended from the goddess *Amaterasu*. The teachers often described the words and deeds of Japan's infallible leader.

Takeshi and his classmates had always looked forward to the military drills, Kendo practice, and other physical challenges designed to cultivate the ideal warrior. They were all taught to fight and to win. The techniques encouraged you to attack and not defend. There could never be failure in battle, only victory—or honorable death.

The hypnotic movement and vibration of the train caused Takeshi to drift in and out of sleep. Short dreams involved his fears for Yuki. His Aunt Keiko would take the guise of a demon, and his sister had become a ghost. Each time the rails below shook him back to consciousness, he had to steady his nerves once again. Only the need to change trains brought him back to reality.

The afternoon had passed and early evening was taking over. As Takeshi left the small train at Uno Port, he stepped into the rain. A blanket of gray clouds rested above the hills that surrounded the small city. The other passengers who had been around him dispersed, leaving him alone to wander through the exit onto a quiet and almost deserted street. The port he would depart from the next day lay ahead, just a short distance away.

He crossed a road and turned to his right; the street stretched out, leading to a cluster of buildings in the distance. The ryokan he was told to go to would be somewhere down there. A neighbor had recommended it and given Takeshi the name of the owner to ask for. He would find it later, for now, he was still in a daze; it seemed the right thing to do was to first head for the sea and take in the view of the next stage of his journey.

The rain urged him to move on. He could see where the ferry berthed. As he drew closer, he spotted the first of the small islands that extended out from the mainland. In many ways, it was like his hometown and felt familiar. He looked around; there was no one else prepared to brave the elements, and he was alone, so he decided to announce his feelings to the world.

"I stand on the edge of the greatest journey. My fate will be glorious, regardless of how destiny shapes its end. I will see you again, Yuki. I promise you that. I will see you again."

Only the sound of the sea responded. Its gentle movement seemed to emphasize how small Takeshi was within this world. A blast of cold air prompted him to walk again.

Moving on among the buildings, it didn't take long for him to find a stranger willing to give him local directions. Before long, he stood looking at the front door of the ryokan, a warm, inviting glow that provided promise of some comfort. He knew that a hot bath and a comfortable sleep would restore him after an exhausting and emotional day. Tonight he would relax. Tomorrow, his war would begin.

Chapter 3
The Imperial Rescript

"Yoshida Takeshi-san, from Sasebo?"

"Yes, *Gunso-san.*"

The sergeant held Takeshi's red card against a checklist. His eyes narrowed as if he were scrutinizing the *outsider* for defects. He stood so close that he seemed to drain all the air between them. His presence was overbearing and threatening, even though he was only checking off the names of the new recruits.

He made a mark and moved on to the next man in line. Takeshi allowed himself the smallest gasp of relief. The rain had only stopped half an hour earlier, and the temperature was uncomfortable. The bad weather and fear shattered any last shreds of optimism that Takeshi may have had about joining the army.

He shifted his gaze back and forth, from looking downward to catching glimpses of the surrounding scene. Around a dozen military police organized three groups of new recruits into lines, each standing by the side of a waiting bus. Each line had a sergeant or a corporal responsible for registering the new recruits' attendance. Two fellow officers accompanied each of those, both brandishing bamboo canes. These were being used to guide attentive people into position, but for those who didn't pay attention, the cane could provide an added sting.

A further group, wearing the distinctive white armbands and black boots, stood beside two army vehicles. Armed with rifles, they smiled in amusement, maybe remembering their own first days, and deciding who was likely to be the first to fall foul of the strict conditions that the Kempeitai were there to enforce.

All the new intake could sense each other's alarm. The waving flags of family and neighbors were long gone. The blanket of gray cloud hung in the air, while the mood of the military police gave an early warning of the life that lay ahead.

Checks completed, the three officers that had been recording the names came together as a group. It was obvious from the way they were speaking that something was wrong. Another head count took place, and all were told to step forward when their name was called.

It seemed that Suzuki Jiro-san had not reported for duty.

The sergeant and his corporals carried on with ordering all to get on board the buses that were bound for camp. The young men followed in a line, taking their place on the first available seat. One larger recruit had stood out from the crowd. He had the air of a wrestler, and a build to match. He looked like he would need two seats to fit his frame, but he chose to press his way into the seat next to Takeshi, squeezing him into the side of the bus.

"My name is Ichiro, Ito Ichiro."

"Hello Ichiro-san. My name is Yoshida Takeshi."

"Silence!" came the call from the sergeant, "The only voice that you will hear before you arrive at camp will be mine. I am Sergeant Watanabe. Listen to what I have to say and follow my instructions. If you can do that well, then you may have the good fortune to never hear from me again..."

Sergeant Watanabe's speech stopped as a commotion outside drew everyone's attention. Two of the cane-carrying Kempeitai were running on either side of a young man, barking instructions at him to hurry and get to the bus.

The sergeant checked the time before sighing and stepping back outside the vehicle. "Suzuki Jiro?" the other officers confirmed his identity as Jiro cowered in fear, "He has disobeyed his first command by failing to turn up on time. Remind him of how many minutes he was late. Ten, I think."

The other officers followed the command. Taking five strokes each across Jiro's body.

Takeshi and the other bus passengers looked on in horror. The force of the very first stroke behind Jiro's knees caused him to collapse to the ground in agonizing pain. The officers then took the time to aim at different parts of the body, maximizing the area of bruising and swelling, while wounding the victim just enough to allow him to carry on with the rest of his day.

Punishment complete, he was then dragged to his feet and hauled onto the bus, before being shoved down on the last vacant seat. Then they cast a small bag of belongings he had brought with him into the trees that were growing by the roadside.

They met his painful calls for mercy with further intimidation. Sergeant Watanabe took over, screaming orders at the recruit's face. Ordering him to sit up with a straight back and to stop causing disharmony among the other recruits. Raising his hand, positioned for a strike, seemed to be enough to convince Jiro to quiet down and do his best to sit upright.

Sergeant Watanabe walked to the front of the bus and picked up the checklist before returning to make his last mark.

"Suzuki Jiro-san, from Takamatsu?"

"Yes, Gunso-san," answered Jiro, stifling his urge to show discomfort.

Sergeant Watanabe nodded his approval of completing the list. He walked back to the side of the driver and ordered him to start the journey to camp.

The bus led off the small convoy of vehicles. Lines of faces pressed against the glass in a series of grim and austere expressions that masked the turmoil of internal fear and anticipation that none could admit.

Sergeant Watanabe stood again to deliver the essential information and his few words of advice.

"Some will tell you, you are here to learn and to train, to develop your skills to fight, and play your part in advancing the glory of Japan. I can make it simpler than that. You are here to serve the Emperor and follow his commands at all times. The Emperor's commands will come through any officer that outranks you. I will make this even easier to understand. You are the lowest of the low. Second-class privates have no authority. You will salute all ranks and obey all orders. Ask Suzuki-san, if you are in any doubt about following an instruction.

"When you arrive at camp, you will receive a medical examination and be awarded a grade of fitness for duty. From there, you will receive your uniform and your section leader will escort you to your barracks. You will receive brief instructions about care of your kit and how to keep your living quarters tidy. Pay attention. Inspections will happen every day and at any time. We will not tolerate failure on any task. There are many ways to earn a beating in the Imperial Japanese Army. If I can give any advice—accept punishment without protest. Know that the army toughens you up to face the enemy dogs of war. You will thank us for educating you on loyalty, respect, and valor."

Sergeant Watanabe ended his brief speech and took his seat at the front of the bus. With his back to the recruits, there was no invitation for questions.

Takeshi and Ichiro glanced at one another with weak smiles, no words were required.

***

> Yuki, how have you been?
>
> The days are growing darker as we move through winter. We train all day. My Kendo has been improving and we also wear traditional armor to practice fighting with bayonets. The instructor always has a longer rifle, which he will use to encourage and correct you if you make a mistake. Sometimes the blows can land outside of the armor, so we all have some bruises, but they are just reminders to improve our fighting...

Takeshi looked through the grill of his Kendo helmet at his opponent. The stakes were high in a competition between rival groups of recruits—a battle that could be over in seconds. For the winners—bragging rights. For the losers—today's reason for further punishment beatings.

Each recruit took it in turns to wield the strange wooden weapon that was half rifle butt and half *shinai* sword. Intended to train for close combat with a bayonet fixed rifle, the participants resorted to the traditional fencing techniques they had all learned when they were young.

Feet placed to move back and forward in a straight line, they lifted the weapons high before striking with brute force rather than trained finesse. The roars and jeers of all those assembled increased the tension in the fight. The breastplate armor did little other than offer protection from blows that hit the target. A small piece of cloth hung below, displayed over the area that was out of bounds. Strikes from an opponent would almost certainly connect with flesh or bone, something you were just expected to absorb as you replied with your own attack. This discipline, in particular, was not a form of self-defense. It was a rehearsal for the natural conclusion of a banzai charge—the point where you are close enough to experience the dying breath of your foe.

The addition of an armed umpire was also a modification of the martial art. He would step in to set the distance between fighters, but chastisement for slow attack—or blatant disregard for training—could see punishment strokes inflicted during the combat. A weak fighter would soon find themselves surrounded by opponent and instructor.

Takeshi was confident with his movement, staying upright while he stepped in and out of range. His opponent was not so skilled, his spine arching back on the retreat while his feet remained glued to the floor. It would have been easy for Takeshi to knock him off balance, but he wanted to win with skill, in the true way of the sword.

Stepping back from his opponent's desperate lunge, he prepared to make the attack, bringing his shinai down on the other man's wrist, before letting it bounce toward a stabbing motion on the small piece of protection that covered the neck. In real life, he would have amputated the enemy's hand, before impaling them on the bayonet. An instant kill.

The umpire stepped in to declare the victory, and a cheer from his comrades watching from the sidelines confirmed his victory. There were still other bouts to take place, but Takeshi had completed his part. His section leader would note his effort.

> ... I have been learning a lot more about the code of
> Bushido. In amongst all the physical activities, we also
> go to a hall where we listen to The Imperial Rescript
> to Soldiers and Sailors. We must commit the words to
> memory and contemplate their meaning. I understand
> more about being a warrior and serving the Emperor
> with devotion because I have attended these classes.
> Our commanding officers test us all the time. Not
> everyone has such a wonderful memory, and they need
> to be schooled further to take in all the information.
> There are certain officers who are very good at
> improving the memory of the men who don't do so
> well. Once they have received extra coaching by them,
> then their learning and memory improves quickly...

Since the very beginning of training, the officers
considered the daily reading of *The Imperial Rescript to
Soldiers and Sailors* more important than hours spent
learning how to march and how to present arms in a parade.
Committed to memory, it was the code of ethics, a rulebook
for the simple soldier to act in the manner of a samurai in the
Emperor's service. A clear understanding of these
commandments emphasized the need for all to act as one.
Failure to adhere to them would turn the soldier into nothing
more than a wild beast or a savage, a lower form of existence
than what they expected as a standard for the typical Japanese
soldier.

The corporal that led Takeshi's section had carried on mistreating Jiro Suzuki since his arrival in camp. Handing out daily beatings to the unfortunate second-class private had become nothing more than daily morning exercise to the officer charged with looking after his troop's welfare.

Jiro was slow to learn. He had struggled to keep up with the intense physical rigor of constant tuition in close combat. Nursing broken ribs, a broken jaw, and a dislocated shoulder, the others commented on whether he would even live long enough to face the enemy. They speculated that he might rush to the facing guns just to find relief from his miserable existence.

Yet there was something in the daily readings that inspired even him. It presented the cruelty he suffered from as a form of care. Conditioning him with the fist, the boot, and the cane into becoming a soldier who ranked among his peers. He would graduate with his class regardless of his failings. His opportunity to serve the Emperor through the toughening of his spirit would make him an outstanding soldier in the end. When he offered his own valiant death, they could assure him he may end his days at Yasukuni shrine with the other heroes of Japan.

For Jiro, that was enough to pick himself up and continue facing his trials without complaint. He had learned who was more lenient with the force applied. In the end, he had a list of officers he preferred to administer the beatings. Being careful to choose who to make mistakes in front of was the best way to survive.

> ...I have made friends with others in my section, most of them are locals from Shikoku Island. It took a few days for them to accept me. They called me gaijin, at first, but my friend Ichiro is the size of a sumo wrestler and he persuaded them to use my real name.

As the corporal on the train platform at Sasebo had warned, Takeshi was an outsider—a gaijin—who became the natural choice for disparaging comments and bullying. Making a first friend in Ichiro had proved fortunate. His larger physical presence intimidated the others, and he was an islander, so entitled to his opinion about Takeshi; this meant he could decide Takeshi's suitability for acceptance into the group.

The support allowed Takeshi time to impress the others with his own worthiness. Takeshi had proved himself to be a good recruit like his uncle had predicted. He was fit and able to handle the extreme tests designed by the instructors. He always played a full part in team activities, and he had a sense of humor that turned the others to laugh with him rather than at him.

Takeshi was grateful to Ichiro for creating the opportunity for him to thrive, and in return, he helped Ichiro where he could. Sharing his food ration was helpful. Ichiro had lost weight under the strict limits on food, and his hunger could cause him to be miserable. Takeshi didn't mind helping. He had been so used to the meager meals in his family home that he felt the army was overfeeding him. He would survive, and it was good to help a friend.

Over the weeks they had endured together, other friendships had formed; Akio had a sister the same age as Yuki, Haru and Ren both had lost parents to tuberculosis, Fuji just shared the same sense of humor.

Takeshi had bonded and found his family. Even the unfortunate Jiro had earned the fraternal loyalty that all now shared. There were those who would cheat at cards or have a tendency to steal from others; some would throw their weight around in an argument or lead others into trouble and inevitable beatings, but they were warriors together, held together by their unquestioning duty to the Emperor.

> I hope everything is going well at home, and our cousins are on their best behavior. Write to me and let me know. I hope Uncle Taro and Aunt Keiko are happy. I was sorry to leave you at the station. I hope you were okay. Please write back and let me know.
> Your brother, Takeshi.

Takeshi folded the single-page letter and placed it in an envelope, ready for posting. He didn't seal it. He knew the military police would read it. He could put up with everything he had gone through over the previous weeks if he could just know that Yuki was safe at home and happy at school.

He had last seen her dragged back by Aunt Keiko at the railway platform. Weeks had passed, and he had heard nothing from home. He was sure that Yuki would have written by now, but what if Aunt Keiko had forbidden her?

Even worse thoughts crossed his mind about her being sold into a forced marriage, but he had to believe that there was a better reason.

Soon he would head off to battle, and mail would take time to find him. As he looked down at the envelope, he just had to hope that the gods would bless him with a message. A confirmation that his decision to leave home was right. He wiped the tear from his eye before the others in his barracks spotted it. That was a sign of weakness, and considered selfish. It might affect the mood of everyone else in the small and packed hut they had all learned to call home.

***

The darkness of a long overnight trek was lifting as the rising sun spread its light as a halo across the distant hill peaks. For three days, Takeshi's section had been marching and surviving on the most basic of rations, and one canteen of water.

The challenge had been to survive on as little as possible, to navigate the difficult terrain without eating and drinking. To prove that they were ready for the demands of the ever-changing circumstances that were required to move an armed force; change position; reinforce a distant unit; or discover and trap an enemy.

The rain had been heavy, so the major enemy on this day was the relentless downpours. Tree cover helped protect from the water descending from the sky, but not the sweat from inside the uniforms or the exhaustion created from carrying full packs of kit.

After almost sixty miles of maneuvers and marching, the closing stages of the task were taking their toll. Tempers were fraying; grudges were being nursed. All had to make it through the test if they were to avoid punishment on their return to camp.

Ichiro hadn't fared well. He was strong, but suffering in the conditions. All the others looked up to him. Seeing him falter caused a gloom that was only matched by the thick blanket of dark clouds.

The corporal who led them had stuck to the same rules as his men and guided them through the challenge. He was safe knowing that he didn't have to face the threat for the man that returned with the least water. The *weakling* would receive punishment at the hands of his own friends. If any of them resisted or lacked eagerness, then their punishment would be worse.

Ichiro had drunk more water than most. A brief rest, five miles from home, saw him drain the last drops from his supply. Takeshi watched him put himself in last place.

"Ichiro-san, take some of my water for your canteen. No one has ordered that we can't help one another. Please, take some of my water."

"What does it matter, Takeshi-san? I am so tired, you will all just kick me into a pleasant sleep. I'll cope with the bruises when I wake."

"I want to give you a chance, that's all. You stopped the others from picking on me all those weeks ago. I owe you a debt for what you've done. Please let me gift you some water."

Ichiro sat contemplating and considering his response. The reluctance to express emotion fixed his face with stern acceptance.

"Thank you, Takeshi-san, but no. I am not the Emperor. If I was, I would expect all of you to give me the water I needed. If I was the commanding officer, I would have already noticed who had drained their bottle. The person who helped me would be guilty of defying the Emperor's command. I would not like to think of what would happen to that man after they had dealt my punishment. If you want to help me, then make sure your first blow knocks me out cold," Ichiro bowed, "It is good to know a good man and call him my friend. We are brothers, but we are all brothers; we cannot expect for one to be more important than the other. We must all rush to death together in the last charge. Isn't that what we have all spent these weeks learning?"

"I understand," replied Takeshi.

He understood all the years of his youth had pointed to this moment. From learning how to salute when he was only six years old, to when the teachers stopped giving exercise classes in favor of a military instructor taking over. Early classes in Kendo, Judo, and Sumo. The encouragement to compete and win. Learning the ancient and near history of his nation. The influence of the divine leader was mentioned every day. It wasn't just the last sixty miles that had led to this moment; it was his entire life. He recalled the words of *The Imperial Rescript to Soldiers and Sailors.*

"Duty is weightier than a mountain."

"Well remembered," said Ichiro, "it is not your turn to fail today."

The corporal summoned everyone back to the march. As they collected themselves, most kept their heads low. They only observed the path ahead, as their boots trudged through mud and gathered pools of water. They knew what came next. An ultimate question of loyalty. Total obedience to the Emperor's wishes, delivered through the order of a commanding officer. That was the only answer.

The weary troop marched through the gate with heads held high—final command to display their strength to all who witnessed their return. The corporal called them to a halt in front of a sergeant major, surrounded by four higher-ranking privates. Each of the privates carried several canes. The threat was obvious. They had seen this same ritual happen with others. It tended to be the only time that someone with such a high rank would appear before them.

The sergeant major had experience in drawing out the fear, a skill designed to make the threat of the beating worse than the event itself. He took pride in the ability to intimidate his own soldiers.

Takeshi looked to his side. Ichiro was nervous and sweating. It was impossible to tell if it was fear or the stress of the march. He resigned himself to his fate, that was clear.

One by one, each man opened and poured the water from his canteen onto the ground. The sergeant major noted the time that it took for each one to empty. All were similar, even Jiro had avoided last place.

Ichiro opened and upturned his canteen, and not a single drop of water appeared. You could hear the sharp intakes of breath from all his comrades.

The sergeant major said nothing at first. He allowed the remaining soldiers the choice to show how well they had done. Then he issued the command for all except Ichiro to arm themselves with a cane and form into a circle around the intended victim.

The officer ordered Ichiro to remove his kit, his jacket, and his boots, which the sergeant major's men collected. They then placed the uniform outside of the circle.

"There is only one command that you should all follow. The last command that you hear. These are the words of the Emperor, of a god. His inspiring presence is the reason that Japan will rule over Asia, and then rule over the world. In a god you must have faith, you must believe in his divinity. Whether he grants you the gift of his mercy or the wrath of his anger, you must accept all in equal measure if you are Japanese."

The rain continued to fall for a few more seconds before the sergeant major raised his sword into the air.

"Tennoheika banzai!"

"Banzai!" shouted the men as they charged upon Ichiro, attacking him from all sides.

His build and strength saw him absorb the first strikes, but as the blows came crashing in, he fell to the ground, laid out on his back, taking a beating to ribs and limbs. Takeshi moved to the end of the group and caught a pain-filled plea from Ichiro's face. Without a second thought, Takeshi brought the cane down with all its force on the forehead of his friend. Blood streamed from the broken skin, and Ichiro's eyes closed as the beating continued and the rain poured down.

Chapter 4
Aki Maru

"Over eleven thousand four hundred tons, and a top speed of seventeen knots."

"What are you talking about, Takeshi?" said Fuji.

"My cousin Ryo likes to know all the information about ships, and planes. I'm just committing it to memory so that I can tell him all about it when I get home."

The conversation ended. There was an instant melancholy whenever *home* came up in conversation. There were times when it served the purpose of drawing friends together with a shared experience, but standing on the dockside waiting to be called forward was the wrong place. Fuji changed the subject, to the rumors that were circulating about their destination.

"Most of the men think we are heading for Luzon."

"I don't know. The clerk who sent me to the eleventh division mentioned to my uncle that they would send me to Burma if I was in the twelfth; I don't think we're going to the Philippines either. All I know is we're heading somewhere with mountains."

They both laughed as they looked at their new uniforms. After training had been completed, Takeshi and Fuji transferred to the 38th Infantry Division as part of a mountain artillery battalion. Both had proven themselves in the skills required to assemble a 75mm gun in just a few minutes. The army also considered them fit enough for the arduous task of lifting the gun parts into remote and hidden locations. Stamina was just as important as firing accuracy.

"Yoshida Takeshi-san."

Takeshi stepped forward at a quick pace to receive the boarding information—his deck allocation. This is where he would compete for a place to sleep, and make the best use of the square foot of space allowed. Enough room to stand upright for inspection, but very little else.

He joined the line. It felt like he was walking into the belly of a whale. The troops remained silent during boarding, but the sound of so many bodies moving together, the loading of cargo and military equipment, and the barking commands of officers rang out in short echoes across the stairways, the galley, the engine rooms, and into every hollow corner below deck.

Takeshi could feel his heart race. It was only a few months since he had incurred his Aunt Keiko's wrath for taking part in Kenichi's game. He felt as if he had lived a second lifetime since then. Home was still important, and still not that far away. His transport ship lay berthed in Ujina, Hiroshima, a place he had only passed through once before, on the train that had taken him away from all he had known.

As he looked back at the dockside, he stared in the direction of Sasebo and thought about Yuki attending school. His letter had not received a reply. He knew that Yuki would write, she would have kept her promise. He felt a sense of shame at even trying to keep in touch. He could never share the worst of what he had witnessed at training camp. His friend Ichiro had been so beaten up that the officers removed him from duty. How could he even admit his part in the punishment, without Yuki hating him for what he'd done?

Stepping on board, he now recognized why few shared much of their experience of war. His father had been a kind person, who had loved his mother with complete devotion. He was proud to have Takeshi as his son, and like any father, he had a special place in his heart for his daughter, Yuki. He had manned a machine gun in Manchukuo. How many had he killed? He never spoke about it. How had he sealed that part of his life from view? No one asked, and no one told. Soldiers of the Japanese army had to become samurai to fight to the death, but they were not the warrior class of old. At one point, many would have to return to the life they had lived before the time of war.

By the time Takeshi entered his mess deck, he had convinced himself that holding on to the memories of his home would not serve him well. The army had done everything they could to remove that for a reason. His new family were here on board; the soldiers of the 38th Infantry were his brothers. These were the people he would live and die with. If the divine will brought victory and success to Japan, he would return a hero and all would have changed for the better while he was gone.

The thought cheered him—the eternal optimism that life would repay him for the austerity and adversity he had experienced. Whether it was with his own future of a wife and family, or his arrival before the gates of heaven, what was there to be worried over? He stepped forward into the crush, ready for whatever came next.

"Takeshi-san, Takeshi-san," Fuji had caught up, "do you want to go up on deck? We're allowed to take exercise as long as we return for inspections and meals. They just said to avoid where they're loading equipment."

"What about our kit? Where do we put it?"

"In at the sides, just try to stow it where it won't move around so much."

The two found suitable gaps between pipes and the deck walls, tight enough to hold everything in place. As they finished making sure the equipment was secure, they came under the watchful eye of Corporal Miyashita.

"Note your surroundings in case you need to find your equipment in a hurry," he advised, "We'll be passing through dangerous waters. I guarantee it. The navy takes responsibility for steering our course, so it's better for us in the army to be prepared, no?"

"Yes, Gocho Miyashita-san," came the joint reply.

"I need volunteers to help serve the officers at each meal time. You will carry their food from the galley, serve it, and collect the dishes, which you'll wash and pack away. Only then will you return to receive your ration. Be in the galley queue at least fifteen minutes early. An officer can still have you flogged if you cause him the discomfort of a missed or rushed meal."

"Yes, Gocho Miyashita-san."

The corporal produced his own checklist and marked off the names of the *volunteers* before stepping back into the crowd.

"I don't think we had much choice," said Fuji.

"It will give us something to do. I think I'll prefer to keep busy."

"Yes, you could be right. The threat of a flogging always keeps you focused."

"Let's go and take in the view," said Takeshi, "our last sight of Japan, for the moment."

The first soldiers on board had already made their way to the top deck, sitting above oil drums and ammunition containers. It didn't matter that they were relaxing next to a vast quantity of explosive materials. It was a small price to pay for savoring the opportunity to breathe in the sea air and escape the packed spaces below deck.

Takeshi and Fuji looked out over the side from the bow of the ship, standing underneath a raised platform with defensive guns already in place. Hundreds of men had boarded, but thousands more still waited on the dockside. Across the port, two other transporters were engaged with their cargo of men and supplies, the Sakito and the Tosan. A destroyer was also nearby, the Asashimo.

"How can the Americans even think they can destroy us?" Takeshi reflected. "They don't know us or understand us. Look at what we are prepared to face them with."

"They believe that the entire world is theirs," said Fuji, "they expect us to surrender."

The two friends laughed out loud with one another as they looked out across the port. How could they ever expect the Japanese to surrender? Such a concept didn't exist.

***

Two days had passed. It was an hour until lights out, so Takeshi followed many others in grasping a last piece of air. His last sight of Japan had taken longer than expected as the convoy had only just edged its way toward the very southernmost part of Kyushu.

He had traveled all this way and still not left his homeland. Another transporter and a further two destroyers had joined the convoy. Those who could read the positions of the stars continued to note the convoy was moving south even after it had left sight of land. Once the fleet changed course, then they would have a better idea; the Philippines lay to the southwest. A southeastern direction could mean any one of the small groups of islands that stretched further into the Pacific.

Somewhere closer to the bow of the ship, a single voice carried across the deck. An old fisherman's song traveled along on the breeze. Takeshi recognized it, from his time of helping to land the fish in Sasebo. It made him feel nostalgic and proud. He caught the smiles and happy glances of others on the deck beside him. Regardless of where the Aki Maru was bound, he had never been more sure of his future. In that moment, he understood what it was to be a Japanese soldier, to be part of the great unifying force of the Japanese army, and to serve the will of the Emperor in a noble conquest over the other inferior nations that stood in their way. His previous life had only steered him toward this moment.

As he descended from the deck to find a small area where he could catch a few hours' rest, he no longer thought about the discomfort of the cramped space. The others laid out on the floor beside him were all there for one reason. They all had shared the same experiences over the past few months. They had all left the places where they had grown up with their families, friends, and neighbors. They were an unstoppable force that would reach out across the world: *eight corners, one roof*. Takeshi found enough floor to stretch out on and fell asleep.

***

The sound of large guns firing woke Takeshi in an instant. He sat upright in amongst a swathe of bodies, all stumbling out of unconsciousness. Officers were barking commands for all to stay calm and hold their positions. No one was being allowed to leave the deck.

A few feet away, Takeshi spotted Fuji. They made their way toward one another, half crawling through the crowd as further bangs sounded over the rumble of their own ship, repositioning itself.

"It's our guns that are firing," said Fuji.

"What are they firing on?"

"Most are saying it will be a submarine. They say we'd know if it was a plane attacking."

The gunfire continued for several more rounds before a silence fell once more. The Aki Maru had settled on its course. They gave an order for the men to be quiet, and an officer announced that he would update all as soon as he had established the facts. He reminded them that this had been a navy incident, and so the army shouldn't be the ones to be concerned. All were to do their best to get back to sleep so they could perform their duties well after first light.

The men did their best to appear to obey, but whispers were finding a way through the room; Fuji nodded to another man as the word spread.

"They're saying it was the Asashimo. It chased a submarine that was nearing us and fired its guns."

"Did they hit it?"

"People say that, but they're not sure."

"They must think the danger has passed, though?"

"I hope so. The navy are not the smartest."

Takeshi cracked an ironic smile. "We just have to hope that they're smart enough."

The two men settled down amongst the crush. The danger seemed to have passed and tiredness began to take over once more. Takeshi closed his eyes, but he remained alert, listening for every creak of metal straining under the power of the ship's engines, waiting for the arrival of more explosions.

***

Troops rehearsed the emergency drill every day. Everyone knew what to do and where to report. The Asashimo had been doing its job in protecting the fleet. Takeshi tried to persuade himself he was safe, but he had still lain awake through the night without further sleep.

Before long, he was making his way with Fuji to the galley, standing in line with others tasked with serving the officers. The word of the night's events was beginning to spread out along the queue.

The Asashimo had engaged an enemy submarine with guns and depth charges. The rumor was that it had caused damage, but no wreckage or fuel had surfaced. The thought that the submarine was still out there among them kept everyone on edge, but the more pressing matter of delivering breakfast to the officers distracted all from further fears of attack.

Takeshi's own breakfast followed his duties. Rice gathered at the end of a long line, you ate the meager meal as you made your way forward to the spot where you washed your bowl. The emphasis of the whole exercise was to consume calories as efficiently as possible, without leaving enough in your stomach to be upset by the roll of the ship. Exercise drills would follow. Each of the sergeants or corporals would gather their own men for an allocated time and space.

The men could join another queue for the optional saltwater shower. Many chose to avoid it, as others complained of feeling dirtier after emerging from their wash, but at almost five days on board, Takeshi had decided he had no choice. Like everything else on the transporter, it was a controlled process, with little time allowed for cleaning yourself. Takeshi often suppressed thoughts of home, but the memory of that last hot bath at the ryokan in Uno Port resurfaced.

A scheduled afternoon emergency drill allowed all out on deck. Every soldier paid closer attention based on the events in the early morning. The rumor spread that the convoy had turned to the east, past the southernmost reaches of Okinawa. There was no doubt in anyone's mind that they were bound on a course for the more distant Pacific islands. Everyone had an opinion on where they would end up, but a popular choice was the Mariana Islands; Saipan, Tinia, Agrihan, Rota, and Guam.

"How do you feel about where we're heading?" asked Takeshi.

"I would have preferred Luzon to get off the ship sooner," Fuji replied, "There's not a lot of good we can do with our bayonets against a submarine. How long will it take to get there?"

"Three days, some are saying. Plenty of time for more inspections, more drills, more beatings for not paying attention."

"You make it sound so good, Takeshi. I wonder why I didn't enlist earlier."

The order to dismiss interrupted their humorous exchange. Small groups pushed past one another as they decided on how to use their time until the next round of rations. Sitting in any available space on deck was one choice. The view was now vast miles of ocean that stretched out in all directions. The ships of the convoy maintained position. Sometimes one of the destroyers would move further away to survey an area for enemy boats. After its investigation, it would return to the rest of the fleet.

Takeshi and Fuji took up their normal view toward the bow of the Aki Maru. It was positioned in the middle of the convoy, while the Sakito forged ahead and the Tanso brought up the rear. Conversation of what the future held fueled excitement. Heading for the palm trees and beaches of a remote and beautiful island was far preferable to the jungles of Burma. A contented and relaxed state descended once again that lasted until the dinner ration was due to be served.

Takeshi and Fuji had returned to the galley line, queueing for the officers' dinner, when the next two explosions rang out. The response was immediate and different from the previous attack. All men were relieved of their duties and told to return and gather their equipment. There was no need to question the orders—the convoy was once again under attack.

You couldn't go anywhere on the ship without navigating through the endless lines of troops, all struggling to reach and take possession of their equipment. In the chaos, Takeshi got to his station along with Fuji. Corporal Miyashita's advice to note everything about where they stowed their equipment had proved useful, even if it had got displaced in the rush.

A barrage of barked commands filled the air. Orders to prepare, but none to attack. They were vulnerable on the vast metal hulk of the Aki Maru.

"They've hit the Sakito!"

The words were being repeated by everyone. Two torpedo strikes on the port side and fire on the decks. Horns and megaphones blared out messages. Takeshi and all his comrades could only wait to see if the navy could respond.

As the 38th Infantry stood in wait, their worst fears manifested. A third torpedo slammed into the bow of the Aki Maru. Ears filled with the noise of the impact and the frantic cries of all now faced with the terror of what might follow.

The orders changed. Troops began assembling toward points for leaving the ship. Takeshi and Fuji pushed their way toward the railings for a clear view of the destruction.

The Sakito was in trouble. Soldiers threw wood, parts of the decking, and fittings into the water, anything that could float alongside. People leaped away from the ship as smoke billowed out. A raging inferno highlighted its outline, with towering flames that were reaching up from deep within the ship.

Screams and cries for help penetrated the air even amidst the sound of battle. The Asashimo once again took on the role of pursuing the unseen attacker, while another of the destroyers began to maneuver its way toward the struggling survivors.

Time stretched out across a disaster that none of them were prepared for; many men disappeared below the waves never to resurface. The smell of burning gasoline filled the air.

Then a barrage of depth charges dropped into the ocean. Each blast causing its own violent disturbance in the scene.

"Who do you pray for, Takeshi?"

Fuji had never looked so serious in his life. A man who never seemed plagued by the stresses and strains of normal life looked pale and drawn.

"I am married. My wife became pregnant just before I left for the army. I pray that I see my child. I just pray that I get to see my child. Who do you pray for?"

"My sister," Takeshi admitted, "I only have my sister."

"Pray for her, pray for her good life. Your family blood will carry on through her."

They stood observing the Sakito continuing to burn, unable to help the fathers, husbands, and brothers being taken from their families. Time seemed to stand still as they awaited a command to abandon ship, yet the order never came. The regiment had engineers among them who could join the ship's crew in attending to the damage. Word circulated of flooding, but no fire. Meanwhile, the Asashimo had reported the wreckage of a submarine surfacing. They fired a final depth charge to confirm its destruction.

All were told to stand down and return to their mess deck. Japan had triumphed in the battle. That was the message, but the search for survivors was becoming shrouded by a darkening sky. Searchlights mingled with the eerie backdrop of a ship still ablaze. Desperate calls for help began to diminish and fade.

Life below decks continued again. The order to resume the duty of serving a meal to the officers surprised Takeshi and

Kenji. It was late by the time they shared in their own meal. There were to be no inspections, but morale-boosting duties instead.

No one slept that night. All lay waiting for another attack. The Americans were among them, operating deep below the surface. The war had arrived before they had even reached their destination.

The Sakito sank before the sun rose on the next day. Aboard all the other ships, they held ceremonies in the name of a high-ranking commander and the other two and a half thousand men who had perished at sea in the previous hours.

A gap in the convoy emphasized the loss. The Aki Maru had survived, but it sailed on damaged, slowing its speed in half.

Officers reminded men of their loyalty to the Emperor. They were told to contemplate the words of *The Imperial Rescript to Soldiers and Sailors* and reminded that death in whatever form was more glorious within the heat of battle. A commanded period of free time followed. With less drill, there was more time to drink tea or play cards. Men bonded together by singing patriotic songs. They distributed paper to those who wished to compose a letter, but on the condition there was no mention of the sinking of the Sakito Maru.

Takeshi and Fuji still had their duties to perform over another two days. It kept them from falling into bad habits by making sure the officers shouted at them at least before breakfast and dinner. The time passed without further incident.

Land came into sight and the convoy began to separate. Troops were told for the first time that they were about to disembark at the Mariana Islands. So the rumor had been true.

For the last few hours, the Aki Maru departed from the main convoy and continued to be shadowed by just one destroyer. Sailing on its last leg, all the men prepared to leave, checking equipment and making ready. Takeshi and Fuji stood to attention as Corporal Miyashita gathered the men of the unit together.

"*Grass sprouts, trees bud*," he said, describing the time of year with a smile, "It is March 4th, shortly we will land on Omiyajima. What used to be known as the island of Guam."

Chapter 5
Omiyajima

Takeshi felt elated at returning to dry land. The island was beautiful. Blue sky and sea framed white sandy beaches and rising hills covered in rich green foliage. It brought a brief moment of joy to Takeshi's heart, as he gazed around, taking in the sights of his new home.

The orders from his corporal kept him moving. The various battalions were being organized together along the road that followed the coast, passing through the town of Agana. Officers patrolled the units. Any sense that you had lost your way, or failed to find your comrades, brought a predictable response from a senior officer. A slap to the head or a whip with a bamboo cane would remind the offending soldier to pay full attention and follow his orders in good time.

Fuji joined Takeshi as they made their way to their appointed location. The officers had ordered the mountain artillery units to gather close to the local school.

"How can we be at war in this place?" asked Takeshi.

"I don't think we are. Maybe the war will stay out at sea, and we can just put our feet up and enjoy the—"

"Hey, you two!"

The gruff-sounding voice belonged to a *jotohei*, a private, who had served at least two years with the army. Although still in the ranks, his seniority demanded a bow in respect.

"Yes, Jotohei-san," they replied.

"Tell me your name and battalion."

"Yoshida Takeshi, 38th Mountain Artillery, second battalion, Jotohei-san."

"Good, I am in the right place. I am Oda. Do as I say, and your time on Omiyajima will be pleasant and trouble-free. Of course, if you don't do what I say..."

Oda paused with a menacing grin. Takeshi noted he was thin, but battle hardened. A scar across his cheek was of the type caused by a mark from an officer's Katana. Takeshi sensed that Oda's disheveled appearance pointed to him being a dishonorable man who had learned to survive by his own set of rules. As he watched the soldier swagger off in the direction of Corporal Miyashita to report for duty, he decided having Oda as a friend rather than a rival would be a wise choice.

Once the disembarking was complete and the troops stationed with their equipment, the order came to stand down for the night. The men organized tents for temporary cover and received instructions about where to collect a meal.

Is this where I will live out my life?

The question rolled around in Takeshi's head as he settled into his new surroundings. The local people were doing their best to guide and provide help for the new arrivals, even when some of his fellow troops didn't return the same respect. He followed others to take his turn attending a hall, where they served rice and pickled plum with a few slivers of dried fish. A strange peace descended with a full stomach and the knowledge that he was at least safe from the enemy submarines.

Corporal Miyashita had appeared with one of his famous checklists. Tonight, it was only for guard duty. Takeshi and Fuji were happy to take their turn.

A further hour lapsed before Oda returned out of the darkness. Takeshi pointed his rifle and bayonet out of instinct rather than training.

"Friend. I am friend," Oda smiled. He seemed drunk, although he only gripped a small can of beer, "Yoshida-san? It is Oda. *Konbanwa.*"

Takeshi returned the greeting and dropped his guard.

"You know it's not such a terrible place. You will like it here. The CHamoru do what you tell them. Whatever you tell them."

"The CHamoru?" asked Takeshi.

"That is the name for the island natives. The Emperor tries to make them learn our culture and our language, but don't even begin to think of them as Japanese. They can never be that."

"How are we meant to treat them?"

"The same as the others we defeat. We treat them with the contempt they deserve. Don't let their nature fool you. They hate you Takeshi-san. They hate us all."

"I understand," Takeshi replied, "We received training at camp about what we would face."

"Use your rage with wisdom," smiled Oda, "Know the right time to inflict pain and the right time to take lives. Sometimes we need them for growing food or building shelters. Sometimes the women serve other needs, if you know what I mean."

"Yes, I know."

"Don't get caught, though. Our commanders know what happens, but they don't want to hear a personal account. You know everything is an excuse for a beating in the Imperial Japanese Army, especially anything that may give you pleasure.

"My advice is to get to know some of the Kempeitai at the Governor's House. They run a club that even a second-class private can visit on a Sunday morning. There are even two fine Japanese girls, but they are very popular. You will need to pay someone even for a place in the line."

"How long have you been here Oda-san?"

"Last year I arrived. I served in China before that. This place is paradise compared to Manchukuo. You're young; is this your first posting?"

"Yes. I volunteered a few months ago."

"Volunteered!" Oda laughed, "what age are you?"

"Seventeen."

"Takeshi-san, you were too impetuous, too ready to die," Oda dropped his voice to a whisper, "Our war is over. Everyone knows that Japan can't last out here. You have become a samurai at the worst possible moment. You will get in line, Takeshi, one way or another. Either for your time with the comfort women or for banzai, the last charge towards heaven. You should have stayed at home," Oda raised his can of beer into the air, "*Kampai*!" he shouted, before wandering further off down the road, disappearing into the darkness like a ghost.

***

The next morning, all rose with the sun. Fuji handed Takeshi a mug of tea as they spent more time taking in the surroundings.

Fuji smiled and nodded his head in appreciation of the view. "If I write to my wife and tell her what a beautiful island I'm living on, she will be jealous and want to come and stay with me.

"My sister would as well. She would like to walk on the beach under the branches. She doesn't like to be under a tropical sun, but she would love being near the ocean."

"They will all need to come on a better passenger ship than ours."

"With no submarines," smiled Takeshi.

Oda appeared behind the two men, slapping Fuji's back and causing him to spill his tea. Fuji could only summon an annoyed look in return. It wasn't worth starting a fight with Oda over such a small thing.

"Breakfast is over you two. We have to pack up and move out."

"Where are we going?" asked Takeshi.

"East of Agat, about ten miles south and a little inland. We'll pick up some of the natives at a roadside and then we'll head into higher ground, under cover of the trees."

"There will be natives with us?"

"We need someone to carry the gun," Oda laughed, "unless you were planning on doing it, but I wouldn't recommend it; the rewards for slave labor are terrible."

It didn't take long to clear up the temporary camp. The one thing that the army was good at was moving from one location to the next. The drill from training camp was still fresh in everyone's mind, so before long the tents were gone, the small fires extinguished, and they carried out last checks on the equipment—before Corporal Miyashita's inspection.

Oda stood at his side, along with another soldier posted to join their battery. Hayashi was the same rank as Oda, but he looked even more intimidating, if that was possible. His role involved assisting Corporal Miyashita with more screaming and shouting for any small misdemeanor. He made Oda appear to be very approachable in comparison.

Thankfully, for Takeshi and Fuji, they passed the examination without further incident. The order to board transport followed within moments, and a small convoy of vehicles and guns began the journey along the coastline. The morale was good. All knew they were here to set up defensive positions and boost the number of troops. They knew the Americans would come one day, but a strong rumor insisted it would be later, maybe November. They had months to prepare, to write letters home, and maybe even receive some back. But Takeshi felt something different as he sat and smiled with the others. There was something about this place, something in the air, that was different from home. As the procession turned inland, the sweeping curves of the surrounding high ground appeared to close like jaws round about them, as if the island itself might swallow them whole.

The transport came to a sudden halt near some small buildings, bringing Takeshi back to reality. As he jumped from the truck onto the road, a large group of soldiers and Kempeitai confronted him. Around the roadside, they had assembled over thirty native men to form the work detail. The island tranquility departed in an instant. Corporal Miyashita barked orders to disassemble the gun, ready to carry into the hills. In the background, the locals were being herded and harassed for no apparent reason. Screams of commanding officers formed into a constant running stream of hatred. The natives kept their heads bowed even as some suffered slaps, lashes from bamboo canes, or even the back edge of a sword. Takeshi carried out his rehearsed part of breaking up the gun, but it was hard not to follow what was happening just a few yards away.

Corporal Miyashita and Hayashi had crossed the road to select their native recruits. As other section leaders gathered from the other gun units, it looked like it was becoming a competition to see who could get away with the best of the workers on offer. Those making the selection laughed and bartered with one another. It was a game as they pushed and pulled men out of the packed group. If a worker looked too strong or imposing, they would receive slaps or punches, just to remind them who was in charge. If they had the misfortune to look weak, then perhaps a solid punch to the stomach might cause them to fall, resulting in being dragged around in the dirt, kicked, or stamped on. This was entertainment for their new masters.

Takeshi flinched at the cruelty. He knew that these people had surrendered to their fate. They had chosen this destiny. If they had fought like the Japanese to the death, they would not have had to endure the misery of life in captivity, and all that came with it. He understood why they had to be shown their place in this new society, yet the mocking laughter and the demeaning insults had more to do with classroom bullying than the code of Bushido. He recognized it, but he couldn't reveal it. Eventually, he broke into laughter with the others to not draw attention to himself.

They allocated six CHamoru to each unit, and the slow climb began. They transported the heaviest parts of the gun with bull carts to carry the officers and the first allocation of ammunition. The paths were narrow and uneven. The ancient trails exposed by natural erosion were never intended for transporting heavy artillery weapons. Smaller less defined areas that had become overgrown with vegetation did present opportunities for the slaves to escape, but if the Japanese bullets didn't catch up with them, then it was probable that someone else among their number would pay the price with their life.

Oda and Hayashi were keeping control. The island veterans had learned enough CHamoru to be able to switch between languages if they had to, but in front of a corporal subordinates delivered all instruction in Japanese. The rest of the unit followed in a stretched-out line. Smaller parts of the gun still needed to be carried by the soldiers themselves. If you didn't have something to carry, then your only responsibility was to keep your bayonet pointing at the nearest islander.

A breeze blew across their path as they veered toward a high road that began to level out above Agat. Branches rustled and boughs creaked. They had climbed the path at a strong pace, but lack of sleep on board the Aki Maru—and the short rations of life on board—was beginning to take its toll. All were tired and desperate to reach the target location, but as they neared the destination, the CHamoru men seemed to move slower, taking longer with each step.

Hayashi's anger exploded because of the lack of effort, but his outrage was a well-practiced charade. He took delight in the acts of cruelty he unleashed, having redirected his rage from his own mistreatment to be re-enacted on others. He ignored the monster that had created him in the first place.

Corporal Miyashita called a halt and stepped forward with a map in his hand. Another section, bringing up the rear, also came to a stop. The unit leaders huddled together to have a brief discussion about venturing off the road to set up the new gun positions. Oda and some of the other longer-serving troops joined the conversation while pointing at maps and positions through the trees. All the time, Hayashi stood at the front, glowering back at *his* slaves.

The breeze picked up into a stronger wind, and across the route in front of them the trees seemed to speak to one another. Miyashita, Oda, and four others walked from the path downhill; in a short time, they were out of view.

Takeshi stared along the road at Hayashi. The anger hadn't left his face, but a sweat was now covering his brow.

He's frightened of something.

Takeshi could feel a presence as well. He had felt it since he stepped on Omiyajima. He had awoken in the darkness the previous night, out of a dream about the soldiers who had drowned at sea. It was a vision of their bodies being pulled down into a deep ocean, arms and legs swaying and writhing in the current, a lifeless dance as they descended. His nightmare didn't leave him as he sat up inside the tent that night, sweat dampening his skin. He considered getting up and out into the night air, but it felt as if someone, or something, was lurking nearby. He retreated and fell back asleep.

Did Hayashi have the same dreams?

The CHamoru stayed with heads bowed, all except one. He could hear the change of pitch in Hayashi's voice; he could sense the fear. He raised his face to look at his captor.

"You feel them, don't you? The *Taotaomo'na*. Our ancestors."

"Silence," ordered Hayashi, "You are here to work, not talk."

"They only want to help us do our work. The trees talk with their voices. Hear them; they are all around us now."

"Silence, or the next words you speak will be your last."

"They want you to know they are on the wind, they are the thunder that rolls across the sky. You are being warned to be on your guard. Your skin will erupt in pain when they bite. A mark will be the only trace, a curse for all you—"

The islander groaned as Hayashi's bayonet plunged into his body. The soldier screamed at his victim, as if he would still follow his commands. Death wasn't instant, a bullet from another gun finished the task. The murderer ordered two of the other CHamoru to throw the body to the side of the road, where he used his boot to complete his display of brutality.

They heard shouts from where the officers were walking back through the trees. Oda led them back. He looked at Hayashi with a lack of surprise.

"Hayashi-san, what do you think you're doing?"

"He tried to escape."

Oda gave a look along the line. As he suspected, no one was leaping forward to verify Hayashi's version of events. "Are you going to carry his part of the gun, Hayashi-san?"

Miyashita was keen to move on. Following commands was always the most important part of showing loyalty. The corporal had his orders, the same as everyone else. The five remaining slaves would do the work of six. It was time to leave the road and take up position. His only comment on the dead man was that Hayashi better watch out, in case his victim's spirit followed him through the jungle to haunt him. The corporal laughed hard at his own joke. Hayashi stayed silent.

The last stretch of the journey took them to the edge of tree cover. A clear path for the shells to rain down upon an invader and enough trees to be hidden from a pilot's view. They were near where the Americans would arrive. Japanese artillery didn't fight from the rear; the commanders expected them to dominate the front lines of any battle—to provide intimidating force and cover for an infantry whose entire approach was to fight close and overwhelm with the ferocity of the charge.

They reassembled the gun, and while they sent some men back with the remaining slaves to retrieve more ammunition and supplies, they tasked the others with beginning the process of digging in and establishing areas of patrol. As the sun descended before them, Takeshi offered a prayer to the seven lucky gods to protect him from the enemy and the island spirits.

***

The sun had risen and fallen for just over two months since Takeshi had arrived in his Pacific home. It was *Boshu*, the time for rice planting. Some of the men in his battery had worked in the paddy fields, so there was a good excuse to share out some sake. Takeshi had developed a taste for it, like his Uncle Taro, but the army didn't provide it in the same quantity as a shipyard worker in Sasebo might expect.

As they sat, reminiscing about life back in Japan, Takeshi noted how he had changed. The pain of being uprooted from his hometown had long gone. He had written home twice since he had reached his post, but was still to receive a reply. Letters had even less chance of arriving than troops, given that the waters were being patrolled with American submarines. It was convenient to think of that being the reason; he was sure that his sister wouldn't just forget him.

Life had settled down, with a daily routine of tasks to pass the time. Everyone took their turn of patrol, even though there were no enemies to discover. A rota would decide who traveled back to pick up rations of rice, barley, miso, and green tea. Foraging for fruit helped everyone's health. It was easy to find bananas, mango, gooseberries, and jackfruit. Then, of course, there was always coconut. They shared cigarettes to make them last. Rivers lay southwest of their position, so washing or collecting water for boiling and cooking was possible. The corporal did not grant permission to swim, but the odd patrol would stray as far as the coastline, affording the opportunity for a quick plunge into the sea.

They had constructed a strong shelter that could house most of them. It offered protection from the rain and so far hadn't been battle tested. It smelled bad, so many preferred to sit around the gun that had been silent through the changing season. They would practice firing, but the commanders were reluctant to waste any valuable ammunition. The excitement of the process only lasted thirty minutes before life returned to waiting.

Oda had turned out to be a good person to be stationed with. He passed on his knowledge along with his own sardonic sense of humor. Takeshi felt that Oda would be reliable to fight beside, but he still wouldn't count him as a friend. There was just an overbearing feeling that Oda would protect his own life before anyone else's. You couldn't trust him.

Hayashi was a different person altogether. The stories he shared were about beatings, rape, and treating the locals no better than dogs. He taunted those of his comrades who had maybe come from a better home or family, and he didn't reserve his violent threats for the enemy either. He operated as an attack dog for Corporal Miyashita, handing out the slaps and discipline on the unit leader's behalf. No one wanted to get stuck out on patrol with him, where he had undisputed control, and the freedom to unleash his short temper. In fact, the camp atmosphere always lifted when he wasn't around, and that is why no one had bothered to look for him when he had disappeared during the previous day and hadn't returned for the morning ration.

Corporal Miyashita started wandering around with his field binoculars, trying to pick out his missing gunner.

"He was over at Agana, I'll bet," said Takeshi, "It was Sunday yesterday. His chance to pay his visit to the *club* run by the Kempeitai."

"Even Hayashi wouldn't get to spend the whole day there," said Oda, "He's disappeared before. He comes back in the end. Then you'll all wish he had stayed away, eh?"

The men all joined in silent agreement, but Corporal Miyashita was now pacing up and down more rigorously.

"Maybe he feels unsafe without Hayashi to do his dirty work," said Fuji.

"He's just upset because he can't cross a box on a checklist," replied Takeshi.

All sniggered at the corporal's insistence on recording every detail, but they hushed themselves as he walked back toward them.

"Oda-san, take two men and search north as far as the road that heads for the coast. Two more should head for the river and another two up onto the high path. Search its length before returning."

"Takeshi-san, Fuji-san. I volunteer you," smiled Oda, "If you have time to bayonet a wild pig, then just make sure it's not called Hayashi."

The rest of the unit offered muffled laughter. Corporal Miyashita was too concerned to reprimand anyone, but he could nurse his displeasure until later when his enforcer had returned.

Takeshi and Fuji split out to the left and right of Oda as they kept each other just in sight. The way forward wasn't clear. Razor grass and thorn-filled branches scratched and attached themselves to clothing. The ground was uneven, with patches of rock and mud mingling. Tusk marks at the bases of trees showed where the wild boar had passed through. It was another danger to watch out for, especially if there were young present. Calling Hayashi's name out was as much for warning off the animals as it was for finding the missing soldier.

Two more hours passed before Oda stumbled on Hayashi's body. Trapped amongst undergrowth, his eyes were open; fear had contorted his mouth into the shape of a last scream. A spider ran across his chest as Oda used his bayonet to clear the creeping plant life away. Hayashi's exposed skin had erupted into large boils and blisters. His arms and hands looked like they had suffered scratches and bites. Yellow and brown marks appeared like old bruises.

It horrified Takeshi and Fuji as they arrived beside Oda.

"What caused that?" asked Fuji.

"An animal?" said Takeshi.

The trees reacted with a powerful breath of wind blowing through the branches. Glimpses of something moving through the undergrowth caused the men to raise their rifles and fire off a volley of shots, but there was no apparent target. It was fear that aimed the weapons and instinct that pulled the triggers.

"Fuji-san, fetch Corporal Miyashita and bring him here. He'll need to arrange for the body to be picked up."

"Shouldn't we carry him back?" asked Takeshi.

"I'm not touching it. I've seen this before. It's like a disease that only Japanese can catch. The CHamoru don't suffer from it like us. They can come and pick him up. We'll guard him until you return Fuji-san, go now.

Oda pulled out a cigarette and turned his back. Takeshi suspected that he knew more. He observed the deliberate silence that followed. It was better to offer prayer than ask more questions. He bowed his head and whispered a few words to wish Hayashi's spirit on its way.

Chapter 6
The Storm-Filled Sky

After almost four months of waiting, cleaning, mending, and cooking, war was arriving. A set of binoculars passed around each member of the gun position unveiled the first American warships sailing in the direction of Orote.

Corporal Miyashita took the time to remind everybody what it meant to be a samurai. An eternal allegiance to the Emperor and an unconditional acceptance of the code of Bushido. This was the day that all had been waiting for. To Corporal Miyashita, at least, this seemed to be the opportunity to be remembered. To take his place with the heroes that had given everything for Japan.

The talk seemed to work. The men cleaned and checked the gun again, as was befitting its status as a shrine. The gun was the whole reason this small group of men were together.

They had all had different lives, careers, and loves. Now they shared the same tiny space for the sole purpose of firing the gun and killing the enemy.

They completed the tasks with typical speed and efficiency, and then all of a sudden it was back to waiting; smoking, tea drinking, and gazing through binoculars. The excitement was starting to wane when the opening salvos boomed across the sky. Distant, muffled explosions followed. Puffs of smoke began to rise into the air. Sirens all along the coastline alerted those who hadn't witnessed the approaching danger.

The shelling lasted for thirty minutes before the ships sailed out of view, making for Agana. In that time, more vessels had taken their place on the horizon. The defenders scrambled planes in response. Machine-gun fire spat out across the sky, spraying over the decks of the warships, but no fire or explosions followed. The Americans were stubbornly refusing to suffer any meaningful casualties on the first wave of attack.

Takeshi's battery might as well have been watching the scene play out on a movie screen. The barrage was falling somewhere else, miles away to the north. The anticipation was all based on what would follow. How long would it be before they were facing an invading army?

"Will they fire at us?" Takeshi asked.

"They'll want to clear the beaches. Start a few fires in the trees," replied Oda, "They can't see us any better than anyone else. If we fired back, then we might attract attention."

"They won't destroy us by fighting from ships," said Corporal Miyashita. "They'll still have to face us on the ground. Our bayonets will pin them to the beaches. They can set explosions amongst us, but they'll still have to meet us in the charge."

"So we wait some more," continued Oda, "that's army life, my friend. We wait, we move, then we wait some more, and then..."

"Then? Oda-san?"

"Then everything happens fast. All the waiting ends, and we rush headlong into victory. Then they move us on, and the waiting starts again."

"I feel excited about the battle," Takeshi replied.

A murmur of agreement, smiles, and nods, passed around the unit. The sound of artillery fire began again, rumbling off into the distance like thunder passing overhead. Too far away to make you feel that lightning would strike.

***

A week had passed, and Agat had come under fire as well. The shells were falling closer now. Acrid smoke blew across the coastal hills, both below and behind the units of the 38th Mountain Artillery. Yet their own guns remained silent. The commanders were aware of limited ammunition stocks and had not ordered a response.

Takeshi was becoming used to the explosions. After a while, it was just background noise. No one flinched unless the shell fell close enough for you to see the flame erupting from its impact. As he made his way through the trees on his turn to pick up more rations, he was careful about his movement, but he was hungry as well.

I'm more likely to die from starvation.

The supply depot was further inland. It was a mass of activity, far away from the prying eyes of the seaborne enemy. Trucks and other vehicles ferried troops and cargo back and forth. Men gathered to share cigarettes and exchange the gossip of what was going on. Stories of places and people hit by the blasts dominated all the conversations.

Takeshi stood in line, waiting for his turn. Supplies were meager at the best of times, but since the start of the American attack, a siege mentality had begun to develop amongst those in charge of the island. Takeshi just stared back at the private who had handed him a small pack of rice and a little pack of salt.

"It's not just for me. I've to pick up rations for ten."

The private smiled. "Funny guy, eh? You think you're the only person to say that to me today. I have my orders, and that is your ration. If you want more, then find Sergeant Abe, he's looking for volunteers to help him make requisitions from a farm."

"Requisitions?"

"Do you like pork?"

"I love pork, who doesn't?"

"Then find Sergeant Abe. He's on a hunt for a pig."

Takeshi walked back outside with his poor offering of rice. His comrades would not be happy if that's all he came back with, and picking fruit would take too long. The shelling had stopped again. Sergeant Abe was a few feet away, still looking for one more soldier to join him. Corporal Miyashita might be unhappy for him taking so long to return, but then again, if he came back with pork...

"Gunso Abe-san?"

The sergeant looked over and in an instant was looking Takeshi up and down, as if deciding his worth based on appearance alone.

"I heard you were looking for volunteers to go looking for a pig."

Sergeant Abe laughed in a deep baritone voice. "Yes, we are hunting for pigs, dogs, anything that can feed us," he gazed at Takeshi's uniform badge, "You are artillery? How is life in your bird's nest? No one has heard you squawk yet."

"We are awaiting our commands, Gunso Abe-san."

"Yes. I think you have time to join us. The farm is a little walk further south. We'll be there and back in just an hour or so. You can tell your officer there was a long queue for rations. Who's heading your unit?"

"Gocho Miyashita, Gunso Abe-san."

"Gocho Miyashita!" he laughed before pretending to mark a checklist in front of the other men, "As long as he can tick a box about your brave efforts to feed your unit, he will be okay with me taking temporary charge of you."

Takeshi completed the group of four men, plus the sergeant. Once out of sight of the supply base, their marching style transformed into a casual trek across the undulating landscape. Their mood was bright and hopeful of what lay ahead. Takeshi noticed that all the men were thin; uniforms looked begged and borrowed. It was common for little to be left for the dead to be buried with. Recycling, trading, and selling were just business between the troops. A better pair of shoes, or trousers, would always fetch a price.

Takeshi stuck out for that reason alone. His new uniform and more youthful appearance marked him out as a new boy. As they continued down through gaps in the rocks and trees toward cultivated land, the questions kept coming in his direction.

"Takeshi-san. You know what we expect of you today?" said Sergeant Abe.

"What do you mean?"

"This is special operations, you understand? We do this to make sure we are fit to serve the Emperor. It is important for an army to forage and take what it needs, every now and again."

"The farmer will give us a pig, right?"

"We will take a pig if he has one."

"And if he hasn't."

"We'll take something else. We're very reasonable with the locals."

Takeshi had an instant sense of foreboding. He scolded himself for being naïve. He frowned as he thought about what the war had forced people to become. He thought of his younger cousin, Kenichi, and how much he wanted to join up, but he was sure he wouldn't want to sign up for this.

They reached the farmhouse and looked around the outside of the building. Two of the soldiers made straight for chickens penned off by a fence. The noise of their farcical attempts to grab hold of a bird brought the farmer out of the door, his wife and son behind him.

"Please Sergeant, stop your men. These hens are for eggs."

Sergeant Abe strode over and without a word, he struck the farmer in the face with a heavy punch, knocking him to the ground and kicking him in the side of the ribs. The farmer yelled out in pain.

"Please, stop. We have chicken already cleaned and ready for the stove. Please let us help you."

"Pick him up," ordered Abe.

Takeshi and one of the other soldiers helped to pick the farmer up, while Sergeant Abe had already pushed past into the house. The two others continued looking around for what they could steal among the vegetables, wheat, and spices that were stored and hidden from view.

Enraged by the assault, the farmer's son launched himself at Sergeant Abe's back. Takeshi responded in an instant, crushing his rifle butt into the back of the young man's head. Takeshi yelled as the boy crashed face down in the dirt.

"Who do you think you are? You are nothing," he prodded his bayonet in between the shoulder blades of the islander. The point caused the farmer's son to cry out in anguish as it pierced a layer of skin.

"You should die. Die! Why shouldn't I kill you?"

Takeshi couldn't quite believe his own words, but they had trained him to be this way.

The mother screamed for mercy for her boy. The father sat beside her, hurt and unable to fight back. All the while there were sounds of furniture and other parts of the house being dismantled and broken apart, as the search went on for anything of worth.

The scream of a young female voice suggested that Sergeant Abe had found what he wanted. He slammed the front door shut, leaving Takeshi and the other men to wait for him. The mother's screams intensified as her daughter's desperate cries filled the air. As she tried to battle her way through the door, the soldiers flung her onto the ground—a boot on her back and a rifle pointed at her head. She cried floods of tears, with an emotional plea for mercy from those who were behaving without remorse. The noise stopped from inside the house.

"Hey, I hope I get a turn," said one of the men.

"If she's still alive," said another, "Takeshi, you could have an enjoyable time with mother here."

The other soldiers laughed. Takeshi looked away, down the line of his rifle, where the bayonet rested among a small pool of blood. The farmer's son was about the same age as him. He wondered if their sisters were the same age. The thought filled him with horror. He wanted to be dead in that moment, but if he couldn't die, then he wanted to kill. To avoid the shame of any surviving this moment that could bear witness to his involvement. He pressed the bayonet harder on the son's back as an uncomfortable rage took over.

"Takeshi-san, let him go."

Sergeant Abe had returned, tightening the belt around his waist, as if to make a statement about his power. He allowed the mother through into the house to stop her wailing from annoying him. Another punch to the jaw of the farmer knocked a tooth from his mouth, for no other reason than Sergeant Abe felt like it. He screamed into the man's face, warning him what would happen if he tried to report their visit.

The farmer's son got to his feet, the gash on his back causing him to groan. Even so, he soon found himself tasked with helping to bag up the stolen food, and then carrying the greater part of it on his shoulders as the party made their way back with the supplies.

Sergeant Abe expected Takeshi to continue motivating the prisoner with the sharp point of the blade. The others exchanged conversation, and Sergeant Abe's voice boomed out with pride in himself. His actions of bringing food back to his own troops would increase their admiration for him. He was a good man for thinking about how to best feed his fellow soldiers. Some would call him noble for his selfless acts of care.

Takeshi kept quieter than the others. His all-consuming anger built with every step forward. He wanted the farmer's son to go, to run away and be out of his life. For their paths to never cross again. He told himself he would try to miss his shot if the unfortunate wretch would only make a break for freedom. Takeshi's frustration only made him more intimidating. When they reached the edge of a jungle trail, he had done such a good job that Sergeant Abe decided to bestow an honor on him.

"Kill him."

Takeshi hesitated for a split second, in which time Sergeant Abe took the rifle out of his hands and shot the farmer's son in the head.

"Don't wait, Takeshi. When the American is in front of you, waiting is the worst thing you can do. If you can't use your bayonet, then use a bullet, but never, ever wait, because then you will die instead. Am I right, men?"

The others agreed and nodded. They then set about splitting up the rewards for the day. A small sack of food and spices became Takeshi's share. Half a chicken, and some sugar.

"Sorry there was no pig," said Sergeant Abe, "You did well with us today, maybe you can come out with us again. You could almost make an infantryman, rather than a bird in the trees."

"He'll need to learn to shoot faster," quipped one of the others. They laughed as they parted, bowing and waving like old friends.

Takeshi walked as fast as he could, back to the road that climbed toward his gun position. When he knew he was alone, he stopped at the roadside to vomit. Tears flowed from his eyes. His self-loathing made him think about ending it all. A grenade held against the heart was the standard method for lowly troops.

"Takeshi-san?" Fuji's voice brought Takeshi back to reality, "Where were you? Miyashita-san is going crazy. He thinks the ghost who got Hayashi has come back for you."

Takeshi sighed and dried his eyes. "I ended up going to a farmhouse with some others. The rations they're handing out are nothing. I just wanted to help everyone eat. We'll be dead of starvation before the Americans ever get here."

Fuji searched through the sack of supplies. "Wow, Takeshi! It will thrill everyone. Look at everything you've brought back. Is that chicken? Where did you get it? Tell me everything."

There was no way that Takeshi was ever going to tell him. Fuji put the tears down to nothing more than exhaustion and hunger. He felt that Takeshi was only expressing the deep relief of being able to help his brothers.

They sat around a small fire, hastily arranged to cook the small chicken half before the sun went down. Everyone enjoyed the flavors of the meal. Everyone except Takeshi.

***

In the days that followed, the first bombs started to fall on the island. The battleship barrages increased. Fire raged across the palms lining the coast and the jungle areas around the hills. News had broken through about the last brave charge of Japanese warriors in Saipan. The American troops would soon attempt a landing, that much was certain.

The waiting for Takeshi's unit was still stretching out over the long days of relentless shelling. The deafening blasts were dulling the senses; only adrenaline and fear of being under the next bomb kept all ready for action. The cramped conditions in the shelter didn't help. They realized too late that they should have built something to accommodate everyone. They felt packed together like cattle for the slaughter. No one had been able to wash, and the temperature was warm. The rising sun was out there, somewhere above the thick shroud of an island, drowning under the constant rain of cannon shells.

"Takeshi-san, remember our first day in training. When they lined us up and told us we must learn to take a punch. Then they hit us all in the face."

"I remember. How could I forget?"

"I would let them do that to me every day now if I could just go back home."

"What are you talking about, Fuji? I can punch you if it makes you feel better," Oda remarked.

The men huddled together, sharing in the joke.

"You know what I mean," replied Fuji.

"This will end soon," Corporal Miyashita sounded confident, "If they bomb the island much more, then it will just sink, and be of no use to anyone. Even Americans aren't that stupid."

"Good, then we'll get our chance," Oda agreed.

The surrounding ground shook. The explosions had been creeping closer to their position. Shells had already hit some of the other units in the battery. If the enemy destroyed the gun, you went one of two ways. The best marksmen would find themselves dug into a rifle pit near the beach, others would end up in a labor unit.

"I pray to the gods each night," said Miyashita, "that our gun will fire in anger. That our time here will end with American deaths."

Takeshi noted that Corporal Miyashita didn't say *victory*, he chose his words well. Another shell landed close to their position. Oda peered out at the gun. Their shrine was still in place. Fire hadn't caught the branches that covered it. For the moment, Miyashita's prayers were still working.

The day passed. The warships would move and launch attacks on different parts of the island, the planes would focus their attacks on buildings rather than nature. It had been days since anything flown by a Japanese pilot had crossed the sky.

The noise and the smoke cleared away from the immediate area. All left the shelter to just stretch out and breathe air that wasn't doused in the stale scent of an unwashed group of men. Cigarettes were lit, but covered. No light could escape. No clue of their existence, and that meant no food either. Takeshi had provided them with the last good meal they had eaten. They had asked him to go again, but he claimed he never saw Sergeant Abe after that day.

He would have ended up the same way as Hayashi.

Takeshi and Kenji shared a cigarette. They could catch glimpses of ships between the shifting clouds. From where they stood, entire areas lay scorched and smoldering. Planes circled and made their way back to carriers further out at sea.

In the background, a lone voice in the shelter hummed a melody that they all knew.

"Is that Oda-san?" Takeshi smiled.

Oda's low voice sang out. "We are the Imperial Army, and our enemies are our Emperor's enemies…"

"Battotai!" laughed Fuji.

As the song went on, each man began to join in with the words, defiant against the military might that surrounded them. All released their frustration by singing the popular patriotic song. Everyone was together by the chorus. "...Until our enemy is destroyed, march on, forward, as one."

The volume increased and in the distance, another unit was singing back. They sacrificed the tune for a final exclamation from those taking part. "We must go forward, prepared for death!"

As laughter and cheering erupted, the engines of a plane roared toward them. The whistle of two bombs increased in pitch as they descended. The unit scrambled for cover. Takeshi turned to follow and found himself lifted into the air. His eyes filled with light, his ears ringing in pain from the explosive blast. A short intense heat, then darkness.

Takeshi's eyes opened. A smell of ammonia caused him to shake himself and sit up. He had avoided serious injury, just pain and aching from being cast aside by the blast. He was alive, at least. He looked around himself for anyone else that might have survived. The gun had taken a direct hit, the second bomb had smashed into the middle of the fleeing soldiers.

Takeshi sunk to his knees again, as Fuji lay dead before him on the ground. Covered in marks from the blast, half of his skin removed from his head.

"Takeshi!"

"Oda?"

"Come and help me. I'm losing blood. My leg."

Takeshi moved as fast as he could. The force had thrown Oda against a tree, impaled against a branch that had penetrated his thigh. The blood was rushing out of the wound. Takeshi looked around for something to stop the bleeding but Oda was breathing hard with his life slipping away.

"Are there others?"

Takeshi looked around himself, and back towards Oda. He shook his head.

"Take at least one life for me Takeshi-san. Make our Emperor proud, make me proud."

Those were his last words as he slumped into death. Takeshi knew he had to get away. Another strike in the same spot was possible. He had to make it to another unit. He lifted his rifle and set off into the cover of trees, heading back toward the high road.

As he fought his way through in the darkness, it was as if the trees were moving around him. Disoriented and in the half light of burning timber, it looked like the jungle was alive with bodies moving in and around the boughs and branches of the trees. He was sure he saw faces peering out from amongst the leaves, and it felt like they were closing in on him. The jungle was following every move that he made, every twist and turn as he ran for the road.

His breathing was heavy, his legs were struggling to keep him upright, and his heart was thumping against his chest. Branches scraped at him as he pushed his way through the tangled vegetation. Thorns ran like sharpened nails across his face and neck.

Then voices, growing in number. He couldn't tell where they were, but as he stumbled on, he began to make out the familiar bark of a Japanese officer shouting at him to slow down and stop.

Takeshi halted and prepared for the jungle to take him, but it was the hands of two other artillery men that reached out. They lowered him on to the ground and started to check for any wounds.

"Yoshida Takeshi-san?"

"Yes," was all Takeshi could say.

"Were you all hit?"

"Yes."

The two soldiers talked, and the officer arrived on the scene. He could hear them speaking to one another, but it was fading into the background. Drowned out by a memory of the last anguished cries of his friends.

"Can he walk?" asked the officer.

"Yes Gunso-san," one of the men replied.

"Good. Don't worry," said the officer, "You will be back on duty tomorrow. We'll soon have you back to being a samurai for the Emperor, eh?"

Chapter 7
Road to Manenggon

Takeshi sat on the high road, told to wait for others who, like him, had suffered the American bombing from the night before. Hour by hour, more arrived. He sat, lighting and relighting a cigarette that he would forget to draw on as his mind tumbled with the aftermath of the attack. The smiles on the faces of his comrades before the bombing struck him as a strange contradiction, but then his army training always had an answer. The divine will of the Emperor would always make sure that the soldier would experience elation before the moment of his death.

How else can we face our enemies? The gods give us the strength we need.

A small group started to build up. Twelve other survivors of the attack had joined him at the roadside. The mood was somber. Most had lost friends in the last few hours. A shared sense of bewilderment permeated, but no one cried out or gave in to any sense of defeat. At least for the moment, officers would redeploy them further back from the front. The Japanese army never retreated, they only repositioned for the inevitable charge.

Higher-ranking officers soon appeared to decide on the direction of travel for the survivors. The word went around that they were moving east, to the other side of the island. Without artillery to fire, other roles would need to be found. It might not be what they signed up for, but most felt that the east was the right direction to be walking in, so they didn't complain.

A weary-looking sergeant found himself appointed to lead the men. The soldier never introduced himself. He had been through this process before, leading defeated units back to work in the prison camps. He knew they were just as likely to die from disease as a bullet or a bomb, and didn't want to know anyone's name or what they did before the war. If his temporary troop followed his directions and orders, then that was all he needed. He made it obvious to his superiors that he considered it too dangerous to just march along the main roads, but his motivation to pursue a path that ran between mountains and hills was quite different.

"Have any of you heard of the American, George Tweed?"

A few of the men nodded that they had. Takeshi also knew the name, a fugitive reputed to be hiding on the island. Corporal Miyashita had urged them all to look out for him. In fact, it had become a game on days when they were patrolling familiar paths and the routine bored them. They had never carried out a search for George Tweed in earnest.

The sergeant continued. "As we cross the island, we'll pass through many places where *the dog* might be hiding. Be watchful, there's a fine price on his head for the man that captures him. Also, be aware that he will be desperate; don't stray from the sight of the party. Think of him as a worthy opponent and keep yourself ready to strike. Now follow me."

The sergeant began his walk at a brisk pace. Takeshi rushed to gather his rifle and fall into line. The first part of the route he knew well, but they soon descended into deeper cover. The explosions began again. The ships and planes were increasing the frequency of their attacks. Although most of the shelling and bombing was happening far behind them, there was still enough activity in the air to make them nervous about revealing where they were. The Curtiss Helldivers often lived up to their name, spreading fire and destruction wherever they flew.

Walking where there was little cover encouraged an increase in speed, while undercover there was the constant obstacle of packed trees. Dense and low branches slowed and obscured the way forward.

The sergeant led on in silence; he had come equipped with a *nata* axe, for hacking and cutting a route forward. The trails could change with weather—or bombing. He knew the area enough to not lose his sense of direction, even if he had to cut a fresh trail.

The sound of engines hummed away in the distance. As Takeshi gazed up to his right, Mount Lamlam rose above the other hill summits. The planes would be on the other side, dive bombing anything that was man made.

"I think the Americans want to flatten everything for their tanks," said the soldier following Takeshi in the line, "Did they hit your position last night?"

"Yes," replied Takeshi, "we were in the trees just off the high road, looking over Agat—and you?"

"I was further down from you, at Ga'an Point. It is hell down there. They never trained us to fight this kind of battle. For every shell we fired on a plane, a thousand would drop in revenge. It surprised me we lasted so long before we took a hit. They had made plenty of attempts."

"I could see it from where we were. We watched it from the first bombardment. We often talked about those stationed along the coast. We wondered if any of you were alive."

"Well, I'm here, but many have died. Our commanders just send others to replace the fallen. When did you arrive here?"

"A few months ago on the Aki Maru."

"So you'll remember the coastline when it was still beautiful. You would have felt you were on a pleasant holiday and asked why are the army putting me here?"

"Yes," Takeshi smiled.

"It doesn't look like that anymore. All the way from Agat to Agana, I don't think there's a single palm tree left, never mind buildings and houses. It is a wasteland now. Only the Japanese army would come here on holiday now, eh?"

A silence fell again, as both men displayed expressions that showed they were considering their thoughts. As he walked on through the narrow trails, Takeshi's mind strayed back to the previous evening, to his escape through the trees. He couldn't shake off the feeling that someone or something followed him. He could have stumbled like Hayashi had done. It was easy to stumble or lose your footing in the dark. His mind had been a blur. Had he seen figures surrounding him? Did they help him, or did they want him dead? The hairs on his neck stood on end at the very thought.

The sergeant led them on without encouragement. You followed wherever he went; it was as simple as that. He stuck to a trail that offered them some protection by following along the line of hills that separated them from the coast. A change of direction followed onto more open land. They began to head toward the east coast. The distant shelling was increasing in ferocity as the day wore on, but it was safer on this part of the island. All remained focused on the way ahead, trusting that the sergeant knew the best way to go.

The ocean began to dominate the view once more. Takeshi's heart sank as he spotted ships of the American fleet patrolling around the island. They were under siege. He had stopped asking himself when their own submarines, ships, and planes would return. No convoy had followed beyond his arrival. If it was true about Saipan falling, then there weren't likely to be others. He cursed the navy under his breath. The rivalry with the army had been a fundamental part of training.

"What was that you said?" The man placed a hand on Takeshi's shoulder, pulling him back.

"Nothing. I said nothing."

"You cursed the IJN. I heard you."

"What are you saying? You're hearing things," Takeshi lied, "The shelling has blocked your ears!"

"Quiet!" shouted the sergeant as he halted the march, "What's going on?"

"He cursed the navy, Gunso-san. He said we were weak. Who is he to talk to me that way?"

"Stop complaining. You are all weak. That's why you're here. You didn't die for the Emperor. None of us are better or worse than the other. We all carry the same dishonor. Where you are going, you will never be proud of being Japanese again. Just always remember you are Japanese. You can never sink as low as our enemies.

"I've listened to so many talking about the hell of war. You are going to be in hell, and your only way out is to follow orders and carry out the divine will of the Emperor. You do not want to attract attention from officers when you are already in such an unfavorable place. Your families back home will never want to hear about your war now. It is better that they have already set up your memorial back home. Your ashes in a box will be the only way you will return now.

"You two. Neither of you look stupid. Make sure you only have one enemy on this island and if you are angry, take it out on them. Beat them, burn them, shoot them. I don't care, but we Japanese cannot turn on one another. The days of the clans are over. Japan fights against the entire world as one force. That is the only way we win."

Takeshi nodded, acknowledging his error. The other man also accepted. They would never be friends, but they understood the lesson, that they should never be enemies.

"I think we need to cool off," said the sergeant, "follow me."

The line formed up and once again found themselves on a covered path. The bombs hadn't reached this area. It was tranquil and pleasant. The rushing water showed the way forward, a flowing river descending from the hills that bubbled over small waterfalls on its journey through lush green jungle. Orchids painted themselves across the gold, bronze, and emerald of the foliage. It was a paradise the worst effects of man had left untouched. A miniature part of the world that war hadn't reached.

As they walked on, the sights became more impressive, larger falls that frothed and twisted into pools, carved out over thousands of years. They reached a point at the foot where multiple showers cascaded into a deep depression in the riverbed, a plunge pool.

The sergeant stopped in his tracks and began taking off his uniform. "This is going to be your last chance of a good clean wash for a while. Get in and freshen yourselves. It's not a hot spring, but it will help you after what you've been through on the last day."

The men didn't need a second thought. Each one rushed to undress and race under the showers that nature provided. Takeshi felt human for the first time in a long while. The water pounded against his skin. It was a massage to relieve every aching muscle, and for a brief moment a feeling of childhood returned. He began to laugh, and the sentiment soon spread. For around twenty minutes, the sergeant allowed all to wallow in the river and the pool. Water splashed and got thrown over everyone. Tired bodies stretched out under the heat. The bombs still fell in the background, but they could be a thousand miles away in that moment.

No one complained when the time was over. They all appreciated what the sergeant had done in bringing them to such a beautiful place. Takeshi understood the improved results that an excellent teacher could make in a class, or even now the role of an outstanding officer. Within a few minutes, he had changed the tension and rage into friendship and camaraderie. Everyone was eager to reach their destination after the refreshing break.

The sergeant gathered them together before leaving the idyllic spot. "Now we head for the village of Inarajan. You'll go on transport the rest of the way, and the Taicho will choose your new jobs. You're going to be at Manenggon Camp. Take a memory of this place with you, you'll need it."

*****

The sergeant ordered the men into a last march as they entered the village. His job was to deliver his troops to the waiting vehicle. He liked to do his best and give the impression that he performed his duties well. This meant covering the last stretch like a military parade. The sergeant improvised his part well by suddenly beginning to yell at the men. Takeshi and the others responded instantly, as if they had never left the training camp.

The personnel carrier was already waiting where they came to an abrupt stop. The driver got out of the cabin when he saw the group marching toward him.

"I have the men for Manenggon," said the sergeant.

"Yes, Gunso-san," the driver bowed, "they have changed the orders. There is trouble with the CHamoru further down the road. They've ordered us to give support to the *Kaikontai* before we go to the camp.

"What kind of trouble?"

"They're executing Father Duenas and two others. The locals are upset."

"Everybody on board," called out the sergeant, "The army doesn't like to have you sitting idle for too long."

The driver sped off along the coast road, his eyes only occasionally on the road as he flicked between checking ahead and checking the sky for spotter planes.

Takeshi also watched the landscape pass by, and sat in silence as the others discussed the Catholic priest who represented the CHamoru. There had been many rumors that he knew where George Tweed was hiding. The Kempeitai had been determined to prove that he was involved with harboring an enemy. It seemed they had made their move.

As they drove on, the first sight of Manenggon Camp lurched into view. It snaked itself around the banks of the Ylig river. There were no fences or gates to keep the people imprisoned. Just a series of covered shelters that spread out in the surrounding jungle. It was fear of the guards and what they would do that kept the prison population in place.

The last twenty-four hours had exhausted Takeshi, but Manenggon made his heart sink even lower. He knew the Japanese treatment of prisoners was harsh and unforgiving, and even passing by the camp, he could already sense the atmosphere of cruelty and despair reaching out.

They carried on moving north, past the farms where much of the island's food was now being produced. The Japanese army had created the *Kaikontai* specifically to oversee the enforced hard labor of the CHamoru people. They had their own reputation for a strict regime intended to bolster the supplies of rice for the army. Long hours and tough punishment beatings were the usual means of achieving results.

The driver turned his vehicle into the Kaikontai field station at Ta'i. The chosen location for the last hours of the three men jointly accused of protecting George Tweed.

They arrived to the noise of sobbing and anguished cries. Despondency echoed out from the center of the gathered crowd. The Japanese quashed the rising protests in an instant. An all too familiar routine of short warnings followed by long beatings played out before the judgement proceeded.

The sergeant ordered his men off of the transport, and walked them directly into the crush, pushing aside the locals as if they were nothing. Each soldier carved his own path ahead, before forming into a guard line with an unobscured view of proceedings.

Takeshi sucked in a quick gasp of air at the sight that met him. Father Dueñas kneeled before the crowd, broken and beaten, exhausted and unable to move. His restraints only allowed him to fix his gaze on the pit that had been dug to receive his body when he fell.

Two others, who also stared towards their graves, flanked him on either side. Behind each of the three men stood an officer with Katana drawn. The drama that was about to play out was a tragedy. Takeshi wanted to look away, but he couldn't. It was his duty to watch. A ring of soldiers surrounded the scene of the looming execution.

The officer in charge checked the paperwork. He read out details of charges to justify the killing. Jostling came from behind as the islanders tried to protest. The army enforced a vicious response, with many locals dragged away to serve their own punishment. The disruption ended with a shot from a rifle, fired into the air. A grim silence followed.

The officer read out his charge sheet. He delivered a notice of authority. A brief statement detailing the crimes of offering aid and support to an enemy. There was no evidence, no confession, but there was also no presumption of innocence. The three men could only hope to avoid beheading with information that would lead to the arrest of George Tweed. The officer made another offer for them to speak.

The scene paused for an agonizing last few seconds. The priest made no movement. His eyes closed, as he made his peace with God.

A command broke the silence and caused a shudder through the crowd. Everyone's blood ran cold as an executioner moved to stand behind the man to the left of Father Duenas. He raised the Katana above his head, and with a powerful shout, brought the blade down on the victim's neck. He separated the head in a single blow, and it fell to the ground. The swordsman stepped back, and two other soldiers rushed in to push the corpse into the open pit.

The commanding officer nodded his satisfaction and waited for another pause. He asked again of the two surviving men, offering them at least a delay before their end. Again, only silence followed, so he ordered the second execution. This time it was the man to the right of Father Duenas, who didn't waver. Takeshi wondered at how he could remain motionless, feeling his executioner step up behind, hearing the shout that announced the strike was about to happen. He must have felt the brief rush of air before the sharp blade struck, but there was no reaction, no scream of terror. As they rolled his body into the grave in front of him, everything about his life, his childhood, his family, his work. It was all gone in an instant.

The commanding officer paused once more. "Father Duenas," he said, "you have done much on this island to help your people. You have caused us no end of trouble during these past three years. You have survived only because of the understanding that many Japanese also follow your God. I am not one of them. I offer you one last chance. You will save no one else with your silence, not even the American. We will find him in the end, and you will have sacrificed your life for what? You can stop this now. Tell us where George Tweed is hiding. My men will do the rest, and we will spare you the sword."

The silence fell again. Seconds of delay counted down. The distant shelling emphasized that all were facing the end of life.

"Execute him."

In one swift movement. The executioner raised his Katana; he uttered a shout, and the life of Father Duenas was over. The CHamoru islanders couldn't fail to react, but they had no way of intimidating their captors. Disobedience only brought further punishment.

Takeshi turned away from the scene and followed the sergeant, leading them back to the transport. There were comments about the victims, but the talk was about how well the executioners performed. They compared and admired the demonstration of ability. The chatter only ended as the engine shuddered into a start and the wheels began to drive forward. During the last day, Takeshi had witnessed death in so many ways. As he gazed out to sea, he knew the horror of war was only going to get worse.

***

The journey ended back at Manenggon. Tents and newly constructed barracks housed most of the Japanese, while the captive CHamoru lived under simple frames covered with coconut leaves to fend off the worst of the rain.

They drew to a halt before a building guarded by Kempeitai. The sergeant leaped out and returned to his aggressive display of authority, ordering his temporary troop into a line at attention.

"You're a ragged-looking bunch," the sergeant grinned, "but you'll do for this place."

A door opened in front of them. An officer bearing the rank of second lieutenant emerged, followed by a sergeant major, who was shouting even before the door had closed behind him. He gave another order to stand at attention and be ready for inspection.

All stood back with the memories of their first day of getting punched in the face at basic training. The sergeant major looked capable. The commanding officer stood back to allow his enforcer to impress on the new recruits their sense of duty and the importance of the camp commander's authority. Laziness, or any form of insubordination, would see the perpetrator confined in even worse conditions than the prisoners.

"Yes! *Socho-san*," was the mass reply.

The second lieutenant stepped forward. He looked up and down the line. Soldiers that had survived attacks on gun emplacements, rifle pits, cave shelters and artillery positions. Their rough appearance reflected the years of service under challenging conditions. Takeshi still looked younger. His uniform still fit. It made him stand out from the rest.

"Your name?"

"Yoshida Takeshi-san, *Rikugun Shoi-san!*"

"Well, Yoshida-san, you look in good condition for a bomb victim. Maybe you are lucky. We need luck don't we?"

"The Imperial Japanese Army will win through the divine power of the Emperor, Rikugun Shoi-san."

The second lieutenant smiled. He was happy that his men had good training. Understanding divine will meant that Takeshi had paid attention, a good sign.

"You will receive new roles for your time here. If you can help with building construction, mechanical repair, or firing a heavy machine gun, then there will be plenty for you to do over the days and weeks ahead.

"We have selected Manenggon to be the most important camp on the island. Our commanders have given instruction for the island population to be gathered here. We cannot afford any of them to fall into the hands of the Americans. They may come here with what they can carry. We will oversee their march to camp, and we will conscript those who are fit to work into our labor gangs. There is much to do before we face the inevitable, and every man should expect to do his duty."

"Do your duty!" echoed the sergeant major.

"I am Rikugun-Shoi, Kimura. I am known in the camp as the *Taicho*. That is how I prefer to be addressed."

"Yes! Taicho-san!" the men acknowledged.

"The rules of the camp are simple. Our rations are poor; find food where you can. Our medicine is limited; don't get sick. And when the hour comes, be quick with the fist, the boot, the bayonet, and the gun. Always know that the enemy fear us, and we must not let them rest from that condition. That is all; Sergeant Major!"

"Yes, Taicho-san. Now find your barracks!"

At double pace, the sergeant major directed them to a new building. The smell of the timber was still fresh. It wasn't so different from training camp, beds packed, with a single table in the middle for the men to share.

They had just selected their spot for sleeping when another corporal arrived. He introduced himself as Corporal Suzuki. More orders and more inspection followed. He dealt the first slap out to the man who was last to stand by his bed. There was no other reason. The corporal only wanted to show who was boss.

A small and brief familiarization followed with the camp facilities; a place to wash, a place to cook, a schedule of work details, and a nod in the infirmary's direction. Striking for two reasons; the corporal didn't want to go near it, and the sheer number of men that were living there.

"Pray that you don't end up in our hospital. Some kind of disease is wiping out our men. There are thirteen of you arriving today. We lost twenty yesterday. Whatever it is, it ravages your body and marks your skin. After so many days, the patients will become delirious. They talk of seeing ghosts. If it gets to a certain state of madness, then all we can do is shoot them. Do your best not to join them. We don't know the cause, but it seems to like Japanese people. Taicho-san believes there are those who are cursing us. The CHamoru believe in a spirit. We cannot allow them to think that this spirit will save them. If you come across anyone worshipping these demons, then kill them. You have my authority."

PART TWO

Tano I' Man CHamoru
"Land of the CHamoru"

Chapter 8
Shadows of the Past

The first day at Manenggon was coming to a close. Corporal Suzuki had already set tasks for Takeshi and some of the other new arrivals. The day had been light on sleep after the American bombing runs the night before. Exhaustion had made them overtired. Their eyes flickered shut for a few brief moments at a time. They felt colder, and their hands shook, as their energy levels dropped.

Corporal Suzuki didn't care. There was a patrol to organize. A trail that wasn't popular to roam through at night. They always picked the fresh troops for the duty, a policy that kept the rest of the guards loyal. Once you had served your time patrolling the jungle around the Ylig River at night, you would find acceptance by the other guards on camp.

Corporal Suzuki was insistent that Takeshi took part, along with three others. He told his young private that the Taicho had insisted on it.

"You are lucky, the Taicho seems to like you. He believes you will give an honest account of what you see in the jungle. He has asked that you report to him at first light. So you will lead the group."

"Yes, Gocho Suzuki-san."

The corporal laid out a map on the table in the center of their barracks. All the men gathered round to look at the route.

"Follow the river south; it will begin to turn west, keep on the trails that run in parallel. Keep it in sight or you will get lost in the darkness. Once you start to break cover, turn northeast and head for the village of Yona. Just keep to the edge of the tree line, and that will send you in the right direction. You will end up back at the river. Carry on east until you are almost at the sea. You'll then find the main road. Turn back toward the camp at that point. Do not cross the road, stay in the jungle to keep out of sight. Once you have returned, the second patrol will be ready to replace you. Are you all clear about your orders?

"Yes, Gocho Suzuki-san," they all replied.

"Gocho Suzuki-san, may I ask a question," said Takeshi, "what are we looking for?"

"George Tweed for one thing, anyone trying to leave the camp and head back to their ranch, and those who roam the jungle looking for us. I'm sending four of you out. I want four of you to come back. There will be no other patrols out on that trail, so if it moves, then shoot. Is that clear?" the men nodded, "Now grab your rifles, fix bayonets, and get out there."

Takeshi and three others emerged into a pitch black night. A waning moon provided an indicator of direction, but little illumination as they pressed forward on the first part of the trail. For a few moments, the faint outlines of the buildings in the military part of the camp provided reassurance of support. With each step into the darkness, that security faded from view.

Takeshi pushed on. The other men followed in silence. In the distance, sounds from the CHamoru people, imprisoned in camp, floated out over the stillness of the night. People in pain. The old and the infirm. Women carrying unborn children who had been force-marched to camp, and those who had lost loved ones on the way there. Voices that rose in a disjointed choir. A backdrop of desperation that chilled the soul.

Takeshi soon led the group to the river. He was relieved to reach his first goal. The sound of the coursing water settled them all. Takeshi brought his men to a halt as they arrived at the river's edge.

"Is everyone alright?" he whispered.

The men nodded back. They all understood that it was important to remain silent. The thought that George Tweed might spot them was enough to keep all on alert, but with the lack of food and sleep, it was difficult to stay ready. Takeshi signaled with a hand for them all to move on.

After only a short while, they were in thick jungle. The river stayed to their left, odd glimpses of the moon and stars helped them judge their direction, but the jungle wasn't an empty place. Animal, birds, and insects were always on the move. Branches would break, an odd gust of air would blow. Although the men tried to move as quietly as possible, it was imposible to hide their footsteps as they walked through mud and pools of water that were difficult to spot in the darkness.

They made it to the next checkpoint and began to break cover. Takeshi stopped for a brief moment. The others stood still beside him, thankful for the brief rest. The smell of smoke still hung in the air, all across the island. A faint glow on the horizon pointed to the places that were still on fire. Takeshi gazed up at the starlight that had found its way through the clouds. There was something powerful about this place. He could feel his skin break out in goosebumps, a shiver moved through his body, and it felt like a hand placed itself on his shoulder.

He spun around in fright, about to chastise one of the other men for scaring him, but they were nowhere near him. They sat perched on some rocks, hiding the light of a cigarette they were sharing. Takeshi looked around himself. He dropped his bayonet as if to face an enemy, but there was no one there. He gathered the men together once more with the wave of a hand. He looked into the distance where the tree line ran next to more open ground. As they moved forward, he knew his eyes were tired. The jungle seemed to merge into a dark cavern before him. The wind began to blow stronger from his back, and waving branches seemed to point to figures in the distance. Takeshi called a halt to his patrol. He nodded ahead for them all to look in the same direction. They crouched low and pointed their guns, but there was no obvious target. After a few moments, they carried on, still half crouching as they proceeded deeper into the undergrowth. Branches dragged against them and thorns caught on their faces.

Takeshi was beginning to feel that he had lost the trail. He was sure they should have arrived at Yona by now. A scream erupted from just a short distance ahead. It was like the cry of a starving baby. They all froze again. Takeshi could feel his heart thumping against his chest.

"What was that?" said one of the men.

"A fox?" said Takeshi.

"It's *Kitsune*," said another, "the fox spirits."

"We have to be careful," whispered the third man, "Kitsune can bring trouble. We must not anger them."

"We will wait for a moment, be quiet," said Takeshi, "Whatever it is, it may pass and go on its way."

Takeshi didn't believe his own words. He only spoke for the benefit of morale. He had experienced the spirits of the island only the night before. He was certain it wasn't Kitsune or *Yurei*. Something else existed in this place. Something that had led Hayashi to his death, something that had followed Takeshi since the raid on the farmhouse.

"Here, I only have a little left, but we all need it," said one of the others.

He passed around a small flask of alcohol. It tasted rough and caused most of them to choke.

"What is that?" asked Takeshi.

"I don't know," said the soldier, "I bought it in Agana, with some sugar. I got the sugar from a CHamoru, so it didn't cost me anything."

"You raided a farmhouse?" asked Takeshi.

"Doesn't everybody?" replied the man. The others nodded in agreement.

Takeshi felt worse. They had all stolen from the islanders, and who knows what else. There was no doubt in his mind that they had angered some kind of spirit.

After a few minutes, the warmth of the alcohol helped them find some courage. They walked through another short stretch of trail that tunneled below low hanging branches and emerged on the outskirts of Yona. Takeshi signaled for the troop to move east. He was happy to be heading toward the ocean. Maybe it had been growing up in Sasebo, but he had always felt more comfortable next to the water.

One last section of jungle remained before part of the camp would begin to emerge. The mood had lightened. All felt the worst part was over for the night. Takeshi turned around to check on his men, as he did, he spied the shadow of a man running toward them at an incredible speed.

"We're under attack," he shouted as the figure ran through between them, sending one of the men spinning and crashing to the ground. The others dropped to their knees and started firing. The man on the ground started screaming as his body seemed to be dragged away by an invisible force. Takeshi ran over and grabbed hold, and as he did, he felt an electric shock running through his body, sending him backward. As he fell, he reached for his rifle, but a hand seemed to descend on his face, blinding him from his surroundings. He yelled out, and the jungle had returned to normal. Whoever had attacked them had gone. A gust of wind seemed to clear the air.

All four men picked themselves up and ran as fast as they could in the camp's direction. As they reached the spot where the first CHamoru shelters were situated, they could see many of the islanders just standing and staring at them.

They must have heard the rifle shots.

"Get back to your shelters!" Takeshi shouted. He was sure that the locals knew what they had just encountered. Some of them smiled to themselves as they turned their backs and returned to their family groups.

The rest of the patrol was quiet, although they ran most of the way. Soon the base was back in sight. True to his word, Corporal Suzuki had a replacement patrol ready to go. Takeshi and his men walked straight past them without making eye contact. They returned to their barracks with all haste. Not one man spoke of what he had witnessed. Takeshi undressed and threw himself into bed, tucking his head under the blanket as if he was a frightened child. At that moment in time, that's exactly what he was.

***

Takeshi took a few moments to gather himself in the morning light. He had slept, but he hadn't rested. He felt cold again, even though the temperature was already warming up for the day. One side of his face felt tender, under his right eye and below on his jaw.

He dressed and went outside into the compound. With the morning light, the military huts and buildings appeared different from his first impressions. The accommodation was better quality than the CHamoru people had built around the river, but not by much. The rest of the surrounding soldiers looked hungry, and Takeshi shared their discomfort. He had not eaten since leaving his gun position in the hills above Agat. The only taste in his mouth was from the home-made alcohol that he'd taken a sip of only a few hours earlier. Those who had food would hide themselves away to consume it.

We're living like rats. Stealing from our enemies and our own, just to survive.

He walked to the outside of the office building. Corporal Suzuki looked better fed than most. Takeshi assumed correctly that he was also likely to be annoying the spirits of the island.

"You have a report about last night's patrol Yoshida-san?"

"Yes, Gocho Suzuki-san, we came across something, though I'm not sure what."

"That's what everyone says. No one has a name for it."

"One of my men thought it was Kitsune."

The corporal laughed. "The Kitsune is in Japan. Why would they leave our beautiful homeland to be with us here? Go in and see the Taicho, he's interested in these shadows that taunt us."

"Yes, Gocho Suzuki-san. Have you seen it too?"

"I don't know what it is, but this is a terrible place to make a stand. In a few days, once we've brought all the CHamoru, we will end their presence on this island. When they go, I hope their spirit protectors will go with them. We should see the Taicho now."

Corporal Suzuki led the way into a small room. The Taicho sat behind a desk. Hot tea filled an army issued mug to the brim. A small plate of rice with dried fish sat untouched beside him. He looked up from the paperwork strewn in front of him.

"Yoshida Takeshi-san", said the corporal as he stamped his foot then bowed. Takeshi bowed with him, careful to bow lower.

"I heard there was firing from your patrol last night?"

"Yes, Taicho-san. We came under attack to the east of the village at Yona."

The Taicho nodded. It was clear he knew of similar incidents. "Can you describe the attackers?"

"They were like shadows, Taicho-san. I don't know how else to describe them. They could strike us and make us fall to the ground, but they were dark shapes, Taicho-san. We couldn't make out faces or anything else. They ran fast. Faster than any man could run. That is how they could get to us before we fought back.

The Taicho stood up and walked round to stare at the bruising on Takeshi's face. "You have fewer marks than the other man who was with you. He is already in the infirmary. How is the other one Suzuki-san?"

"The swelling has increased on his back and legs. He looks bad and screams as he wakes up from even a few moments of sleep. I wouldn't give him long."

The Taicho shrugged and returned to his seat. He took the time to sip some tea and taste a little of the fish and rice before sitting back.

"We need to solve this problem soon. I'm losing more men than the infantry units on the front line. At least they can charge their attackers. We do not have that luxury. They say they are the spirits of ancestors of the locals.

"In a few days' time, most of the island's population will be here at Manenggon. I do not want to think that all of their ancestors will travel with them. I'd rather face a thousand Americans with my Katana, and not have to fight with a single ghost, who can attack you without fear of their own death."

"Taicho-san," said Takeshi, "we did fire on them, but our bullets never stopped them."

"How do you kill a spirit?"

The Taicho was becoming angry. Takeshi stood to attention and looked ahead. He thought it better to be silent than cause added displeasure with his commanding officer.

"Suzuki-san. Take Yoshida-san and some others into the camp; try to find out anything you can about the jungle near Yona. Use any means you must. Dismissed."

"Yes, Taicho-san," they both replied before exiting the office.

***

"Do not tolerate any disobedience. It is your duty to strike or wound a CHamoru who doesn't answer a question or attempts to show even the smallest form of rebellion. This is my order and so it is an order from the Emperor. The only thing worse than an insolent CHamoru is an insolent Japanese soldier, who should know better. Am I clear?"

"Yes, Gocho Suzuki-san," said the troops in return.

As he followed his corporal into the encampment on the Ylig River, Takeshi still hadn't had food or decent sleep. The day had just started, and he wanted it to end. He'd been told that he wasn't required for the patrol at night, so he knew that at lights out in the barracks, he would at least get some rest.

This time, the troop comprised Corporal Suzuki, Takeshi and four others. They proceeded from the hard standing outside the military compound onto the dirt track that led to the main part of the prison camp. They ordered the CHamoru to keep within their shelters during the day to avoid the gaze of American planes. The inmates stared back at the patrols with eyes that bore a mixture of fear and contempt for their keepers.

Takeshi noticed that women and children, as well as the ageing and the sick, made up most of the inhabitants. He knew they would conscript the healthy men for labor, and he knew what happened to them after the work was over. It was too dangerous to have survivors that could reveal information about gun positions or ammunition storage. They would suffer execution at the completion of their work. They ordered many to dig their own graves first.

The muddy ground extended from the river to the shelters, and many times it ran inside the shelters themselves. As the patrol went past, mothers and grandmothers hugged the children close, stopping them from crying out or drawing attention. All except for one. A young boy ran out into their path, pleading for something to eat. He made the mistake of running toward Corporal Suzuki, who lashed out in response, holding the boy and punching him several times before shoving him onto the ground and sinking the bayonet of his gun into the child's chest. The mother was subdued by others around her in the shelter. All knew that any protest would only result in more death.

Suzuki snarled back at the rest of the boy's family in Japanese. They couldn't understand most of the words he was using, but his intent was plain for all to see. He kicked the child's limp body towards the river's edge before walking on as if nothing had happened.

The brutality horrified Takeshi. He could feel the anger of the jungle rising around all of them, why couldn't Corporal Suzuki? The sun was rising higher, and the bombing and shelling had begun again. As they reached a busier part of the camp, the effects of overcrowding were clear. Everywhere they turned, disease was spreading, and thirst forced people to drink from the same water that they washed with. There were no beds to lie in, only the ground. Any blankets they had were there only to wrap the dead.

The smell was overpowering. Takeshi couldn't hide his distaste for the way the islanders were being kept, but

Corporal Suzuki chose to interpret it as Takeshi sharing his contempt for the prisoners.

"They make me feel unclean too," snapped Suzuki, "Look at them. It was the same in China. They live in their filth rather than die. I know what I would prefer. Always keep a grenade close by, Takeshi. What can be worse than ending up like this? They wallow in the mud like wild pigs. We will have done them a great favor when this all ends."

Takeshi noted that Corporal Suzuki was making no attempt to question the prisoners about the events around Yona. His tour of the camp was only an excuse to unleash his frustration on those who couldn't fight back. After stabbing the young child, he had continued slapping and screaming at any who attracted his attention. If it looked like a family had good food, then he ordered his soldiers to steal from the supplies.

Takeshi became embroiled in the madness when an older woman questioned why he was at war at all. She referred to him as a young boy. Corporal Suzuki yelled at the old woman and then yelled at Takeshi to pay her back for insulting him. Caught in a dilemma requiring him to strike the woman with force but not wanting to strike her where he might end her life, he chose to drop his rifle before he beat and kicked her.

As he picked up his rifle and walked off, he couldn't turn around to check if she got back up. Suzuki seemed satisfied with the retribution, but complained to Takeshi that he would need to use his bayonet more. Maybe the next time.

He set others in his troop the same challenges. In a scant hour of encircling the camp, there had been a killing, an amputation of a hand, faces and bodies beaten out of recognition, and one person knocked into the river and drowned. Once again, Takeshi decided to save face and provide the mercy of a quicker killing. As the victim struggled under the water, Takeshi used the opportunity to bring down his rifle butt hard on the victim's head, ending her life with more haste than the others would have allowed.

He was physically and emotionally exhausted when he made it back to barracks. It was still late morning. There was other work to be done. He had an hour before he was to join the corporal once again. This time they were leaving the camp to head out toward Talofofo. The mission was to visit as many ranches as possible and hand out warnings to the families. They were to move to Manenggon. There was no negotiation.

Takeshi sat at the table, alone. He watched the smoke spiral from his cigarette, following its pattern as it climbed through the air. He rubbed at his face and his forehead. He hadn't looked in a mirror, but he could tell that the bruising on his face was beginning to swell. He had seen the prisoners watching him on his patrol. They knew what had happened to him, of that he was certain. He closed his eyes to escape the emotional pain of the camp, but every time he did so, he would see Yuki staring back at him. She looked frozen and cold in the image in his mind. Her lips tinged blue.

Takeshi smacked the table with his fist and yelled out in rage; like the night before, something trapped him. All his thoughts had turned dark. He had never witnessed so much human suffering. Death was anything but noble. Heaven would never be a certainty for the acts he had committed. He wanted to cry to let the tension out, but he couldn't. The weakness if discovered would bring too much shame, and there was nothing worse than shame to his people.

He finished his tea and extinguished some of the cigarette for later. He rose to his feet and picked up his rifle. His feet felt like lead as he stepped outside to join with the next work detail of the day.

The instruction had come down from the island's Japanese rulers. All CHamoru had to be told to pack up and leave their homes. They would have twenty-four hours from receiving instructions to get out. The CHamoru could take as much as they needed, but any failure to leave by the end of the warning period would call for an instant execution.

Chapter 9
The Death March

The day was becoming warmer and uncomfortable. The clouds of smoke from burning buildings and jungle trees had begun to fill the air again. The pounding of the battleship cannons and the distant fire of airborne machine guns were all reinforcing the urgency amongst the Japanese defenders.

As Takeshi walked through the jungle on his next patrol, he noticed the pressure affecting all the surrounding soldiers. Corporal Suzuki was acting as if he was in a race to complete his orders. Each farm that the patrol visited made him quicker and more organized at giving out instructions to the families they visited.

At first, the violence only happened after some initial resistance, but as he became more experienced dealing with the locals the beatings came first. He would rotate which soldiers carried out the violent assaults to make sure everyone had their turn at handing out cruelty. He seemed to enjoy selecting the easier targets. The fit young men were required for slave labor, so they were less likely to be beaten. The children or older adults, made for more persuasive targets. Threatening daughters reaped better results than threatening sons.

Takeshi could understand the commands from on high. There was a strategy to stopping the Americans from getting access to the locals. They had to be moved to make sure of control, but the methods of implementing the policy were anything but honorable. From the comments of the others patrolling with him, he knew many felt the same way. It didn't change the mantra of always following orders. The order of rank meant that as soon as Corporal Suzuki had achieved even a modest promotion, then his extreme approach could thrive and prosper.

Takeshi noticed how Corporal Suzuki would gather all the family members together in the main room. It wasn't to make issuing orders easier. It was so he could note where objects of value, or food supplies, might be inside the house. Then, each official patrol would lead to an unofficial follow-up to loot anything of use. A nice little black-market business could then sell the stolen goods.

The cold and unfeeling approach to the islanders was having a profound effect on Takeshi. He had always respected his elders, his teachers, and the wise words of those who could share their experiences, but he disrespected Corporal Suzuki with a passion. If anyone was to be killed, he wanted it to be him. For each broken jaw or slashed neck that Takeshi had handed out in the last few hours, his anger grew.

Like the other soldiers, he had to give in to circumstance. He was no more worthy than Corporal Suzuki. He was no better. Corporal Suzuki had avoided touching anyone. He had left himself with a clear conscience that he was only issuing orders based on the orders that he had to follow in turn.

It reduced the people that were threatened to nothing more than hostages being moved as cargo. The families being split up represented an efficient use of resources to aid the war effort. Sons and daughters became commodities. Stolen food became supplies, and in amongst it they reduced the CHamoru people to something less than Japanese, something less than human. Control wouldn't work if you thought any other way.

As the patrol approached the last farm for the day, Corporal Suzuki was happy. He had completed his orders well, and on time. He was ambitious and with the number of sergeants dying off in the infirmary, he was confident that promotion was only one or two more deaths away.

The sky was beginning to darken again. They were nearing the road that led back to camp. They could radio for transport to collect them from there. One more farm, finished early, would be a chance to take a break and share a cigarette and rumors of what was coming soon.

Takeshi had been silent for much of the day. Most of the men had kept quiet. Corporal Suzuki and a couple of his more loyal followers had dominated the conversation. They mixed a dark humor in with the constant justification of their actions. They were heroes, not demons.

As they laughed at the front of the pack, Takeshi experienced a rush of air go past him. Something brushed against his face. He could feel the pain in the bruising that was already there. He shuddered as he saw a dark, formless shape move past him. The branches moved as it sped through, and then a scream of pain called out from the front.

Takeshi and all the rest of the patrol rushed to surround the corporal. His arm was bleeding from below his elbow. It looked like a knife wound, but there was no one nearby. Bloodied razor grass seemed to be the likely cause, with its sharp edges, but as one soldier applied first aid, the corporal ordered the rest to go looking for a potential attacker.

Takeshi and the others stepped deeper into the surrounding trees. The men called out every now and again, but the thought of George Tweed nearby kept the communication to the smallest level.

The trees began to move around Takeshi again. The strain in his eyes caused him to rub the water from them. Each time he did so, something seemed to encircle him, watching him. It moved through the branches like a snake, not like a man. It was quick and he couldn't focus enough to know what it was.

Whatever it was, it had attacked Corporal Suzuki; he knew that much. A further yell came out of the trees, and Takeshi dashed to the source. Another soldier had fallen in the darkness onto rocks by a river bank, his ankle broken because of his accident.

Panic was setting in amongst the men. Two mysterious injuries, minutes apart? It felt like an attack. Corporal Suzuki prioritized his own lack of safety and shouted for his men to return. Takeshi stood guard as two others lifted the soldier with the ankle injury.

"It was a dog," shouted the corporal as they returned, "Look, there are teeth marks."

He held out his arm for all to see. With the first flow of blood cleared away, the men could pick the imprints out.

"We move on to the roadside and radio for a truck to pick us up."

"What about the last farm?" asked one of the others.

"They'll survive for one more day," replied the corporal, "Though if I find out it was their dog, then they won't survive any longer.

Takeshi held back as the others moved toward the edge of the trees. He could feel a powerful force. It was nearby. He was sure it could strike him at any moment. His feet became rooted to the ground, and sweat dripped from his brow. His rifle was ready to fire at anything that moved in the darkness, or so he thought. Dark shapes started to emerge around him. The same shadows from the night before, but more of them. They stepped closer, becoming no clearer. The surrounding darkness was obscuring the jungle from view. Time slowed down for Takeshi. The formless shapes were closing in, edging to within inches. One reached out as if to touch Takeshi's face.

"Takeshi!"

A soldier's voice cut through the air.

"I'm here."

"The truck is coming. Where are you?"

The figures were gone in an instant. The jungle trees were just as before. Everything had returned to normal.

"I was just looking for the dog, I'm on my way."

He turned around and jumped in fear as an old CHamoru woman confronted him, facing him in defiance."

"Na'para" was all she said, before turning and heading into the jungle.

"Takeshi!" came the call again.

"On my way, I'm on my way."

***

The bombing had stopped again. The conversation in the barracks had turned to any form of distraction. All the men were now involved in either guarding or moving prisoners. They had all had their turn of handing out punishments for no good reason. Many could cope, and others may have enjoyed the power, but they kept it out of barrack room conversation.

Some men could sing well, playing cards or other games was popular; they shared tea out with the *kanpan* biscuits that were hard to eat, but popular all the same. Reminiscing about the life they had come from and the girls they had dated, whether it was true. It all helped to spread a sense of calm in amongst the chaos.

A new intake that day had brought some unfamiliar faces to the barracks. Takeshi noticed a soldier sitting alone. He had been watching the various antics and smiling, but his manner was weary. Takeshi felt that the war was taking a toll on him, making him look older than he was.

"Do you have a mug for some tea?" asked Takeshi.

"Yes, I do," the soldier reached into his kit bag and produced the mug. Takeshi took it and poured tea for both of them before returning.

"I am Takeshi, Yoshida Takeshi."

"Hello Takeshi-san. I am Hasegawa Hiroshi."

"Hello Hiroshi-san."

They bowed at one another and sipped some tea. Hiroshi just smiled in response.

"Hiroshi-san, can I ask how you ended up in this place? We're all just survivors of our original units."

"I was near the airfield at Orote, or what's left of it. I've forgotten what a Zero looks like in one piece. The American planes swarm everywhere."

"Hellcats?"

"Hellcats, Helldivers, B-14's. Orote was a big target. The commanders thought we would be okay. We had bayonets, right? Cigarette?"

"Yes, thank you," Takeshi accepted the cigarette and the light, "I was in the hills above Agat. We were there for the American tanks, but we never fired a single shot.

"Agat?"

"Yes, just near the high road."

"Then you'll have seen the spirits that walk on this island."

"Excuse me?"

"If you hadn't seen them, you would have asked me, what spirits?" Hiroshi paused and lowered his voice, "It's alright, I've seen them too; you're not going mad."

"Not just in Agat, they are around here, too," confirmed Takeshi.

"That would make sense, they are everywhere on this island. The CHamoru say that they will help you, but you have to be careful not to offend them."

"What do you do to offend them?"

"Oh, most things that we Japanese do. I can see they have touched you on the face."

Takeshi had forgotten about his bruising, the pain had disappeared since he had returned from his last patrol. As he reached up with his hand, he could feel that the swelling had gone down.

"It seems to have got better today."

"Better? I've seen terrible marks and blisters erupting on the skin after they attack someone. The CHamoru call them Taotaomo'na. Many soldiers are terrified, and lose their nerve to fight after encountering them."

"I've heard that word before."

"The CHamoru are aware of them all the time. They pay their respects before stepping into a place where the spirits are present. To you or me, or any other Japanese, we're just walking from one part of the jungle to another. We don't know where we need to ask permission, so it guarantees we cause offense."

"I saw them tonight, as we finished our patrol. I was alone for just a few seconds. They gathered around me. As close as you are now."

"Then I'll need to make sure I'm on your patrols from now on. You're lucky."

"When did you see them?"

"Most places I'm afraid to say, but if I'm honest, they have left me alone as well. Others I have known were not so lucky. I know that the infirmary here is full of men that have fallen to them. They think it's a disease. It's nothing like a disease. It's not just the injuries. Things go wrong, equipment fails, people have *accidents*."

"Two of our patrol had *accidents* tonight."

"Then cheer up Takeshi-san. It sounds like they like you."

Hiroshi clashed mugs and finished his tea.

"Talk to the CHamoru people when you can. We shouldn't be here, Takeshi. I think you know that, as well as me. Time for lights out. I'm sure it will be another busy day tomorrow, waiting on the Americans arriving with their C-rations. I could do with a good meal before the last charge."

Hiroshi smiled, patting Takeshi on the shoulder as he rose and walked outside to the compound. The room had quieted around him. Some of the other men had already gone to bed, stealing a final few minutes to write part of a letter that would never leave the island, never mind arrive home.

He had eaten a small bowl of rice and some breadfruit that was stolen from a prisoner, but his stomach still ached as he undressed and climbed into bed. He thought of home, his house in Sasebo. Not his Uncle Taro's house but his own, with his mother and father, and Yuki taking her first steps, bringing everyone joy as they watched.

He turned to his side to hide the tear that rolled onto the pillow. He promised himself that he would see Japan again. That he would return home as a hero. People would wave flags in celebration of their glorious victory. There would be parties and rejoicing.

He sighed as the feeling of isolation returned. He prayed and closed his eyes.

***

Takeshi stood at the top of a hill, and the sky was clearer than he could ever remember. The heavens sparkled above him and a shooting star crossed the sky. The island was calm and the ships out at sea were silent. He looked around.

How did I get here?

He was alone, with no sign of a patrol. The sound of an animal eating nearby made him start to descend below the summit. All was in darkness, but he could see what was around him. He took a few more steps and the sound of grazing stopped. A deer stood looking back at Takeshi. Its eyes seemed to look deep within his soul. It drew his scent from the air.

Takeshi couldn't believe that the deer was letting him stand so close. He started to walk toward it, reaching to touch its back, when it charged at him, knocking him to the ground. He tumbled over and over as he rolled down the hillside. A vision of the world rotated around him until he came to a stop. When he stood up, he was perching on the edge of a waterfall. It dropped from a great height, where the river stretched out ahead of him, cutting through the jungle.

A way forward or a way out?

It tempted him to jump, but he sensed a great danger if he fell. He looked around for a way to climb down; there seemed to be convenient places to place his feet and hands. He felt relaxed as he began his descent. The first few steps were easy, but then the water started to fall with more force. The rock under his hands and feet became harder to hold on to. He started to fear for himself. His heart was thumping in his chest. As he looked up, he saw the dark shadows lined across the top of the waterfall. The water started to run into his mouth, flooding into his body. He choked and couldn't hold on any longer. Plunging the last few feet into a pool, he felt as if he was drowning, but something grabbed him, pulling on the collar of his uniform and dragging him up through mud onto dry land.

Takeshi fought to free himself, only to realize he was still alone. He stood up, the river and the waterfall had gone. He was in a clearing in the middle of the jungle. A farmhouse sat at the center, perched high on stone pillars, with a single light on in the window. Takeshi looked down at himself; he was still soaking wet. He knew the farmer would help him.

I'm Japanese, but he will still help me. He will see I need dry clothes.

He looked around the clearing. The jungle surrounded him in a circle. Every direction he looked, he could hear a voice telling him he couldn't cross out of the clearing. Forbidden ground that belonged to the Taotaomo'na, surrounded him. The voice persisted; *you cannot cross, you do not have permission.*

Takeshi shivered, he was cold, and the farmhouse looked inviting. The voice faded to a whisper before disappearing. Takeshi stepped forward and climbed the steps up to the farmhouse. He felt it was unusual looking, but it was welcoming. He knocked on the door three times. There was no reply, but with only a gentle push it swung open.

Takeshi walked inside the home. There was a smell of cooking, the aroma of chicken and spices, but the farmhouse seemed empty. He called out, but no one responded. He looked around and found a blanket to dry himself. He only dried his face, but his uniform also dried itself. The smell of the food warming in a pot was calling him. His stomach ached from hunger.

There is no one around, will they mind if I eat?

He stepped toward a stove, a covered pot bubbled away. He found a plate and a large serving spoon. Opening the lid, he stared down at a blood-drenched head still seeping from a cut on the neck.

Takeshi crashed backward in shock. The plate smashed on the ground and the light extinguished. The front door slammed shut. Takeshi scrambled to his feet. He searched for something to protect himself. He had no rifle or bayonet. He couldn't remember where he had laid them down, and then from outside a low chant began.

Takeshi searched for a knife. He knew he had to defend himself. Searching the house presented him with a large knife.

He held it close as the sound of running around the house started to increase. It sounded like there were many people. Just like a patrol. The door and the windows started to rattle and vibrate. Shadowy figures were banging on the walls, the chant continued along with the stamping of feet. It reached a frenzy as the door started to push. Takeshi knew the door was already open, but whatever was outside was using force to break it down.

Takeshi prayed for forgiveness for whatever he had done wrong.

With knife in hand, he rushed toward the door. It swung open and there was the same old woman he had seen out on patrol.

"*Na'para,*" said the woman as a clawed hand struck him on the chest.

The pain tore through him as he sprung from the doorway into the jungle. Racing through thorns and twisting branches, he knew he was being pursued. He knew this was their land. Takeshi jumped and rolled. From beside him, sling stones crossed his path, clubs knocked against rocks and wood. The noise was terrifying.

On he ran, but the figures chasing him were never more than a few feet away. Hands were starting to grab him; he could feel bites and scratches tearing into his flesh. The jungle never changed, the same endless path of dense foliage closing in around no matter how far he ran. He knew he had to accept his fate and stopped.

He was in another clearing. Whoever or whatever had pursued him was gone. Intense and humid heat caused him to tire, and he collapsed on the ground. He closed his eyes and heard a deer grazing once again.

He took in a breath and sat up. The deer was searching out food as a Japanese soldier stood stroking its back. Takeshi was relieved to see a friend. He stood up and walked over as Hayashi turned to face him.

"*Konichiwa* Takeshi-san."

Takeshi sat bolt upright in bed, soaking with sweat, but thankful that he hadn't screamed. The rest of the men were still asleep. He was shaking with fear, and didn't want to risk returning to the nightmare. Dressing himself, he slipped outside the barracks, making sure he had a cigarette to calm his nerves.

The compound never slept; there were always guards on duty. It made him feel better to see other faces. The world had returned to normality. He walked over toward the edge of the Japanese part of the camp. He could see that the latest prisoners were making their way in under cover of darkness. The number of shelters since his first patrol were growing larger by the day. The gaps between the temporary homes were dwindling fast. The sounds of pain, discomfort, and hunger were growing.

"What have we done?" he whispered under his breath.

He stepped back toward the door of his barracks. A patrol was just changing over. The same one that went around the Ylig River. He examined the faces of the guards that were returning. He could see that they had met the Taotaomo'na. The worried expressions with their heads kept bowed gave it away.

"We are bringing the CHamoru to Manenggon; we are bringing the Taotaomo'na, too."

Chapter 10
Elena

The Taicho stared from the opposite side of a large wooden desk. It looked out of place within the constructed timber building. Transported from the Governor's House at Agana, it represented authority, a division between the rank of a commander and his men. If a mere private sat at it, then it showed trouble ahead, so Takeshi was nervous as he awaited the Taicho's opening remarks.

"Where are you from, Takeshi-san?"

"Sasebo, Taicho-san."

"You see, I'm trying to work out why you are not suffering like others. Maybe the spirits of this place just hate troops from Shikoku, but don't mind other Japanese. If I knew that for certain, I would make sure all my guards came from around Sasebo."

"Yes, Taicho-san."

"We have to solve this problem. It is bad for morale. Men can mutiny or they can look for someone to blame. Rumors can spread and flourish."

"I have heard no rumors, Taicho-san."

"That's because the rumors are about you. Some say that you have signed a contract with these spirits of the island, others say that you are in contact with the Americans, that they've given you a cure that they supply to their own men."

"None of that is true, Taicho-san."

The commander seemed to ponder Takeshi's truthfulness for too long. There was a sense that he could turn at any time, order a flogging, or worse. The young soldier felt his mouth go dry.

"I have a report on yesterday's incident. Corporal Suzuki has sustained a severe injury to his arm. Not good for firing a rifle or wielding a bayonet. Though I'm sure some of the CHamoru will be pleased about that. Then there's the other man with a broken ankle. He will be useless in the banzai attack. Half of the Imperial Japanese Army has died from disease and starvation in this war, but we have the added problem of these...?"

"Taotaomo'na, Taicho-san."

"Taotaomo'na? Whatever they are called, they are causing more sickness than normal. We lose half our men, plus the ones that these Taotaomo'na send mad. I cannot sit back and watch my men grow sick and die. We have to defeat this, don't you agree?"

"Yes, Taicho-san."

"I'm putting you in charge of a unit of men. You will take the river patrol each night from now on. You can survive better than most. I see that you have spent almost a year in the army, so I can allow your promotion to Private First Class; this will allow you to lead a small group. I want you to look for the Taotaomo'na. I want you to do whatever it takes to confront them. I will assign you an interpreter. Go into the camp and find out what you can. Use any means necessary to extract information from the prisoners. Any questions?"

"No, Taicho-san. I will find out what I can, Taicho-san."

"Good. I will divide some of today's new intake to your command. It is better that we use men that do not already believe you have sold your soul to these demons. Dismissed."

***

Takeshi stepped outside into the strong sunlight. Corporal Suzuki stood by a group of men, his arm bandaged and hanging by his side.

"Has the Taicho given you an order?" he said.

"Yes Gocho-san. I have to gather information from the camp about—"

"Yes, I have told the men here that you are to find out important information for the Taicho. I just want you to find whoever owns the dog that did this."

Suzuki pointed to his arm; he couldn't even lift it. Takeshi said nothing in response.

"Your interpreter, Kindo, is at the gate. Make sure he tells you everything. If he looks like he's deceiving you, then your men can kill him. We'll find another interpreter. Now get started, *Ittohei* Yoshida-san."

"Yes, Gocho-san."

The corporal turned his back and headed toward the infirmary. That left Takeshi with four soldiers to accompany him. They had the same appearance he had when he had just arrived in camp. They had been marching through the night for their reassignment at Manenggon. They would have slept little, eaten little, and may well still be in shock from whatever explosion had removed them from the front line.

"Follow me," said Takeshi, with his first command.

He led them to the gate that opened up into the wider camp. A local man was standing waiting for them as they arrived."

"Kindo?" asked Takeshi

"Yes, sir."

"I am Takeshi-san. You must help me today. I need to find out information for the Taicho. Do you understand?"

"Yes, sir."

"No, my name is Takeshi-san."

"Oh yes, I am sorry, Takeshi-san. What information do you need to know?"

"I am to investigate the Taotaomo'na."

"Oh? The Taotaomo'na? I'm not sure what the people will tell you. The Taotaomo'na scare CHamoru as well. The spirits can get angry if you offend them."

"So, how do the people treat them?"

The interpreter looked puzzled. "Treat them? We do not rule over the Taotaomo'na, we respect them, we honor them.

We ask permission from them to even enter their lands, and then we hope. Hope that they say yes, to whatever it is we ask."

"Can you take me to someone who can tell me more?"

"You will need to speak to a *suruhana*. Someone who works to remove harmful spirits that cause poor health."

"They can cure the effects of these spirits. So, they can cure our men?"

"That's a different matter, but I can try to find you a suruhana amongst all of this."

Kindo drew everyone's gaze over to the prison camp stretching out in front of them. Thousands were now arriving every day. Shelters were stretching back further from the river's edge. An entire island population was being forced into a small strip of land.

Takeshi couldn't believe it was the same place that he had arrived in just days earlier. Manenggon was becoming a small city of broken families, separated from those selected for forced labor.

"Where do we even start?" he asked Kindo.

"Perhaps we should ask the Taotaomo'na for help," came the interpreter's reply.

Takeshi led the party forward. It was daytime, and the guards confined the prisoners below cover. The Americans were more confident about flying over the entire island to search out defenses and buildings to target. Most realized the aerial attacks would begin to move toward the east. Every engine sound overhead caused a step into the trees to avoid being seen.

Takeshi's group reached the point where the first of the shelters were standing. The rows of simple frames and coconut leaves resembled an ancient village. It felt to Takeshi that he was stepping into a world that would have existed centuries ago. Kindo held his arm out to stop him from moving any further forward.

"Guella yan Guello, dispensa ham lao Kao siña ham manmaloffan yan manmanbisita gi tano miyu sa' yanggen un bisita i tano'ma mi faloffan-ha' sin un famaisin." said Kindo.

"What are you doing?"

"I'm asking permission of the Taotaomo'na to enter their land."

"This is *their* land?"

"All the jungle is their land. You can anger them by not asking for permission."

"Are you a suruhana?"

"No, but everyone here knows how to ask permission, and a suruhana is a female healer. A suruhanu is male, but I think most of them are constructing defenses or working on the farms."

"So, how do you know when the Taotaomo'na grant permission?"

"Do you feel anything? A shiver, the hairs on the back of your neck?"

"No."

"This is foolish!" said one of the other soldiers, "Kindo is making a fool of you Takeshi-san."

The others sniggered in agreement, but the Taicho had promoted Takeshi. It meant that the men under his command should never question his authority. He laid his rifle down on the ground and turned to the man who had commented.

"My orders are from the Taicho! Do you think you are better than him? His orders are the orders of the Emperor. Do you think you are better than him?

"No, Takeshi-san, no."

The man stepped back, but not fast enough, as Takeshi launched a punch at the man's jaw, sending him sprawling onto the mud. As the soldier tried to scramble to his feet. Takeshi kicked him in the stomach with all his force.

Takeshi's army training was now complete. He stood firm as his subordinate picked himself up. The man was thin and hadn't eaten for days, yet he still coughed up bile and clutched at himself in pain.

"You will do as you are told at all times. You will be loyal at all times. You will respect all ranks above you, or granted authority over you. If you insult me you insult all above me. Do I make myself clear?"

"Yes, Ittohei-san. I'm sorry."

"Ittohei Yoshida-san. That is how you will refer to me, and show respect."

"Yes, Ittohei Yoshida-san."

Takeshi directed his stare to the other men. All of them bowed their heads, to show deference, but also to avert any further wrath.

What have I become?

He became conscious of many eyes peering out from the shelters. The prisoners were used to the treatment being handed out to them, but it was an unusual sight for a Japanese soldier to suffer the beating.

"Shall we enter the jungle?" said Kindo.

"Yes, we will go ahead."

Takeshi picked up his rifle and straightened his back. He walked forward, knowing that all his men would now follow him without question.

They stepped forward in amongst the prisoners. He could smell the fear and the filth. Faces stared back with empty expressions. People had lost so much in such a brief space of time. Takeshi could sense that loss as he walked among them. From those that could remember happier times before the war to children who could understand their surroundings. All seemed to recognize that the hell they had found themselves in was a place of no return.

Kindo asked for a suruhana amongst the crowds of people. All shook their heads. Others said there were no suruhana. That the Japanese had killed the last of them, and no one could get medicine for their relatives. Some were even brave enough to challenge Takeshi. He didn't order their beating. His men were already noticing that he was happier to hand out violence to another Japanese rather than a CHamoru.

They patrolled around the course of the river; the word traveled faster than they could, and people knew what they were going to ask before they got there. As they came to the end of a fruitless exercise, a woman stood in their path.

"Who is looking for the Taotaomo'na?" she said, as they approached her.

"The soldiers," said Kindo.

"They are all around you. Can't you see them?"

"How can I see them?" said Takeshi.

"You will see them if they want you to see them. You can find the Taotaomo'na around the Latte stones. You must visit them there. I sense they have chosen you."

"The Latte stones?"

"They mark the burial sites of our ancestors. It is where the veil that separates our world and theirs is the thinnest. The ancient CHamoru built their houses on stone pillars. You will have seen them in places still standing in pairs."

Takeshi felt a shudder run through him. "They built the houses on stone pillars?"

"So that they could bury the dead beneath their houses. These are the places where you can meet the Taotaomo'na."

"Are there latte stones nearby?"

"Yes, but you must learn to ask the Taotaomo'na how to enter their world. They will guide you forward. You are never lost when you follow the path they want you to walk. On your next patrol, I'm sure they will find you. Anyone with you will need to show the same respect. I think you already know how dangerous they can be."

***

Takeshi sat on his bed, alone in a room full of people. He could see the side looks from other soldiers. Conversations would stop or become more hushed if he walked closer. They would be polite with him, but no more. They didn't trust him, that was obvious, but if they believed their own gossip, then they were also frightened of how he could converse with ghosts and demons. Leaving him alone seemed to be the best way to handle it.

Hiroshi appeared with two mugs of tea, and the one smiling face in the room. He lit a cigarette and passed it to Takeshi.

"It looks like you need this more than me."

Takeshi bowed before inhaling the smoke. He passed it back and sipped on his tea.

"I admit I'm frightened. I have to go out looking for the Taotaomo'na now. The Taicho ordered me to do something about it."

"Yes, I know. Everyone's talking about it. They're having trouble getting men to join you. So many are saying, *Oh, Corporal, I'm so sick tonight.*" Hiroshi laughed.

Takeshi looked around at the others in the barracks.

"No one wants to go out with you and meet the Taotaomo'na. I fear the very worst of us will accompany you tonight. The soldiers that are in so much trouble they can't refuse."

"Will you volunteer?"

"I'm the only name on the list so far."

Takeshi felt better, knowing his new friend would be beside him. He spent the hours in between contemplating what lay ahead. The memories of his dreams had returned to him—the fear he had experienced on the patrol with Corporal

Suzuki and the knowledge that he had already been outcast by his own people.

He considered that the Taicho was making a strategic decision. It would have been easy for him to transfer Takeshi back to the front line, to leave him at the mercy of American planes and ships, but he recognized that Takeshi had a use. He knew that if Takeshi solved the problem of the attacks on his guards, then he—the Taicho—could take the credit. If the Taotaomo'na killed Takeshi, then he would just be another casualty. Nothing to report other than the notice the army sent back home for the family. It would present them with the box of their son's ashes. It was an open secret that the boxes were often empty.

Takeshi poured one more mug of tea, then it was time to go. As he prepared to leave with Hiroshi, the others kept their distance. A silence descended that only sprung into conversation once they had left through the door.

Hiroshi was right about the other men assembled for the patrol. They all looked like they belonged in jail. Their uniforms didn't fit because they had found them on the bodies of dead or dying comrades. They had many scars across their faces, and they had the collective presence of a gang, with their own loyalty to one another outranking loyalty to a figure in authority.

They walked together in silence to the edge of the jungle that began outside the confines of the camp, Takeshi laid down his mug of tea on a rock, before offering a small prayer.

"What are you doing Takeshi-san?" said the largest and most unkempt man in his patrol.

"I do not know the CHamoru words. These spirits are not so different from the *Kami*. You know that we offer food and drink to them. I hope that the Taotaomo'na can see the offering in the same way."

They met the offering with the disrespect that Takeshi expected. He swallowed his pride for a moment, as he felt that the men that accompanied him would relish a fight. They had walked on another few paces, when the same large man started laying out some ground rules for the night.

"Takeshi-san. We all heard about what you did today. Giving one of your own men a beating. I warn you now, don't think of doing that with *us*, tonight."

Takeshi swung round, ready to take on the challenge, but the bigger soldier was prepared to back up his threat. His friends were confident enough to snigger at Takeshi's efforts.

"I am called Kyota. I am very easy to get along with, Takeshi. Just don't ask me to do that much and we'll get along fine. We can get to a pleasant spot, sit down and wait, and then go back in the morning with whatever story you want to make up. I don't believe in demons, but if they do exist, then I'm not keen on meeting them either."

The soldier laughed along with his comrades. Hiroshi just gave a frustrated look.

"Very well," said Takeshi, "but you know why we're here. If you want us to sit and let the demons encircle us, then that's up to you. I'm sure they will find us."

He laid down his rifle and sat on the ground. He knew the feeling would come that they were not alone. As he stared back at his men, he could see dark shapes forming in the trees behind him. He could see the branches moving under the weight of a slithering creature, and he knew the men of Kyota's gang could feel it too.

Strange sounds began to travel across the darkness, branches snapped, and boughs creaked. The surrounding jungle didn't appear to be so asleep.

"It is better if we walk on," said Takeshi, "Trust me, they can gather anywhere we are. This is their island, not ours."

"That sounds like good advice," said Hiroshi, "You should all listen to him."

The other men looked at one another, then agreed, with nods of their heads. Takeshi stood up and followed the river, and then the stretch of jungle that led toward Yona. It felt different. He was walking through the same place where he had been attacked before. He could still feel the spirits, but it was as if they were holding back. As he strained to look through the darkness, he felt as if glowing eyes were watching his every move.

He kept quiet. He wanted to hear every sound and follow the path of every shadow. This time, they were walking away from him.

They're leading me.

They walked past more shelters and more new arrivals as they crossed by the far side of Manenggon. The camp was more alive at night. The prisoners could leave their shelters, wash, or eat from the limited supplies they had brought with them. They watched as Takeshi and his party walked past, but they would look away if he caught their eye.

The trail they were on led a little further north and they started to leave the camp behind once again. A few minutes later, they were at the main road. It was the point they would typically turn back home, but tonight Takeshi decided to carry on. He felt he was being pulled to the jungle on the other side.

Ylig Bay had revealed itself before they disappeared back under cover. He could hear the ocean breaking in the distance. The feeling was strengthening again. Takeshi was sure it wasn't only him that was feeling it. The others must be, too. He cast a glance behind. Hiroshi nodded to urge Takeshi to carry on. The others just looked scared. It seemed they had lost their bravado some way back. Takeshi pressed on.

He chose to take a route that followed the coastline, around the northern side of the bay. The air was heavy, and it was becoming harder to breathe as they crossed a rocky surface where some of the stones worked loose, tumbling from under their feet. Takeshi felt that the Taotaomo'na wanted to test him, to see how brave he would be walking on a path that shifted like a snake in the darkness. The others behind him also had difficulties, with slips and falls to give them bruises for the morning.

All of a sudden, through the tight mesh of foliage, they could see flickering flames, torches blowing in the wind. Takeshi brought the troop to an immediate halt.

"What do you think?" said Hiroshi.

"It could be Americans," said one of the others.

"No listen," said Takeshi.

A soft chant blew up from the shore. A group of voices in unison.

"I think this is what we are looking for."

With no more hesitation, Takeshi moved forward. It didn't matter to him if the others followed or not. He knew he had to go down to where the fires were burning, in a clearing just ahead.

As he broke through from the last line of jungle, he could see a gathering of women, chanting around four pairs of stone pillars. The women screamed and huddled together, surprised by Takeshi's arrival. The other soldiers arrived behind him. They didn't wait for Takeshi's instruction. They started knocking out the torches, harassing and striking at some of the women.

"Stop!" shouted Takeshi, but they chose not to hear his voice. Hiroshi tried to get in the middle of the commotion and ended up being caught up under the chaos of both sides struggling. The women were shouting back at the soldiers, and the soldiers were screaming orders and insults in return. Neither in a language the other could understand.

"Stop!" shouted Takeshi yet again, but the soldiers were too determined to hand out punishment. They didn't hear him over their own raised voices.

Takeshi spotted a young woman caught up in the middle of the violence. Hands were pulling at her from both sides. She looked straight at Takeshi, her eyes pleading for help.

Her eyes.

Takeshi thought he saw Yuki looking back at him, he saw Yuki in need of his help. Why would no one listen to him?

At the top of his voice, he yelled out, "Na'para!"

Everything stopped as his voice appeared to travel around the edge of the clearing. He felt a large force around himself, as if a party of warriors had assembled around him, hidden within the line of the trees.

"These women are witches, Takeshi," said Kyota. "They are the ones who are making everyone sick at the camp. Let's show them how that ends."

He turned to start grabbing at the young woman again.

"I said stop!" Takeshi lowered his bayonet and rifle against his fellow soldier.

"*Watashi wa nihongo o hanasemasu,*" she said, as she stepped out from the crowd.

"You can speak Japanese?" he replied.

She nodded. "My name is Elena. We are only asking our ancestors permission to take some food and bamboo from their land. To help us survive."

"Don't let her fool you, Takeshi," insisted Kyota, "She is tricking you. I'll beat the truth out of her."

"You won't do anything unless it is under my command!"

"But look at these torches, they are signaling to the Americans."

"So now they're Americans, and not witches?"

Kyota stepped back. Even he knew he was making a fool of himself.

Takeshi turned to Elena and the group of women.

"Tell me what you're doing here. Or my friends here will just make something up."

"We are here to ask permission from our ancestors. We only need to take some food for ourselves, leaves for medicine, and bamboo for our shelters. We would be stealing if we did not perform our ceremony."

"Your ancestors? The Taotaomo'na?"

The group of women behind Elena murmured at one another. Takeshi was using CHamoru words, and he knew about Taotaomo'na. He was different from the normal Japanese guards.

"Yes, the Taotaomo'na," said Elena, "We come to this place, to these stones, because we know they will be here. They are around us now," she paused, "Can you feel them? They are here now."

The air felt fresh. A vast sky sparkled with starlight above them. Takeshi remembered part of his dream. The pillars that the house stood on. These were the stones in front of him now. All his life he had grown up being told about the divine Emperor, but in this place he was experiencing something that you couldn't read from a book or learn in a classroom. He could have stayed in the moment forever, but the other soldiers were getting restless, and Hiroshi was looking winded and in pain.

"What are we going to do with them, Takeshi?" said Kyota.

Takeshi sighed. "We will return to camp and leave these CHamoru to complete their ceremony. They can gather their food and medicine. We have to cross back through jungle before home. I'm sure allowing them to complete their task is the safest way for us all to get back to camp."

"Well, if it was me—"

"Well, it is not you. I am leading this unit."

"I don't know what I'm doing here," Kyota complained, "I want to take my place in the banzai charge, not live out my last days under the stench of Manenggon."

Takeshi frowned. "You are forgetting I have a meeting with the Taicho in just a few hours. I'm sure your request can be granted."

He led his men back to the jungle. They were unhappy and would probably report on how he once again got involved to stop the CHamoru from being hurt—how he threatened his own men first. As Takeshi glanced back, he suddenly didn't care. He locked eyes with Elena. He could see Yuki, not just in her face, but in her soul. In that moment his heart ached, for home, for Yuki, and for Elena.

Chapter 11
Crossing Enemy Lines

"So what are you saying?" asked the Taicho, "that we must bow and ask permission to enter the jungle?"

"It is what the CHamoru people do, Taicho-san," replied Takeshi.

"That would never work. It would turn us into a laughingstock. These CHamoru are making fools of us. We would be better rid of them, and we will be if they don't serve any use."

"The interpreter told me about the suruhana, Taicho-san. They are healers. They can cure the people, those suffering from attacks."

"That is better news. If we can cure our sick, that is something. Where can we find these suruhana?"

"Some said that we had killed them all. They gather plants from the jungle, perhaps I can find out where? Taicho-san."

The Taicho considered Takeshi's proposal. He sat back and closed his eyes as the days bombardment began in the background.

"Yes, of course, we are running out of time. We will need all the help we can get to make every man fit for battle. You must work fast. What do you need?"

"Just Kindo, the interpreter, and another soldier, Hasegawa Hiroshi, from my barracks. He was the first one to explain the word Taotaomo'na. He understands a little about it."

"See to it. Though a word of warning. The commanders cannot see that I am involved in this matter. I will be careful not to look too hard at what you need to do, but I can only do that for so long. I will have to act if others think you are helping our enemies. I am not known for a merciful reputation."

"I understand, Taicho-san."

"See that you do. As soon as you find one of these suruhana, bring them back here and put them to work. If they can cure the men, you will be a hero. If not, then I cannot save you."

***

Takeshi and Hiroshi stood at the barracks gate. Kindo hurried forward out of the crowds toward them.

"Good morning, Takeshi-san," Kindo performed a low bow, "I was happy that I could help you today."

"I asked for you especially. The Taicho wants me to stop the guard from falling ill. He wants the medicine that can cure them."

Kindo gave a discouraging look. "I will not try to put you off, but look around us. Why would the CHamoru seek to help the Taicho?"

"I'm sure the Taicho does not expect to ask for help," said Hiroshi.

"That is what I mean, Hasegawa-san," said Kindo, "The suruhana do not have to help. The cure that you want is not just taking a medicine. They must investigate how you offended the Taotaomo'na. Sometimes they will work on parts of the body."

"We have to do something," said Takeshi, "I'm worried about what happens to your people next. If they helped the Taicho—"

"They might help *you*, Takeshi-san. The talk of you has spread throughout the camp, of how you defended and helped some of the women last night."

"Don't I know it," said Hiroshi, pointing to a swollen eye.

"And you too, Hasegawa-san."

"There was someone among them, Elena, can you take me to her shelter?"

"I will ask amongst the people. There will be a few Elena's."

"I'll know her when I see her. Let's go."

"Ittohei Yoshida-san!"

Takeshi knew the owner of the voice before he turned back to face him.

"Kyota, reporting for duty, Ittohei Yoshida-san."

Takeshi's heart sank. "What do you mean, reporting for duty?"

"The Taicho has asked me to join your work detail. My reporting of events from last night impressed him. He has asked me to follow you and keep giving him my reports."

Takeshi couldn't hide his disappointment and disgust. "You will follow my orders at all times."

"As the Taicho and our Emperor commands. I am only to report on the orders you give, and help provide some muscle when it's needed."

"We won't need your muscle."

Takeshi invited Kindo to say the CHamoru words that asked for permission. He kept his coldest glare on Kyota as the interpreter spoke.

"How do you feel Kyota?" asked Takeshi.

"Me? I feel fine. I'm hungry, that's all."

Takeshi hoped that a shiver or two would have shuddered through Kyota's body, but then he doubted if he was sensitive enough to even know.

"Alright, Kindo, lead us into the camp."

Even if the Taotaomo'na were around, it would have been almost impossible to sense their presence in the growing chaos of Manenggon. The prison guards had made the latest arrivals crowd their shelters closer to one another. Mothers held their smallest children near to stop them from wandering into the paths of the soldiers. Kyota walked a few steps behind the others so that his rough handling wouldn't be so obvious.

Kindo was making slow progress in trying to locate Elena. Everyone knew what happened to the younger women and girls that the Japanese came looking for. Even though Takeshi didn't know the language, Kindo was meeting a lot of resistance from the other islanders. He seemed frustrated with the lack of help. The only thing that seemed to have an impact was Takeshi's name and Taotaomo'na being mentioned in the same breath.

"What are they saying?" asked Takeshi.

"They say that they know that your heart is sincere, but they can't trust anyone after all they've been through with the Japanese. They are telling me about their journeys here. Family members killed for no reason, beheaded or shot, mothers losing their babies on the road, those that can no longer walk left to die on the road, and rape. You understand why no one wants to help you?"

"Kindo, find one that will listen. The Taicho has set me this task; I believe if we can cure his men, he might be better to the CHamoru for helping the Japanese."

A woman started laughing to Takeshi's side. She was mocking him. Kyota was quick to move in and threaten her.

"No, Kyota, wait!"

Takeshi walked over to the woman. "You understood me. Do you speak Japanese?"

"Yes, I speak it," she replied, "many of us do. You taught us when you first came here. We were all to become Japanese.

We had to study hard to learn the words, we had to learn about your money, and your glorious Emperor!"

"What do you think you are saying, witch?!"

"Kyota!" shouted Takeshi.

Kyota spat on the ground. "They are all witches."

"You heard me speak to Kindo. You know that I don't mean harm. The Taicho needs some of the medicine to cure his men. I'm sure he will repay the good deed."

"How did you end up here?" asked the woman, "You do not belong in this place. Your face is young and kind. Your eyes give away your heart. You have fallen for the beauty of an orchid that only blooms for one day. No matter how hard you try, you cannot change its fate."

Takeshi let his shoulders drop. The others awaited his reply, but he had none. He knew she was right. Tragedy encircled them. He looked into the crowds, to see so many faces staring back. Then the world seemed to stop.

He gasped as he saw Yuki looking back at him. There was a sorrow about her. He just sensed that the beatings and abuse had never stopped. In the moment, he could recall her distress as fate separated them at Sasebo. He knew that the violence had continued the moment she had returned home. Keiko had tricked him into joining the army.

"Yuki!"

A silence fell around him, apart from Kyota, stifling a snigger. The girl walked out of the crowd toward him.

"Takeshi-san."

"Elena."

"You are looking for me?"

Takeshi rushed to compose himself. He took in a deep breath and paused before speaking.

"I thought you would be able to help. The Taicho needs medicine."

"Is the Taicho ill?"

"No, the Taicho seeks medicine for his men, all of his men."

"Of course, it's not like we don't need it," scoffed the other woman.

"Susa, we can do something. We can make *palai*. They could try it."

"Why should we, Elena?" said Susa, switching to CHamoru, "The more of them that die, the less there are to kill us. Let the Taotaomo'na do their work."

"It is the Taotaomo'na who allowed Takeshi to find us. He allowed us to complete our ceremony last night. We cannot trust the Taicho, but we have to trust the ancestors."

Susa looked angry, but she had to consider that Elena was right. "We can only help Takeshi. The Taotaomo'na have chosen him, no other. If they want a cure for their men. Takeshi must come alone. Kindo, tell them that is our condition to get the medicine they seek."

"They don't negotiate," replied Kindo.

"If we die, then they die. The Taicho is not stupid. Tell them."

"What are they saying?" asked Takeshi.

"They will help you get medicine for the guards, but you must come alone. They fear that the Taotaomo'na will not help or grant permission if any other Japanese are present."

"Especially the stupid looking one," said Susa, continuing to speak in CHamoru.

"Susa is saying that they will not grant permission to those who do not show respect."

Kindo glanced to his side, toward Kyota, his real meaning obvious to most.

"I understand," replied Takeshi, "I will need to return to the Taicho and get his agreement. We cannot leave the camp during the day. Can we collect what we need tonight, Elena?"

"We can find the herbs we need, close to Turtle Cove."

"Good. Then I'm sure the Taicho will allow it."

Takeshi looked over at Kyota, who didn't look happy that he would have to report a successful result for the young ittohei.

"Alright, Elena. I'll report back to the Taicho. I will arrange a time and place to meet you. Kindo will return to tell you the arrangements. Is that clear?"

Elena had to bite her lip to stop herself from smiling. Takeshi was uncomfortable speaking with the authority that he wanted to appear to show. It might fool the others, but she could see his true nature.

***

The darkness brought Manenggon to life once again. Prisoners could move out of their shelters under the cover of night. To meet with one another, to wash in the river that was also their only source of drinking water, and to bury their dead. Starvation sapped the little energy that many had left.

Dysentery was spreading amongst the packed population. If you needed medicine for a major illness, then you had little chance of survival.

The bombardment was intensifying. The American ships that were holding the island under siege no longer stopped. The distant explosions had become nothing more than background noise. The only concern it created amongst the prisoners was how much island they would leave when the troops arrived.

Elena walked through the mass of people. She recognized many, but it was impossible to know all. Random patrols of Japanese wandered among the shelters, but she avoided them. The guards were interested in the new arrivals, instructing them where to build a shelter, while stealing part of the fresh food supplies for themselves.

As she approached the dividing line of the gates that separated the Japanese section of the camp, she was pleased to see Takeshi already standing next to Hiroshi.

"Hey, Takeshi!" shouted one of the guards, "Is that your girlfriend?"

"Hey, Takeshi, I've got ten cigarettes that say you can make her my girlfriend," laughed another.

Takeshi ignored them as Elena arrived beside them at the gate.

"Tell her to come into the guardhouse," continued the guard, "She can meet a real man, and not a boy."

"What do you mean?" said another, "She can meet real *men*."

"I think you two should go now," said Hiroshi, "good luck."

Takeshi and Elena walked off into the darkness without a second look back.

"Hey, Hasegawa-san. How did he convince the Taicho to let him have a date with a girl?"

"They are going to collect ingredients for medicine."

"Oh sure, they are, but she could do better than him. Takeshi is weird. He loves the CHamoru more than his own people."

"Takeshi is a volunteer. The Kempeitai had to come looking for you!"

"Watch your mouth, Hasegawa. You've heard what everyone says about him. He talks to the dead and the witches that summon them. Be careful that we don't start talking about you the same way. At least you are from Shikoku, that's the only thing that's saving you at the moment."

Hiroshi drew on the last of his cigarette and cast it to the ground. He knew the guard was right about the word around the barracks. Takeshi was upsetting the harmony of the men. They couldn't understand why the Taicho seemed to allow him freedoms that the other men couldn't expect.

Corporal Suzuki was stoking the fire of resentment more than others. He was convinced that it was Takeshi who had caused his injuries by summoning a demon dog to attack him. At first the idea had seemed to be ridiculous, but as time went on, more and more were starting to believe it.

It was Suzuki who was waiting outside the barracks as Hiroshi returned.

"Has he gone with the girl?" Suzuki's eyes narrowed as if he was interrogating an enemy.

"Yes, they've gone. They will return with ingredients for medicine. Then maybe you will all give him a chance."

"I'll give him a chance until this medicine has cured my arm. Once I can hold a rifle again, he better watch his back."

***

Elena asked for permission to enter the jungle.

"How do you feel, Takeshi?"

Takeshi smiled. "I don't think I have felt happier. With you beside me, I have nothing to be frightened of."

"I am not special, any of us can offend the Taotaomo'na. Perhaps I should ask; have they granted you permission?"

"I think so."

"Then we can step into the jungle."

The sense of being watched hadn't left Takeshi, but this was different. There was a strong sense of power. A feeling that they were not alone, but he felt privileged rather than afraid—privileged to enter the ancestral lands.

He followed Elena through trails that he hadn't walked before. They seemed to travel further north than the previous night, but he knew he could trust her. He wanted to show she could trust him, too.

"I don't understand why the Emperor wants to hurt the people of Guam."

"Does he even know of the people?" replied Elena. "Has he ever met someone from our island? The Japanese army arrived here the day after Pearl Harbor. I was at a festival at the church in Agana when they arrived. I became separated from my parents. Many were in tears and screaming, trying to get their families together as over five thousand men arrived on our island, armed and brimming with confidence. The world was going to become Japanese and we would be one of the first islands to become a part of greater Japan. Omiyajima was to be the new island name. I'm glad you chose to use Guam instead. I was only thirteen years old when it happened."

"That was the age of my sister when I left home to join the army. I've missed her fourteenth birthday."

"Yuki?"

"Yes."

"You called out her name when you saw me today. I didn't know what the name meant to you."

"You remind me of her. You resemble one another, but there's a strength and a kindness that both of you share. No matter what happened, she could always survive. I'm sure her life will carry on without me, but I miss her. I'm sorry that I called you by her name."

Elena stopped walking for a moment. The sound of the ocean filled the silence as they looked at one another.

"I am happy that you could see something of her in me. Your parents will look after her."

"My parents died two years ago from an illness. Yuki and I had to move to the home of my Uncle Taro."

"I'm sorry, I shouldn't have spoken."

"No, how could you know? Do you have family?"

Tears formed in Elena's eyes. Takeshi yearned to offer her comfort.

"They took my father and older brother to work at Orote Point. I haven't heard from them since then. My grandmother was very ill. When they started marching us towards Manenggon, she couldn't walk. People tried to help, but we had to keep stopping, she was in so much pain. Trucks full of Japanese soldiers would drive back and forth along the road. If you were taking too long, they would beat you. They told me and my mother that we were able to walk faster, and to hurry, or perhaps they would just take me in the truck. My mother and grandmother knew what that meant. For my sake, my grandmother asked to be left at the roadside. She was asking to die. She told me of the joy I had brought to her and no matter the cost she would always try to keep me safe."

Elena paused as she sobbed. "My mother and I continued on the road alone. We had to give up on everything we held dear in an instant. There was no time to think—or worry about what awaited us at Manenggon."

"Elena, I am sorry for everything you have suffered. If there's anything I can do to help you, I will."

Elena dried her tears away. "I don't know how we can solve this. We can only make the best of each day and snatch a moment of happiness where we can. Our world is different from those that seek to change it. Only the ancestors have the power to fight on our behalf. Our daily prayer is to survive until we win the battle."

They spoke no more words. It felt to both that there was little hope. Instead, they fell into an embrace. Elena buried her head into Takeshi's chest. As they wrapped their arms around one another, Takeshi looked into the darkness of the jungle. His heart was full of love, tempered with a great sadness. Emotions overflowed that he had never experienced before in his life.

Everything about Elena was perfect to him. His only wish was a way for them to escape. A way to be together. He wondered if everything that had happened in his life had brought him to this place and this point in time. Why was this moment only allowed after all these years? There had to be an answer.

"We better move on and gather the herbs that we need," said Elena, pulling back and continuing to walk on.

"Maybe not all the herbs," Takeshi replied.

"What do you mean?"

"We need time. Don't you want to get away? We could hide like George Tweed in the jungle, the Taotaomo'na would protect us and keep us safe from harm."

"I can't do that. They would go after my mother. They would kill her out of revenge."

"We just need time to think, to work out a plan. Just give me a chance to think of something. We can come back to get the missing ingredient. I'll have worked something out. Maybe I can say we would need others with us."

"The Taicho would suspect something. He wouldn't let you leave with a group of CHamoru on your own."

"My friend Hiroshi will be sympathetic. I only need to find two or three others to help. A normal patrol group. It scares most of the guards to go anywhere near the spirits. They always have trouble getting others to go with me. I always get the day's new recruits for my patrol around the Ylig River. They will have to follow my orders for directions. In the moment, they will have to decide their fate, but Hiroshi and I will be ready if they don't make the right decision."

Elena hugged Takeshi once more, but this time she looked up into his eyes. "I have prayed to God so much in the last few days. I have called on angels and Taotaomo'na. I don't know who I should thank. I never expected them to answer me."

"I also prayed. The gods have shown me they do not wish the death and destruction that some men crave. They've brought us together, and they've given me the reason to live. The Emperor only values my death—to serve his own ambition. His generals bury all of us with their own greed for power. Where can we ask for the help of the Taotaomo'na?"

"The latte stones. We can go now. We're not far."

They raced through the jungle. The branches that would grip on to you, the undergrowth and the rocky surface that would cause you to slip or trip up seemed to disappear. The jungle opened up to grant them safe passage. Within minutes they had arrived in the clearing, The latte stones generated a power of their own, embedded with centuries of ceremony and ritual—the centuries of the CHamoru race, going further back in time than either Takeshi or Elena could imagine.

A vast canopy of stars shone out above, the power of the ocean lay just beyond the coastline, the jungle wrapped around them in a circle of trees, and the latte stones sat in the center of it all. The center of a universe.

Elena took Takeshi's hands in her own and closed her eyes. She began to speak in a language that he didn't understand. Yet he knew everything she was asking for. The sound of Elena's voice, speaking without fear, was like music to Takeshi. He could feel the power of the place course through him. He felt *at home*.

Elena smiled as she stopped and took a long breath of air. She slowly released the breath as her eyes opened. As she stared up at Takeshi, she saw hope for a future, far away from the pain and the torment that had fallen upon her island and her people.

"We can only hope now. I have made a wish to the ancestors for help. I have asked that the Taicho will do what you ask of him."

"It will not be easy," said Takeshi, but he couldn't hide his excitement. Elena had turned around his life in an instant. He felt that with her by his side, his life had a new purpose. Yet he had to acknowledge that he would never return to his homeland.

As they stepped back into the jungle to gather the herbs that they needed, Takeshi hoped that Yuki would be happy for him. He prayed that she would understand that he wasn't turning his back on her. He was only moving forward on the path that life was offering. If he could survive the madness of war with Elena, that was better than charging into a hail of American gunfire.

As Elena worked, she smiled back at Takeshi. Behind her eyes, he could see his sister looking out, smiling with approval. He was sure Yuki would tell him he was making the right choice. She would encourage him to be brave, and she would insist that he followed his heart.

Chapter 12
The Glimmer of Hope

Takeshi opened his eyes to a commotion within the barracks. Hiroshi was shaking him awake.

"Wake up, Takeshi. We have to be ready for inspection. General Takashina is visiting the camp this morning."

"The General? Coming here?"

"Yes, get ready. We have to be outside in ten minutes."

Takeshi jumped from his bed and rushed to get dressed. There was no time to wash. They lay a few bowls of cold water out on the table to allow a quick and unsatisfactory attempt at shaving.

Corporal Suzuki had recovered enough to bark an endless stream of orders at his men. Failure had a habit of spreading blame further up the ranks. He would not suffer a punishment for lack of effort.

In the chaos, they made beds, floors got swept, mugs and bowls were cleaned or hidden away. They made it, standing to attention with rifles, outside and ready for the Taicho's approval.

The residents of the other barracks were also flowing out into the main square in front of the Taicho's office building.

"Who's guarding the CHamoru?" whispered Takeshi.

"No one," replied Hiroshi, "It looks like they have summoned all of us here."

After the rush, the Taicho took several minutes to appear, allowing more time for the NCOs to berate their own men for a variety of reasons. An unfastened button still earned punishment, even though the uniforms themselves were a mismatch of clothes that didn't fit or even belong with one another.

The last few months had seen supplies dwindle. They kept anything of any use for the troops at the front line. The guards at Manenggon were a lower priority, and it showed. Most still wore the insignia of their original units, the uniform they had arrived with. The food ration was worse, so many were in a uniform that was too large for their shrinking bodies. If you didn't look so thin it was a good sign that you bullied or stole from others to keep your weight up.

As Takeshi cast his eyes around, he could only see an army that was facing its end.

When are the Americans coming?

In the light of day, his mind was beginning to have doubts. If he escaped with Elena, he would still have to face the prospect of captivity from the next wave of invaders. His only hope might be to pretend he was CHamoru. He would get Elena to teach him the language; maybe she would be able to ask for his release. The complications of the plan started to fill his head. Last night, everything had seemed straightforward, but now he had time to think. The Americans would capture him as a prisoner. Would they even leave him on the island? He knew he still had to take his chance. If all he did was save Elena and her mother, that was good enough, but what would Hiroshi have to gain? Could he even ask him to help?

The Taicho emerged from his office. His presence was enough to prompt a series of further commands to stand at attention. The troops obeyed as one. No matter how long you had served, you never forgot the basic disciplines.

He carried out his inspection with the expected ceremony, but with few demands on his soldiers. The guard was already a beaten force. The last days of their war would not be ending in glory. The Taicho already had some sense of what was coming. The General's visit to the camp would outline the last commands. They would then leave the Taicho to contemplate his own path to heaven, be it dying in battle or on his own blade. Surrender would never be a choice.

Before he had completed his own solemn walk around the rest of his troops, the General's convoy was already driving in through the gates. A first car preceded the General's own car. A truck loaded with better equipped troops swept in on the rear. The men on board disembarked to present a guard for the high-ranking officer.

The Taicho marched to greet General Takashina with a low bow, then escorted him inside the office. The door slammed shut, leaving the square in silence.

A murmur began to pass around the men as they wondered what was coming next. Takeshi was nervous about what this would do to his plans. Whatever was being decided in that office was likely to impact the next moves. He started to fear for his chances.

Only a few minutes passed, but it felt like hours to Takeshi—too long to keep the doubts from creeping in. The door opened from the office and the General departed with the same speed of his arrival, and without the slightest acknowledgement to the guards. As the convoy circled and drove back out the gates, the Taicho walked to stand in front of his men. He paused, allowing a silence to dominate the camp before starting to speak.

"Today is a glorious day. General Takashina has just given me new orders. The enemy ships are building in force. The commanders are all in agreement that the Americans are about to attempt an invasion. This will be our opportunity to rush our enemy and show them the strength of Japanese steel."

It was a predictable message to the men, which prompted a rousing cheer in response. The Taicho accepted the encouragement before continuing.

"There is much to carry out, and little time left. We must re-double our efforts to bring all the CHamoru to Manenggon. We must leave none to aid the Americans. The army is moving ammunition and supplies to the hills that look down over the coast in readiness for the attack. We are being ordered to organize the work parties, and I should impress on you we need to keep secrecy at all times. We must use the CHamoru men that are left; we cannot allow them to return with information that would embolden our enemy.

"There will be casualties. We will receive the men from the front lines who require medical attention. We need to have somewhere to put them, so again we must work harder. Trees will need to be felled to allow us to build on to the infirmary. With all that work, there will be fewer patrols. I will order more machine gun positions around the camp. The guns will be permanently manned and trained on the prisoners. If there is a bid for escape, it is a death sentence for all that try, and those that surround them. Let the CHamoru know that their disobedience will have consequences."

The Taicho turned and walked back to his office. When he was gone, the calls rang out to dismiss.

The men were glad to relax as they walked back to their barracks, while their officers gathered to sort out the work details.

"What do you think, Takeshi?"

"It looks like the waiting is over. They used to say November before an attack. We had plenty of time. Some that traveled in my convoy went to Saipan. Will any still be alive?"

"Time for a smoke?"

The two soldiers walked to a quieter spot. A few of the guards had the same idea, so they didn't stand out from the crowd. Once they were out of earshot of the others, Hiroshi opened up about how he felt.

"I don't want to die for my country," he said.

Takeshi nodded. He was glad that Hiroshi trusted in him enough to confide in him. Such a thought would cause untold punishment if it became known.

"I feel the same. I'm sure there are others. How do you feel about leaving here, without permission that is."

"Desertion? I don't know. What would they do to us if they caught us?"

"Only what they have done to us already. We've both survived bombings, and for what? To charge at a tank? You know your rifle will break if you try to beat it to death."

They shared a smile.

"But, Hiroshi. You have shared this with me. You are trusting me, and now I must trust you. I do plan to leave, with Elena, her mother, and others if I can."

"That's madness, Takeshi. They would search high and low for you."

"Now, yes, but when the Americans land, they will have other things to focus their attention on. It is just about timing. You don't believe that Japan will win this war, and I agree with you. Maybe we will never be able to return home, but the dead don't get sent home either, you know that."

Hiroshi broke into a quiet laugh. The relief on his face was clear.

"Yes, Takeshi. I believe you are right. Count me in on the plan, and tell me what you need me to do."

"You still have some trust for the others. They don't talk when I'm around them. Keep amongst them and pick up any information that will be useful. We can meet on the Ylig River patrol. You're still the only one that volunteers to do it with me."

"Alright, I'll do that. Watch, Suzuki is coming over."

The corporal marched over from the Taicho's office.

"Hasegawa, get to the barracks. I have the work rotas for today; I will be there to announce them. The Taicho's favorite here has special duties. I don't know how you can even talk to him. He surrounds himself with demons."

"Ah, he always has cigarettes when I've smoked my ration. He's useful for that, Gocho-san."

Hasegawa walked off. Corporal Suzuki did as much as he could to contain his hatred for Takeshi.

"The Taicho wants to see you now. Do not slip up, Takeshi-san. Do not make a fool of the Taicho. His wrath would be a thousand times worse than mine, and that is something I would pay money to see. Go. Now!"

***

The Taicho tapped the blade of his Katana on the ornate desk. He sighed and spent time in thought. Takeshi could only await his response in nervous anticipation.

"The CHamoru have run out of time, Takeshi-san. As soon as the Americans make landfall, the CHamoru will become a danger to us. That will have to be dealt with. One more trip?"

"Yes, Taicho-san."

"And what about the suruhana?"

"There is one that my contact can bring. There might be others, but they have to be persuaded to help."

"Persuasion is something I am good at," the Taicho replied, "I hope you can understand Takeshi-san, that nothing has changed—other than the fact that the army needs all the men it can muster. General Takashina is planning to make a stand. He will never concede defeat. I share his views as must we all."

The Taicho rose from his desk and extended his sword arm to his right, looking along the line of the blade, and studying it.

"Corporal Suzuki tells me that your contact looks very like your sister?"

"Eh, yes Taicho-san. She does."

"She is not your sister. Try to remember that. She is a CHamoru; she can only ever be useful as long as she is serving the cause of the Japanese army and its soldiers. Your sister in Sasebo? She deserves all of your kindest thoughts. She waits at home for news of your victory. I would hate her to suffer shame from her neighbors. It would be terrible if they accused her of putting treasonous thoughts in your head. Who knows where that may end? Value your family, your country, and the Emperor. Become a hero in his name and know that we will honor your name as you look down from heaven.

"Yes, Taicho-san. I understand, Taicho-san."

"Good, Takeshi-san. I will be honest; if we find victory, I'm sure you can have a wonderful career in the army. If your initiative works out, I would consider it prudent to recommend you for officer training. Then you can kick Suzuki without fear of revenge."

"Yes, Taicho-san. Thank you, Taicho-san."

Takeshi managed a weak smile for the benefit of letting the Taicho know that he had a good sense of humor, but it was a day he knew would never come. The threat of execution for the CHamoru was more than he could stomach.

"I will give you one more night to find the missing ingredient. Bring it and the suruhana to the infirmary tomorrow. If the treatment works, then maybe the CHamoru will survive a little longer. If it fails, then I think it's best that we move you nearer, Asan. You are not popular here, but you are strong and fit and ready to look into the eyes of an American. Provide the army with men that are ready to fight, or take their place yourself. I think you find that a reasonable offer."

"Yes, Taicho-san. Thank you, Taicho-san."

***

Yuki, how have you been?

I am sorry I have not written recently. I do not know if my letters have even reached you. I am doing well and the commanding officer says he may recommend me for officer training. He has trusted me with a very important task that I can carry out in the Emperor's name. It has made me very proud.

All the men in my unit are very excited about fighting the Americans. It may be that, or the generous rations of sake. I think I can see why Uncle Taro liked the army so much. I have made a good friend. I can tell you his name is Hiroshi. He is someone I would like to have as a friend when this is all over and Japan has secured a glorious victory.

I think you would like him too; he makes me and others laugh with his jokes. We share cigarettes to make them last longer. I should have said, I've started smoking. I know you won't like that, but please understand it is very hard to avoid when you are a soldier.

I don't know when you will read this Yuki, but knowing the army, you will probably see me first. Your letters haven't reached me yet. Maybe it's best if you keep them, and I'll read them all on my return. You are always in my thoughts, no matter how far apart we are.

Your brother, Takeshi

He stood up from his bed as others returned from their duties. Takeshi was just getting ready to depart, to recover the leaves required for the medicine. The other men seemed happy that he was leaving just as they were arriving. He was used to being ignored by now. Only a few of them would acknowledge him with a small bow, but only because they feared the demons that Takeshi could talk to—or conjure.

Hiroshi entered last. He looked as if he was in pain, as he crossed to his own bed and lay down without talking. Takeshi walked over to him.

"Are you alright?"

"Ah, I think so. It's been a long time since I chopped down a tree, and they asked me to cut several down today. I'm aching all over to be honest," Hiroshi lowered his voice to a whisper, "Are you going back out tonight?"

"Yes, you know, for the last part of the medicine. We'll be ready soon."

"That is good. I'm sorry. I have to sleep now. I'm so sore and tired."

"Of course, my friend."

Takeshi returned to his own small part of the barracks to check he had what he needed. He picked up his rifle on the way out. Corporal Suzuki barged into him as they crossed in the doorway.

"Hey, Takeshi-san. Give your sister a kiss from me."

Takeshi walked on without turning back, to the jeers and laughter of the others in his barracks, mocking him as he left. There was nothing much worse in Japan than being rejected by your community. Standing out from the crowd was shameful in many ways. In Japan, you advanced in society through ageing. Becoming older would bring rewards without you having to prove yourself. Society would make sure you could progress without having to appear special or different. Takeshi had broken the rules.

The taunts continued until he left the camp. They aimed most at his sister. It filled him with rage, but the words of the Taicho had fresh meaning. He had made a threat against Yuki. She would suffer for anything *he* had done wrong. He hadn't considered that risk. It was something else for him to contemplate. He would have to plan the escape well, and there was so little time to do it.

He walked to where the shelters began, and he laid down some Kanpan biscuits on a tree stump. He said a small prayer that would appease the Kami at least and carried on. There was a lot of activity underway. The CHamoru were being organized to dig pits by the side of their shelters, and it was Kyota observing the work. He spotted Takeshi approaching.

"What's going on, Kyota?"

"The Taicho has ordered everyone to dig pits for their," he paused, "protection."

"Protection?"

"Once the Americans arrive, there will be many bullets and mortars. The Taicho only wants them to be safe. Do you understand," Kyota sneered.

"I understand."

"Are you going to meet your girlfriend? Or is it your sister? I can't remember. Your sister is beautiful, Takeshi. Maybe I will call on her when I get back to Japan. I would be a good husband. I'm sure you know that."

Takeshi couldn't stand to be in the presence of Kyota's gloating a moment longer. He scolded himself for not standing up to him, but Kyota wanted the fight. He couldn't take the risk of being caught out in a brawl. He couldn't ask the Taotaomo'na for help, but the thought revolved around his mind. He hoped that Kyota would be one of the first victims if they decided to strike.

Soon, his temper had settled. Elena stood before him. Takeshi's troubles disappeared in an instant as soon as she was near.

"*Pue'ngen maolek. Na'an hu si Elena.*"

"What?" Takeshi smiled broadly.

"That's your first lesson in CHamoru. Good evening. My name is Elena."

"I will try to learn it as we walk."

"Are we allowed to leave for the last ingredient?"

"Yes, but we *must* get the ingredient for tomorrow. The Taicho expects me to turn up with medicine and a suruhana. Have you found someone?"

"Yes, Mariana will help *you*."

"Good. The Taicho has assured me he will do something good in return. Let's go."

The night took over once again. Each time they went out, Elena went a little further north, putting more distance between them and camp. This part of the island was less populated and far from the defenses that were being moved to the hills in the west. A coral reef that surrounded the island was a layer of protection that meant the Japanese could be confident about how the Americans would approach.

"How do you say, *star*, in CHamoru?"

"Estreyas."

"Estreyas, I like that."

"You should learn more practical words, but it's an easy one to remember."

"You will need to teach me how to ask permission."

"That might take a little longer."

"I know, but it's costing me rations every time I enter the camp."

"What?" Elena smiled.

He loved making her smile. Her face lit up. The strain of living in Manenggon left her for a while. The comparison with Yuki was there again. He could see that Elena would handle Aunt Keiko just as well.

Elena picked herbs as they traveled. The mysterious ingredient seemed to grow in abundance if you knew where to look.

"Don't find it too soon," said Takeshi, "I don't want to head back to Manenggon right now."

"Don't worry. I want us to have time together, too, but in a nicer place."

"Alright, in that case, I'll help you gather more. Show me what to do."

They worked at harvesting the leaves they needed. Takeshi loved this island and its people. He only wanted to be here now, and he knew that for certain. He was over a thousand miles from home, but it could be a million miles, or home could be on a distant planet. It didn't matter. He could only see his home being Guam from now on.

After they had collected enough of the herb, Elena started to lead Takeshi over the rocky ground. The trail lay near a deep cliff, and she took his hand to guide him through the darkness. Then they climbed down one slope, then another.

"Where are we going?"

"You'll soon see."

Takeshi could see they were getting closer to the ocean. The waves were calm, lapping against the shore.

They descended to ground level, and a short strip of sand and rocks separated the cliffs from the ocean. They sat down together and gazed out.

"This place is ours. No one will come here tonight," said Elena.

"Not even the Taotaomo'na?"

"Maybe, but even they leave you alone at times. I meant that no one will be around to hear us. We can talk about our plans without fear of being overheard."

"Yes, of course. We don't have a lot of time. A few days at most. If the suruhana can cure someone, then that will give us some more time, I'm sure of it. But the commanders believe the American attack is coming. I think we have to wait for that."

"Won't that be too late?"

"The Taicho threatened my family today, my sister."

"How does he know her?"

"He doesn't, but he doesn't need to know her. A letter to the local police in Sasebo would be all it needed. They would do the rest."

"That's terrible."

"You see why I need to know that the Americans are here. I need to know that Japan will lose before we make a move. As soon as darkness falls, they'll send me to the patrol around camp that runs over to the south of Yona. The shelters have grown so much, they are almost at that point. Meet us at the edge of the camp, the closest point. It will be dangerous, but

Hiroshi will be with me. If we have the Taotaomo'na as well, I'm sure we can get away."

"The Taotaomo'na are everywhere around the camp. Mariana has spoken to me about it. There is going to be a war that the Taicho hasn't planned for."

"What do you mean?"

"There are signs everywhere. Many people can feel them moving amongst us. Children point to *men* that the adults cannot see, and many of the guards are having accidents. Injuries are becoming more common. Your infirmary must be full."

"They've asked us to make more buildings to house stricken soldiers. They sent Hiroshi to cut trees for them today."

"Cut trees?"

"Yes, he was a woodcutter in Shikoku before he joined the army."

"Did he have CHamoru with him?"

"I don't know. He was tired and sore when he came back."

"Then maybe he will need some of our medicine."

"I hope not. I'm relying on him."

The conversation dwindled as they gazed out into the dark ocean. Elena rested her head on Takeshi's shoulder and he placed his arm around her.

"Can we build a house here?" asked Takeshi.

"Maybe it would get a little wet." she giggled.

"How do I say, *ocean*, in CHamoru?"

"Tasi."

"What if I want a fish? How do I say, *fish*?"

"What kind?" she laughed, "Mahi-mahi, lapu? What else do you need to know?"

Takeshi looked shy and gazed into Elena's eyes. "How do you say, *I love you*, in CHamoru?"

"Hu guaiya hao."

"Hu guaiya hao," he replied.

Chapter 13
The Suruhana

Takeshi had only slept for two hours since returning to the barracks. Most of the others were still asleep, but a gray light was creeping into the building; it wouldn't be long before the call came to start the day. He pulled on trousers and boots, grabbed a cigarette and matches, and went outside to breathe in the mix of fresh air and calming smoke.

Bad weather was closing in around the camp. The clouds were thick, and the rain would follow soon, just to add to everyone's misery. The coconut leaves that topped the shelters were only useful for a while. Heavy rain would turn the soil floor to mud. Even so, rainwater was cleaner than the river; there was a benefit to being able to collect it and use it for drinking or cooking. The prisoners made use of every drop of clean water they could find.

Takeshi exhaled and tried to settle himself. There was so much resting on today. The medicine had to work and help persuade the Taicho that the CHamoru could help his men to recover.

It has to work.

The sirens went off around the camp. A rumble from inside the various buildings signaled the charge to be first. Everything about the army was about standing in line. Eating, washing, going to the toilet; all involved a queue. It had been like that from the very beginning, especially when you were in a camp. He started to appreciate being posted on the hillside with the artillery gun. You had more freedom to make the best of your day.

Takeshi had months to learn the area around Agat. He knew it well, compared with other parts of the island, but he couldn't escape to there. The fighting would be bad. The Americans had to attack near Agat. Then he wondered about the cove that he had visited with Elena. He had joked about living there, but maybe for a short while, they could build a shelter, just like one from the camp. As the rain started to drizzle, he knew that was a bad idea too.

If they met near Yona, then there was jungle nearby that would cover them for so long, but then the trail crossed the main road to Agana. Soldiers on the move swarmed around there. They had to head for the coast, back to Turtle Cove and beyond, heading further north along beaches and cliffs. Pursuing a route through the narrow middle section of the island seemed like the safest path to follow.

A yell and a groan from inside the building drew him out of his thoughts. He recognized the voice crying out in pain.

"Hiroshi?" he called out as he ran back inside the building.

Some of the others were standing around the bed. They cleared away to allow Takeshi through, but they couldn't hide their disgust for him.

"Look what your demons have done, Takeshi," said one soldier.

"We warned you, Hiroshi-san, not to hang around with him," said another.

They had pulled the cover back from Hiroshi. His lower legs had deep scrapes on the flesh. Takeshi had seen the markings before, the kind left by wild boars that had rubbed their tusks against trees. The skin had cracked and stained red. It wasn't hard to see why Hiroshi was in so much pain.

Corporal Suzuki arrived, as ever, at the wrong time for Takeshi.

"What have you done?" he demanded.

"I have done nothing. You still don't understand."

"I understand that you have brought these demons here. Not even your one friend in this camp is safe. How do you expect others to treat you? I am taking this incident to the Taicho. You have two minutes to put on a shirt and look respectful before your commanding officer."

Suzuki stormed out to give his side of the story first. The other men kept out of Takeshi's way, but the complaints against him were growing louder. The barracks was becoming a more threatening place to be. All agreeing that maybe Takeshi should move to the CHamoru side of the camp.

He straightened himself as he got dressed. He reminded himself that in a brief space of time, most of the surrounding men would be dead. An American bullet—or a Japanese hand grenade—would not change the outcome. He had to focus on his own plans. He was an outcast already. There was no longer any honor with his death.

He checked on Hiroshi before leaving. "How are you? Can you walk?"

"I think so," Hiroshi groaned.

"I am bringing the suruhana over soon. I will make sure you are the one to get treated."

"I appreciate that," he smiled.

Takeshi turned and walked to the door, barging past the others, much to their annoyance. It was only a short walk to the Taicho's office. In those few brief steps, he had to get his story straight. The plan was already in danger, before they were anywhere near escaping.

He stood outside the door. A stern-looking Kempeitai barred the way. He didn't utter a word. Everyone knew who Takeshi was by now. The military police officer turned and walked through the door. In the split-second that it was open, he could hear the raised voice of the Taicho. It was never a good sign.

He stood as the rain became heavier. Other guards walking past sniggered and assured Takeshi that he was *in for it now*. He could feel his heart race with anticipation. There was never a moment you could feel safe in this army. The punishments were severe and calculated to deter others who might dare to undermine authority.

The door flung open. The Kempeitai officer held it for a miserable looking Corporal Suzuki to march past without saying a word.

"It's your turn," said the officer at the door.

Takeshi entered. The Taicho was sitting with his eyes closed and taking slow breaths. He said nothing for minutes. The Kempeitai had followed him into the room. If there was a beating to be handed out, then the duty would fall to him.

That is, if I get away with a beating.

The Taicho opened his eyes, already staring at Takeshi.

"I regret this situation, Takeshi-san. I have not taken enough control. You understand that I have much to organize, and our rules don't make provision for dealing with an army of demons. Corporal Suzuki wants you flogged. In front of the entire guard. I think you have made him angrier because his arm injury stops him from doing the flogging himself. I am considering his proposal, as it would make the camp *happier*."

Takeshi felt himself start to sweat under the threat of the punishment. Soldiers that were dealt with in such a way were seldom able to do much for days afterwards. The chance of getting away from Manenggon was slipping away fast.

"Then I also have to consider, if Corporal Suzuki is correct, and you are working for these demons, then a beating is going to do little more than encourage their revenge. Who do I seek to appease? Who will serve me better?" The Taicho paused again, "Do you have the medicine and the suruhana now?"

"Yes, Taicho-san. I arranged everything. I can bring the healer to the infirmary as soon as you want."

"Very well. I will side with the demons one last time. Do not let me down, Takeshi. I cannot grant any more favors until I see the results."

"It takes another day for the healing to show."

"Takeshi-san. My patience is running very short. These delays won't help us, but they especially won't help you. The Americans are coming to kill you. Your own men might kill you first—at best you might kill yourself. I'm sure the other men would acknowledge you for that. These Taotaomo'na appear to be the only ones that want you to stay alive. I will allow your release back to the front line of your regiment. It's still positioned around Agat, awaiting the inevitable attack. I'm sure that will keep the camp more content until you leave."

"But, Taicho-san—"

"Do not question my orders or I will have you flogged before you go to the front! You will complete your task today. Tonight, you will resume your normal duties and lead a patrol around the Ylig River. There is a lot of activity between here and the line that General Takashina is establishing. I'll hold you responsible for anything that happens to any man crossing the jungle near Yona."

"Yes, Taicho-san."

"This better work, Takeshi. Time is running out for all of us, but especially for you."

***

"I will be your contact today," said Susa, "I can speak Japanese and translate for Mariana."

"Thank you, Susa," said Takeshi, "You aren't coming, Elena?"

"Of course she isn't. Do you want her to go to a place full of Japanese men?"

"Oh, yes, of course not. I'm sorry, Susa-san."

Takeshi smiled. He looked shy and embarrassed as he met Elena's eyes. Susa shook her head at the small display of affection.

"Will the Taicho let us collect more medicine tonight?" said Elena.

"No, they have put me back on patrol. I will be near the edge of the camp, walking down from Yona."

"I'll watch out for you."

"Be careful you two," Susa warned, "Now Takeshi, we have brought *Amot Tininu*, and palai."

"What is that?"

"A drink and an ointment. Mariana will invite the soldier to take the drink, then she will apply the ointment. She will take him to the place where he offended the Taotaomo'na, and she will ask him some questions."

"And it will work?"

Mariana stepped forward. He hadn't noticed her before now, but he sensed a great power around her, an ancient knowledge.

Mariana spoke to Susa in CHamoru.

"She says the Taotaomo'na have gathered here. Your friend may glimpse them when he is being healed. He should not fear their presence."

"How does she know it's my friend?"

Mariana smiled and didn't say any more.

"She knows. Are we ready?" said Susa.

Takeshi carried the drink and ointment, accompanied by Susa and Mariana. He noticed that the other prisoners knew the two women well. Comments and good wishes followed them through the maze of shelters that led down to the camp.

Kyota grinned over from a distance. Reunited with his gang, they watched more pits being dug. New arrivals were being told to do it before even building a shelter.

"Hey, Takeshi, do you like grandmothers now!"

Kyota's gang howled with laughter as Takeshi and the others kept their heads down and continued walking. Mariana spoke to Susa.

"Mariana says the Taotaomo'na approve of you. She says they will spare you when the time comes."

"They are talking to her now?"

"They always talk to her. She comes from a long line of suruhana. They have talked to Mariana all of her life."

"And what do they mean when the time comes?"

Suza talked to Mariana.

"She says all the CHamoru are under threat. This has never happened. The Taotaomo'na will not allow it to happen. Do you believe in Yurei, Takeshi?"

"All Japanese believe in ghosts. Our ancestors stay near their descendants."

"It is the same here. The Taotaomo'na are our ancestors, and they care for those who carry a small part of them from when they were in life. Would your ancestors be happy about how the other soldiers treat you?"

"No, my father would be furious."

"Well, how do you think our ancestors feel?"

They arrived at the gates of the military section. The guards eyed Susa and Mariana with suspicion, but everyone was aware of what was happening, whether it was from commands or gossip. A small crowd had found the time to gather around and watch.

The guards allowed them and Takeshi to enter. More sneering and laughter, but you could sense a fear. Takeshi noticed Corporal Suzuki standing further back. He wanted to keep his distance.

The door to the Taicho's office opened, and the commanding officer appeared. It wasn't unexpected, but his arrival caused all the men around to stand to attention, including Takeshi.

The Taicho nodded, and a command followed to stand at ease. He walked over toward the two women.

"So, Takeshi has informed me you will help heal some of our troops. I am happy with your efforts. We plan to defend you and your island. We need to have as many fit men as possible. The Americans have arrived with their ships and planes, but they do not care as we do. They say they come to save you, but they bomb your homes, your schools, your church. Please understand, we are happy to return to normal when the war is over. Manenggon exists for your safety."

Susa translated the Taicho's welcome to Mariana. In turn, Mariana responded with words that Susa felt were best not translated.

"Mariana says she is happy to help. Show her to the patient, please."

The Taicho looked over at the army doctors who had gathered outside the infirmary.

"None of the men want to be treated by the witches," said the senior doctor.

"I asked you to bring me a patient!" ordered the Taicho, "I did not ask that it should be a willing patient."

"Taicho-san," said Takeshi, "Excuse me, Taicho-san. Hasegawa-san will accept the treatment. He is in my barracks. We need him to cut trees for our work."

"Very well. This cannot take all day."

The Taicho began marching towards Corporal Suzuki, who snapped to attention once again, outside the wooden building.

"Suzuki-san. Maybe you would like to receive the treatment. Your arm still looks useless."

"Yes, Taicho-san. It is getting better, Taicho-san, I do not think I need the treatment."

"No, I thought you wouldn't."

The Taicho pushed past him and walked inside the door. Hiroshi, surprised by his commanding officer's sudden appearance, did his best to get out of bed.

"Stay where you are," commanded the Taicho, "Let's get this started."

Takeshi rushed over and laid down the prepared drink and ointment. He helped Hiroshi sit up. His wounds looked angrier. The pain was terrible as Hiroshi settled himself.

"This is Mariana. She is the suruhana. She is here to heal you. Susa will interpret for her, she will need to ask you questions so that she can help you."

"Please ask me anything," said Hiroshi, "Just take this pain away."

"First, he must take the drink," said Susa, "Hold your nose while you take it. It doesn't smell so good."

The Taicho and his personal guard watched as Hiroshi picked up a tin can containing the brew. He choked and wretched as he tasted it."

"Keep drinking," said Susa, not impressed with the over-reaction.

Hiroshi drained the can and reached for his water bottle, to take some of the taste away. Mariana continued speaking to Susa.

"Mariana says that by looking at your wounds, they shine. She can tell Taotaomo'na caused them, and the spirit is male."

"Can you see the spirit?" asked the Taicho.

"The spirits are all around Manenggon. That is why your men are so ill."

"Just get on with it."

Takeshi could tell the Taicho was becoming nervous.

Mariana took the palai and applied it to Hiroshi's legs. She was careful to not hurt him and spoke as she performed the healing.

"What is she saying?" asked the Taicho.

"She is asking for help with the healing, she is describing the spirit who is angry. She says that Hiroshi walked into the spirit's land without permission, and cut trees that had grown there for many years. This angered the spirit. Hiroshi must go back to the place and ask the Taotaomo'na to forgive him."

"Suzuki-san!" called the Taicho, "Where were the trees cut?"

"Not far. We can walk there. Taicho-san."

"Yes, but can he walk there?"

"I think I can, Taicho-san. My pain is easing."

"Do we need to do this?" the Taicho complained.

"Yes," said Susa, "this is a very important part. Without the Taotaomo'na's agreement, his wounds will not heal."

"Very well, be quick. I shall wait here. Takeshi-san. You will also wait. Take the suruhana to the trees that were cut down."

"Yes, Taicho-san."

Takeshi helped Hiroshi struggle into his army trousers and boots. Hiroshi dressed in his shirt and army jacket before struggling to his feet. Mariana kept talking in the CHamoru language while he was getting ready. She seemed in conversation with the spirits during the entire process.

Hiroshi stepped forward as Corporal Suzuki waited at the door. Within a few steps, he was starting to move with more ease and left the barracks along with Susa and Mariana.

The Taicho ordered his guards to leave as well. When he was alone with Takeshi, he chose to make an admission.

"I believe in the spirits. I believe they are real. I have seen them almost every night since I came to Manenggon. Their eyes watch me from a distance. I see their black formless shapes moving through the shadows. They never come near me. They only watch. They are waiting. They are gathering, and yes I feel their anger. My interest in you, Takeshi, is how you have made peace with them."

"They are the guardians of the latte stones. We are in their land. We have to show respect. Taicho-san."

"I do not have time to give them the respect they need. Japan is at war. Our enemies must fall, whoever they are, whatever they are. They do not fight like a normal enemy. They pick us off when we are alone or in small groups. They move with great speed through the jungle. We cannot catch them, we cannot shoot them. Yet they can hurt us with scratches, bites and sharpened tusks. They can surprise us and strike terror. They break our men or drive them mad. They are wearing us down."

"Perhaps we could ask Mariana to do something, a ceremony or a ritual at the latte stones. Maybe they would leave us then, Taicho-san."

"It is too late, Takeshi-san. The orders came through from the General himself. From tomorrow, I am to organize death squads. The work will begin to remove the CHamoru for good. In a few days, they will be gone. What do you think the Taotaomo'na will do then? Believe me, Takeshi, I think you will be better at Agat. I believe I am paying you for your work, for carrying out your special project. I am giving you your one chance to kill an American. If I cannot do that, then what has your life been for. To die for the Emperor is the greatest honor you may have."

"Please, Taicho-san. I wish to stay at Manenggon. I am prepared to face whatever happens here. I will carry out my orders. I will make sure my patrol protects the soldiers moving into the hills. I can serve the Emperor by keeping men safe as they move through the jungle. If I could have more time to question the prisoners, maybe I could raise a patrol of suruhana to protect our army. Maybe even to attack the Americans."

The Taicho smiled. It unnerved Takeshi—for a moment it reminded him of his Aunt's smile. It never meant that she was happy underneath it all. He sat in silence for a moment longer.

"I cannot indulge this any longer. If the General even knew of this conversation, they would expect me to commit Seppuku, to at least die with one last grain of honor. I will see the Taotaomo'na tonight, like I have seen them every night, growing in number, and building their rage. When they come, I will draw my Katana. I will fight for my country and my Emperor, but I fear my next sight will not be the light of heaven. The darkness is where these creatures thrive. I think that is where I will go. Go to Agat and forget what you have found here."

"Please, Taicho-san. I only ask to remain here for the sake of the one moment in my life that has brought me true happiness."

"The girl? Think of the others who are here. Many have wives and families. I have a wife and family. My daughters are married and hoping for their own children. Don't you think that I deserve to see them one last time?"

"I am sorry, Taicho-san. I have been disrespectful, Taicho-san."

"There is no one here to witness your disrespect. I see no point in a beating. Stay on your patrol, do what you can, and stay out of the camp. You will not have the stomach for what is about to happen. When the transport comes, leave Manenggon for Agat. That is an order. We will not speak of this again. Where have they got to?"

The Taicho stood up and left the barracks. Takeshi felt tears well up; he was inconsolable. He sat at the table, burying his head under his arms. The thought of losing Elena was the only thing on his mind. He knew he had to try. There was no time left.

A commotion sounded outside. It caused Takeshi to jump up and dry his face, though his distress would show in his eyes. Susa re-entered the room, noticing that Takeshi was upset. She didn't comment, but she offered a nod of comfort in his direction.

Mariana followed her and then Hiroshi, who was walking with a spring in his step. He didn't just look better; he looked happy.

"Takeshi! I feel great. Mariana has worked a miracle. I'm almost back to normal."

"Then you can join me on the patrol tonight?"

Takeshi seemed suddenly excited. He was asking more with his facial expression that he was with his words. Hiroshi knew his intent.

"Well, yes—"

"Well, no," said Susa, "He will need a good night's sleep. If his marks have gone in the morning, then he can return to duty."

"But—"

"No," said Susa, "give your friend a chance to heal."

Corporal Suzuki wandered through the door. "I will take the suruhana back to her shelter. Takeshi-san, organize men for your patrol tonight from the new arrivals. The truck will arrive soon."

"I can—"

"That's an order."

"Yes, Gocho Suzuki-san."

***

The rest of the day turned against Takeshi. As night fell, heavy rain descended. The trail by the river started to flood, and the mud made it difficult to go ahead through the jungle. The Taotaomo'na had stayed away, although he could feel a powerful presence whenever the patrol was going past the camp.

His disappointment grew when he didn't see Elena. He tried to walk past the point where he expected her to be standing, but his men were grumbling and eager to complete the last part of their journey. It was time to head back, before climbing into bed.

My bed?

As Takeshi walked towards his barracks, a bed lay outside in the rain, with sheet, blanket, and pillow soaked. Under the covers, they had placed a mop as if it were a person. They attached a painted piece of wood to the top. The message read, *Takeshi's bed, and his sister's.*

Takeshi was heartbroken. He had never felt so alone, or such a weight of sadness. He walked back out of the gate, the mocking laughter of the guards on duty ringing in his ears. He walked as far as the tree stump where he had left the biscuits for the Kami. They were gone, though he was sure it wasn't the Kami that had taken them.

He pulled his last cigarette from his pocket and laid it down.

"This is all I have," he whispered, "This is all I can offer to the ancestors. I ask you to kill all of them. Kill all of them, before they kill your children. Leave none unharmed. Kill them all.

Chapter 14
Letter from Home

The heavy rain poured down on Takeshi. It dripped from his brow, running into his eyes and obscuring his vision as he lurched from shelter to shelter. He had to find Elena. He had to know what happened to her. It was still two hours until the sunrise. He had to warn her.

He staggered through the mud, sliding and losing his balance more than once. The CHamoru people were more active at night. Some helped to pick him up and steer him in the right direction. They knew who he was. Everyone knew who Takeshi was. The CHamoru trusted him because the Taotaomo'na trusted him. His fellow Japanese soldiers hated him for the same reason. Only the Taicho's support had saved him from worse treatment by his comrades.

His heart raced as he worried for Elena. If he thought they could make it, he would leave now, but he knew that she wouldn't leave her mother to suffer the consequences. He wouldn't leave Yuki if his family was in the same position. His mind kept searching for an answer as he stumbled onward.

Elena spotted him first. She ran out and pulled him toward her shelter, racing to bring him undercover and out of the rain. She guided him to sit down amongst the group of CHamoru she was sharing her living space with.

The eyes of three young children stared back in silence. They were old enough to know that his uniform meant fear and panic. Older men and women coughed and nodded toward him. Mothers of children lost, sat with expressions that displayed pain and torment, rather than anger. They knew Takeshi wanted to save them, but he was only one in an army who wished them dead.

"Let me dry you," said Elena.

She produced a blanket to rub against his head and body. She worked fast, but her touch was gentle. Her care was something that Takeshi had never experienced in his life. She didn't need to speak to tell him of her affection. He just experienced it every waking second that he spent with her.

One of the older women looked more welcoming. She used hand signals to ask if Takeshi wanted to eat.

"Takeshi, this is my mother, Maria."

Takeshi moved onto his knees and gave a respectful bow.

Maria spoke CHamoru to Elena, who giggled at her mother's words.

"She says you are a handsome-looking boy, with very good manners."

Takeshi smiled and bowed again, glowing with embarrassment.

"Tell your mother I am very pleased to meet her."

"You tell her. Magof yo' sa' umali'e' hit."

"Ma-gofyo…"

Elena and her mother both laughed. Elena confirmed what Takeshi wanted to say.

"Are you hungry? We have breadfruit and papaya."

"No, I can't take food from you."

"Please," said Elena, "it is our culture to welcome and share what we have."

"I'll take a little then."

Takeshi's shyness took over once more when Elena went to get the food. He didn't know where to look as the center of attention. He switched between watching the rain and back to Elena's mother who continued to look at him. Elena returned with the food.

"I didn't see you from my patrol; I was worried."

"Soldiers were here last night. They ordered us to dig pits for our safety."

"Don't go near these pits, Elena. Tell everyone not to go in them, they are…"

He looked at the faces of the children gazing at him. They were gazing at the food in his hand. He took a small piece and held it out to the nearest child. They were wary for a few moments, but their hunger overcame their fear. Once one had been successful, the other two stepped forward. The older people in the shelter grinned with approval.

"The pits are dangerous, Elena. They are not what they say they are."

"We know what they are, but what can we do? If we refused to dig, then they would still shoot or behead us. All we can do is pray that someone will save us, before they decide to put us in our graves."

"I will save you. I will save as many as I can. I need to get Hiroshi, he will help. I just hope he is better."

"Don't worry about that," Elena assured, "Susa told me that when they took Hiroshi to the tree, Mariana spent a lot of time instructing the Taotaomo'na spirit that he had been wrong to injure Hiroshi. She told the ancestor he had no right to harm one of the few Japanese that wanted to help us. She is a very hard person to refuse."

"The Taicho just wants me out of camp. He is sending me back to Agat to rejoin my regiment?"

"When?" Elena panicked.

"I don't know. I suppose when there's transport there to take me. The Taicho said my duty in the meantime was to patrol around Yona, to help protect troops that are moving to the front line. He admitted to me he believes in the Taotaomo'na. He has seen them. Many of them."

"So, what will you do?"

"At dawn I'll head back to camp to check on Hiroshi. If he is fit, I can put him on my patrol. If we can get out on our own, we can look for the best route for escape so that we know where we are heading. Be ready to go at any time. I don't believe we can expect to wait for the Americans."

"It is being kept quiet, but the people are gossiping about the Americans saving George Tweed. They have already neared the island. We all feel it won't be long now."

"You just have to stay safe—however you can. If you need to run, go to our cove. I will know how to find you. I will find a way to bring your mother."

Elena wept. "My mother has said if I can escape alone with you, then I have her blessing. She says if the spirits wish it, we will be reunited. She says it is not a large island, she will find me."

Elena cuddled into Takeshi, seeking the comfort of his embrace. The others in the shelter, including Elena's mother, smiled sympathetically.

"Thank you, all of you," said Takeshi.

Elena fell asleep in his arms. The safest place she had known for a long while—the comfort of Takeshi's loving embrace.

***

The rain lifted as Takeshi walked through the gates. The morning alarm sounded for all in the camp. He had shut his mind off to the barrage of insults that followed everywhere he went. They couldn't hurt him anymore, and if his wish came true, they wouldn't be around to hurt him for much longer. His mind was becoming calm and focused. He had one task to do—complete the escape route, using his patrol to spot the gaps in the path they would have to take.

His face lit up when he saw Hiroshi standing by the door of the barracks, looking healthier than he ever had. He strode over to Takeshi with a confident swagger, proving that the suruhana had healed the wounds on his legs.

"Look at me, Takeshi. The healing has worked!"

"You don't have any wounds?"

"Just pale marks where they were now. It's healing by the hour."

"And no pain?"

"No, no pain. I'm ready," he said.

Once again, there was an understanding between them. Takeshi knew what *I'm ready* meant.

"Let me help you move your bed. I'm afraid I still wasn't well enough to stop them all last night."

"Thank you, my friend."

They lifted the bed frame and its bedding as one. Some dragged through the dirt, but it was a straightforward job for the two of them working together. They dragged it into the busy barracks. The other soldiers didn't know what to talk about first, their pet hate, Takeshi, or the amazing recovery of Hiroshi.

"Why are you bringing that thing in here?"

"The bed?" said Hiroshi.

"No, Takeshi."

The other men laughed at the jibe.

"I'm tired of you all insulting my friend," Hiroshi responded, "Look at me. I am better in one day. How long would it have taken in the infirmary? You all saw me. You saw my wounds, and now they are gone, because my friend, Takeshi, did something about it. He used his brain. Something the rest of you don't have. Takeshi has done nothing to any of you, but you treat him worse than a dog."

"He is a dog. A lap dog for the Taicho!" said another.

Takeshi rushed toward the man giving the insult, but Hiroshi held him back.

"Do you want to repeat that in front of the Taicho?" said Hiroshi.

"What is going on in here?" said Corporal Suzuki, rushing into the barracks.

"I am cured," replied Hiroshi.

"Cured?" the corporal couldn't quite believe it.

Hiroshi performed a high step to attention. "Look, there's no more problem with my legs."

Suzuki looked perplexed. It was an amazing recovery. He put his left hand on his own withering right arm.

"You are not in pain?"

"No."

Suzuki took longer to process the thought. "It seems I was wrong about you, Takeshi."

You could hear a pin drop in the room. The shock of the corporal's sudden mood change surprised everyone, especially Takeshi.

"I will be next to be cured. I will tell the Taicho about the success of the suruhana. You will organize it, Takeshi."

"Yes, Gocho Suzuki-san."

He turned to the other men who were still standing dumbfounded.

"Who made this mess with the bed? Are you all animals? I want to see it scrubbed and cleaned, with a fresh blanket when I return. Or someone will face punishment."

From the men's reaction, the ringleader looked like it had been Corporal Suzuki, himself.

"Yoshida-san, Hasegawa-san, follow me."

The two marched out behind the corporal. Hiroshi allowed himself a small laugh back at the dejected-looking soldiers in the barracks.

As was normal, the corporal entered the Taicho's office for his own private meeting first, with Takeshi and Hiroshi forced to stand and wait.

"What do you think, Takeshi? Does this give more time?"

"I hope so. Can you believe Suzuki-san?"

"That's what I mean. If we can change his mind."

"Yes, you're right. I believe the Taicho may well give us more time."

Machine-gun fire rattled through the air. It was small arms fire.

"What's that" said Hiroshi, half-ducking.

Screams and wails followed in the distance. More machine-gun fire followed, and then silence.

"I don't think it's the Americans," said Takeshi.

The door swung open and Corporal Suzuki ordered them to march into the Taicho's office. The Taicho studied Hiroshi as he entered.

"They tell me that your wounds are gone, Hasegawa-san?"

"Yes, Taicho-san. I am ready to get back to my duties, Taicho-san."

"Well done Hiroshi-san, and you too Takeshi-san. Now what are we to do? This requires a plan. We must work fast."

"We will need more medicine, Taicho-san," said Takeshi.

"Of course we will. I will send more men with you tonight."

"More men, Taicho-san?"

"So that we can take more medicine. As much as we can carry. We cannot leave it just to you."

"But, they will need to respect the Taotaomo'na, Taicho-san."

"You will have my full authority, Takeshi-san. Your orders will come from the Emperor himself. You have my permission to punish anyone who shows disrespect or disobedience."

"Yes, Taicho-san."

"And we need more of these suruhana. Corporal Suzuki, organize a search party to go through the camp. Take interpreters, and of course you can also use any means that you believe to be necessary. I believe I just heard our death squads beginning their work. So please find the people we need."

"Yes, Taicho-san. Excuse me, Taicho-san. Is it my turn to be healed?"

"Yes, of course. Takeshi-san, you have your next volunteer patient here."

"We will need transport to take Gocho Suzuki-san back to where the incident happened."

"Organize it, Gocho Suzuki-san. Hasegawa-san, you will accompany Takeshi-san. The demons now approve of you too it seems. If any of you make them fight on our side, then I'm sure that would lead to a nice promotion."

No one followed with a response to the idea.

"I suppose not, then still, we must do what we can. The extra men will help our cause at least.

"You are all dismissed."

They left the Taicho's office together.

Corporal Suzuki departed to plan for his own needs. A small building beside the Taicho's office was responsible for administration. Takeshi remembered the letter he wanted to send. He pulled a sealed envelope from his pocket. It was wet, but still intact.

"I just need to send this. I'll be over in a minute."

Hiroshi walked away, saying he would make some tea, and that they could discuss their plans. Takeshi knocked on the administration door, and entered on command. A stern-looking sergeant stared at him and sighed. The good news hadn't spread to him yet, that Takeshi was back in favor.

"I have a letter to send home."

The sergeant snatched it from him and looked at the envelope.

"You know I have to open it and read it?"

"Oh, yes. I'm sorry, I haven't sent many letters home."

The sergeant looked at the address. "Yoshida Yuki, in Sasebo? Your sister?"

"Yes Gunso-san."

"Do you write about your other sister?"

"No, Gunso-san."

"A pity. I might have enjoyed reading that."

"I will put it with the others."

He walked over to a pile of letters that were scattered, and disorganized, tossing it without care on to the top of the pile. Then he picked one up and returned to the desk.

"It seems that we have a letter here for you."

"For me? From home?"

"Yes, Sasebo."

"When did it arrive?"

"The last post arrived on the Aki Maru."

"Wait, I arrived on the Aki Maru. That was months ago."

"These things take time. We are fighting a war, and soldiers move around a lot. It has caught up with you at Manenggon."

"Please, may I have it, Gunso-san."

The sergeant toyed with the idea of not handing it over for a moment, but then relented. Takeshi snatched it as quick as he could and ran from the office onto the main square of the camp. His fingers scrambled at the paper to open and unfold the news from home.

> Takeshi-san, how have you been?
>
> This is Ryo writing to you. I wanted to let you know how things were at home. It is very quiet here at the moment, but we have enough food and my mother is doing her best to take care of cooking the rice. Though it's not as good as Yuki's was.
>
> Yuki is no longer with us Takeshi. After you left, my mother gave Yuki extra duties to help look after us.

She said because you were gone. Yuki needed to sweep, and light the fire for the stove, and make the hot bath for us all to use.

She worked very hard and never complained; she seemed to eat less after you were gone. My mother insisted that Kenichi and I needed more, as we were growing men. We would need to follow you and be strong for the army and the war.

One night she ran the bath late for my father. He came home in a good mood. I think he had won money from someone and had drunk more sake than usual. He was dancing and singing. We were all laughing, more than we had laughed for a long while.

Yuki told him his bath was ready, and he went through to relax. He fell into the bath and screamed. The hot water burned him. He jumped out and came through screaming at Yuki. I'm sorry Takeshi, she was in tears and very sorry. My mother sent her to bed.

The next day my mother said that Yuki was forgiven for her mistake, so my mother would heat the bath water from now on. Everything went back to normal, and that night my mother said that Yuki could have the first bath, like an honored guest to the house. Yuki was very happy and my mother went through to help her.

The water was too hot for Yuki as well. She screamed, and we heard splashing and struggling. My mother kept shouting at her not to struggle, but the splashing and choking continued. Then it all went quiet. My mother ran out in tears, she said that Yuki had panicked in the bath and hadn't let her help her. She said that Yuki kept fighting against her.

My mother ran out of the house to try and get help. There was only Kenichi, and I left. We went through to see what we could do. She was unconscious, but breathing. Her skin was burned and swollen.

My mother came back with a doctor, and he quickly organized to have her taken to a hospital. We visited her for two days, but then one night, only my father was allowed to visit her. It was hours before he came home. He told us that Yuki had died. I'm so sorry Takeshi. I have written this letter in the hope that you see it soon. Maybe they will let you come home and pray for her.

Kenichi and I hope we can see you soon. We miss our big cousin and we want you to be happy. I say a prayer to Yuki every night, Takeshi. I hope now you can say a prayer for her too.

Your cousin, Ryo

***

Hiroshi poured out two mugs of brewed tea. The room was empty. They would be able to talk about their plans. The door swung open and slammed against the side of the wall. It startled Hiroshi, and he looked up to see his friend entering.

Takeshi could not hide his pain. Hiroshi seemed to know without asking when he saw the letter hanging from Takeshi's hand.

"Your sister?"

Takeshi could only nod. His breathing struggled, and he choked as he sat, retching and gripping onto the letter with a clenched fist.

"Can I take that from you?" said Hiroshi, pulling at the letter.

"Yes," was all Takeshi could say.

"Can I read it?"

"Yes."

Hiroshi scanned the letter. He felt his own emotions rise on reading the words, but he had to be strong for his friend. He placed an arm around Takeshi's shoulder.

"Takeshi, you have to do the best you can now. Make Yuki proud. Your sister will want you to live and prosper, to only have happy memories. You must use this Takeshi, use it to find a strength within you. That is how you honor your sister."

He pushed the mug of tea in front of Takeshi. "Drink this and gather yourself. You will not forget her, and you will always make her proud wherever she is now."

Takeshi drew a long, deep breath. "I knew when I left her at Sasebo railway station. I knew that Keiko had tricked me. I should have left then. I should have got off at the next station and went back. What would it have cost me? A few days in jail? A beating? I could have confronted my Aunt. I could have ordered her to leave Yuki alone. My aunt killed her. You can tell, too? It's not just me? She killed her before I even left Japan.

Hiroshi nodded. "I see what you see."

"There is nothing there for me now. There is nothing for me to fight for. Last night after they played the trick on me, I prayed for the Taotaomo'na to kill all of them. Today for a little while I regretted my prayer, but now I know more than ever. I want the spirits to rise. I want them to take their revenge."

"Remember Takeshi, we are not the only ones hating this war. It could be most that hate it, but everyone is too terrified to speak. Even if they agreed with you, Takeshi, they would not say. They sit in corners with an old photograph, or a letter like yours. The army has told them not to see what is obvious. We are fighting for a few to have more land and more wealth. Does that make any sense? That all of us are told to die to keep a family in power."

"That talk will get you killed," said Takeshi.

"Or thrown in prison. I know, but it is the truth. You have found something very special here, Takeshi. The CHamoru are different. You have found love here? Am I wrong?"

"No."

"Then that is the thing you should be fighting for. Gather yourself. We will make our escape. Who knows what will happen, but if we are fortunate, then we will make it. You will build a life with Elena, and that is where you will belong. I hope that I find what you have found. I too want to settle in this place. Even though I made a spirit angry."

Hiroshi helped to calm Takeshi, his breathing slowed and his tears subsided.

"That's better. Take heart and find strength. We need our wits about us more than ever. Let's plan our patrol tonight. We are getting out of here."

***

The patrol took longer than usual. The two friends had escaped onto the trail around camp without bringing others with them. As they followed the Ylig River, the shelters were meeting them.

The entire island is here.

Or what was the entire island. Every now and again, there would be shrieks and cries for help. The dull explosion of a grenade, the crack of a rifle, or the repeat of a machine gun. The familiar cry of an officer using the power of his voice with the sharp blade of his Katana, after some time, a silence followed. A lull before the horrific murders would begin again.

Even executioners have to sleep.

As they reached Yona, they kept walking forward. Takeshi asked the Taotaomo'na for permission in Japanese, and cursed himself for not learning the CHamoru words. He hoped that his intent would be clear all the same. They reached the road that stretched west to Agana. It was busy, as Takeshi had thought. Army vehicles were racing back and forward through the night. Cargo of ammunition and supplies, and cargo of CHamoru slaves with only one purpose each, to carry boxes of bullets to the top of the hill, before receiving one in the back of the head.

Takeshi and Hiroshi headed back along the far side of the camp. They took notes, made observations about places to hide and caves where they might shelter for a while. Their direction would be north and east. Some deserted farms they knew of lay in that direction. The army had raided many, so their soldiers could loot and feed themselves.

They stopped in the distance before the road that crossed at Ylig Bay, and headed back to camp. In the distance, Takeshi caught a figure moving through the darkness. It was Elena. He was relieved to see her, even from afar. As his eyes narrowed and he peered into the darkness, he could make out dark figures gathered around her. Tall, dark figures without faces. For a moment, he panicked, but then he realized they were protecting her.

He turned and headed back to the gates. Hiroshi gave a smile and an acknowledgement of passing Elena. Takeshi wondered if he had seen the Taotaomo'na too.

Chapter 15
The Ga'lågu

"Takeshi, it is time to go."

Takeshi's eyes opened. It was still dark outside the shelter, but the sky was beginning to lighten in the minutes before sunrise.

"Yes, I'll go."

He scrambled to his feet. The other inhabitants of the shelter were asleep, or at least politely pretending to be asleep as Takeshi and Elena shared a last hug.

"Go."

"Yes. I'll see you later."

Takeshi rushed through the camp until he was just out of sight of the guardhouse. He began to stagger, pretending to be drunk for the benefit of the guards.

They let him wander through in silence. There were no jokes today. Takeshi pondered why. Was it the fact that Hiroshi had recovered? Had word got round about Yuki? Maybe even the cruel soldiers that he shared his accommodation with would give him a day off from insults.

He crept back below the covers. There wasn't a point to getting undressed; he would be back up on duty within the hour.

When the siren went off, he felt as if he had just gone to sleep. He had a dream about the latte stones on a sun-soaked summer day. He was alone in the dream, but he could feel a power around him. The light shimmered between the pillars, which stood aligned in pairs. The air was still. The ocean was like glass.

The calm disappeared in an instant as he sat up. Many noticed that he was already wearing his uniform, but not so many were ready to take him on today. They ignored him by getting on with their own preparations.

Corporal Suzuki barked in his usual style. He was always ready early so that from the very first moment of each day he could make life miserable for his men. He headed straight for Takeshi.

"Find the suruhana this morning and the interpreter. We will head back to Talofofo this afternoon."

"If she is still there, Gocho Suzuki-san. There was a lot of killing yesterday."

"Then leave a sign anywhere you find suruhana. The Taicho will issue orders for marked shelters to be left alone."

Takeshi's heart missed a beat. The corporal had just given him a way to protect Elena and her mother. She was the one going out for the medicine after all. He thanked Yuki in his head. He felt that now he knew she had passed on, she was looking over him and helping him. He resolved as soon as this was all over to commemorate her in a place near some latte stones, with a beautiful view over the island. She would appreciate that. His spirits began to lift again.

"Yes, Gocho Suzuki-san. I will organize it right away."

"Good. Have them here by noon."

Hiroshi joined them. "My wound is gone, Gocho Suzuki-san. The medicine works. I feel stronger. If we could make all the men in the infirmary feel this way, it would be like adding a new division to our army."

Corporal Suzuki smiled, this came as a shock to Takeshi and Hiroshi.

"Yes, the Taicho will be very pleased. Keep me informed of your patrols and your progress. I will keep the Taicho informed at all times."

You mean you want to take all the credit.

Suzuki stood up and went back to shouting at the others getting ready for their assigned duties.

"We have a good chance now," whispered Hiroshi.

"Yes, you're right. Let's get organized."

***

Takeshi and Hiroshi wasted little time in heading back to Elena's shelter. They carried small wooden boards that they had marked with the Kanji script for *Taicho*. They felt that would make it obvious enough not to go near certain shelters. As they passed through the gates, Kyota was also heading out with his own patrol of willing followers.

"Good morning, Takeshi-san. Another busy day?"

"I am on business for the Taicho. I didn't see you bow Kyota-san."

Kyota made a brief gesture of respect. "You are right, of course, Ittohei Yoshida-san. I believe I will also gain a promotion soon. It will be good to share the privilege. Maybe we can beat up the new recruits together, like friends?"

Takeshi couldn't hide his disgust and carried on walking.

"I'm going to need more grenades than that!" Kyota shouted to his men, knowing full well that Takeshi would hear him.

The level of fear in the camp was spreading. The presence of any Japanese soldier, even Takeshi, was causing alarm. Selection by the death squads that were roaming the camp seemed to be random.

A cycle of killing played out time and time again. An officer would order a group of CHamoru to go into the very pit they had dug. They would pack them in so that they couldn't move, dropping in children to fill smaller gaps. The screams and cries for mercy and help sounded around the immediate area. Then the grenades would go in, two or three at a time. The explosions would kill the nearest to the blast. Others would suffer terrible injuries, but they would only survive a little longer. A machine gun would follow, and then troops would step over the mesh of bloodied bodies, using their bayonets to extinguish any last signs of life. The soldiers would then move on. They were following orders. That is all they had ever trained them to do.

Takeshi was glad to see Elena and her mother were still safe when he arrived at their shelter. They hugged. It was a disquieting sight for many around, but their feelings for one another were too strong to hide away.

"Are you alright, Takeshi?"

"Yes, I am better. I feel different now like Yuki is closer to me. I think she's helping us. We have just received the Taicho's authority. If we can find more suruhana for him, then everyone in their shelter will have his protection."

"But how do you choose?"

"If we can save some people, maybe others will survive. We have to act fast while the Taicho will make this offer. Look at Hiroshi. They believe that the medicine will work for all. We have to try."

"They healed you, Hiroshi-san? Let me get Susa. I need to tell her what has happened."

Elena disappeared into the mass of people that surrounded the shelter. Hiroshi organized one of the signs, placing it on to the top of the frame. Takeshi looked at the faces staring back. Elena's mother smiled and nodded, but she was weaker looking now, exhausted from the misery of life in Manenggon. The other older people were showing the same signs of being worn down. Life being sucked from them. Two of the children walked over. They knew Takeshi now, and they trusted him because he had shared his food. They were dirty and malnourished, but they smiled at seeing him.

Takeshi looked for the third child, and then he noticed the quiet sobbing of a mother holding her son, wrapped in a blanket, as he gasped for his last breath. All she could do was draw him closer. A last effort to provide comfort and safety as the young boy struggled through his last minutes of life.

Takeshi offered a prayer in Japanese. Although no one around him could understand the words, they understood the thought he was sending.

Elena returned with Susa, who first attended the grieving mother. She whispered words of comfort and hugged the woman and her son. She stared with an anger she couldn't disguise.

"So, Hiroshi-san. You believe in the Taotaomo'na now?"

"I always did, but now Corporal Suzuki believes in them as well."

"Susa-san," said Takeshi, "We can save some people, but we need to send more suruhana to the Taicho; we need to gather more medicine. They can see the healing works, but we must help them, to give us a chance of stopping the killing."

"So then they will kill us a few days later when we have cured their soldiers?"

"The Americans are coming," said Elena, "We only need some extra time."

"The Taotaomo'na are coming too. I have never felt a power like this on the island. By the end, it will be like the Japanese never existed. Why would the Taotaomo'na help us with this? We cannot do anything without their permission on this matter. I cannot agree to this desire of the Taicho without asking our ancestors. We will need to be allowed to meet at the latte stones, first."

"Susa-san, I'm sure I can arrange it. The Taicho wishes me to lead a patrol with Elena to gather more herbs. He will allow us to escort you to the latte stones at the same time. I'm sure of it."

"Japanese soldiers gathering the medicine. How much do they want to take? We can only pick the medicine in small personal amounts. The Taotaomo'na will never agree to their jungle being ravaged or harvested like a paddy field. The Taicho will only make more trouble for himself. And you Elena, what if the Taotaomo'na are angry with you for being part of this?"

"We have to try. Look at how fast they are trying to get rid of us. The Taotaomo'na haven't attacked them yet, even though death surrounds us."

"It will happen!"

"Yes, but do we just wait for our turn to be placed in the pits, or do we try to do something?"

Susa gazed down at the mother soothing her dying child. She also knew that saving others from a similar fate was the best they could do.

"Very well. What is the Taicho looking for?"

"Suruhana and medicine are to be gathered at the infirmary tomorrow, but today we need Mariana to return and heal my corporal. He was attacked near a ranch at Talofofo. He has organized transport for noon to take us there. Mariana will be asked to cure him, the same way that she cured Hiroshi."

"The Taotaomo'na may not view your corporal in the same way as Hiroshi, but you are right, we need to do what we can to save at least some from this nightmare. I will fetch Mariana."

"Let us come with you. The Taicho has given us signs to place outside shelters where we can find volunteers. It will protect everyone in their group while they carry out the work."

"We can trust this?" asked Susa.

"Yes, I believe the Taicho will keep to his word, if we can just heal his men."

Elena's mother began speaking to Susa. The conversation between them was rapid, and it sounded to Takeshi like she was chastising Susa in the CHamoru language, but the words ended with smiles. Susa said nothing, but Elena explained.

"My mother asked Susa what was happening. She explained what we had to do. My mother then said that it is the CHamoru way to help good people in need. She said you were a good person, Takeshi, then," she paused, "she told Susa that if she helped, then she could come to our wedding ceremony."

Takeshi didn't know where to look. "Yes, Susa. You will be very welcome on that day."

"Eh, I think we should get started," interrupted Hiroshi."

"Yes, I agree," said Susa.

***

The cloud was heavier once again—the rainy season ever threatening its downpours to make navigating the land harder, and ensure the living conditions were even poorer.

Corporal Suzuki was in a rush to get going, as he ordered Takeshi, Hiroshi, Susa, and Mariana into a personnel carrier. The truck exited the camp at speed, making the journey tough and uncomfortable, but for Susa and Mariana it was harder still as they looked out at the places they knew and loved.

The regular sights of home were not so familiar. Truckloads of soldiers moved back and forth on the road. The soldiers had chopped trees down. The odd glimpses of the ocean revealed American ships patrolling in the distance. Ransacked ranches lay empty.

"They are locusts!" said Mariana. Susa chose not to translate.

As they neared the part of the road where the attack on Corporal Suzuki took place, Mariana seemed to recognize something.

"He suffered a bite?" she said to Susa.

"Yes, that's what they said.

"There is *ga'lågu* in this place, they bite. "

"What is she saying?" asked Takeshi.

"The Taotaomo'na in this place take the form of dogs, and they bite."

The vehicle pulled to a halt close to the farmhouse they had been heading to on the day. The driver decided he was staying where he was in the cabin, while Takeshi and Hiroshi helped the two women onto the ground.

Mariana asked for permission to enter the jungle.

"Be quick," shouted the corporal, "I wish to get this done."

Then, the suruhana looked around herself and started to laugh. "*Ga'lågu, many ga'lågu.*"

"She is talking about dogs," said Susa, "Taotaomo'na dogs, the worst kind."

"We shoot dogs." said Corporal Suzuki.

"Not these dogs," mumbled Susa.

Mariana began talking, addressing something that was in the jungle with them.

"You are to stand still, Gocho Suzuki-san," Susa instructed.

Corporal Suzuki looked nervous as Mariana began to walk around him, casting a circle of salt on the ground with him at its center.

"What is she doing?"

"The ga'lågu will not cross the salt. It seems they still want to eat you."

"Tell her to hurry. Yoshida, Hasegawa, be ready with your rifles."

"Stay calm. Now drink the Amot Tininu," Susa was enjoying this moment.

Mariana handed Corporal Suzuki the tin can of brewed herbal medicine.

"Hold your nose. It stinks," then she whispered to herself, "well something stinks."

Just like Hiroshi at the previous healing, he gagged and choked on the drink, almost bringing up the contents of his stomach.

"Hold on to it. It won't do any good on the ground."

"It's horrible," he complained.

Mariana seemed to talk to an entire pack of dogs. Holding her arms out to demonstrate there was more than one present. She began asking questions in CHamoru for Susa to translate.

"Why do you think you angered the ga'lågu?" asked Susa.

"We were only doing our duty. They ordered us to send the CHamoru to Manenggon. We were heading for the last ranch. I was only marching."

"They do not get angry about how you walk it's where you walk. What did you take?"

"Take?"

"You entered the jungle without permission, but then you stole from the CHamoru that you visited?"

"We may have taken food and other supplies."

"Who allowed you?"

"The Taicho."

"This is not the Taicho's land. This jungle belongs to the Taotaomo'na. Did they allow you to steal?"

"Are you going to heal me or not?"

Corporal Suzuki pushed Mariana to the side and went to walk forward.

"Do not leave the circle Gocho Suzuki-san. They are surrounding you."

Mariana pushed him back to where he had been standing and started to unwrap the bandages on his arm. He yelled in pain as the fabric pulled at a still open wound that glistened raw in the jungle light. His arm looked withered and dead. Even Mariana looked shocked at the extent of the damage. Takeshi and Hiroshi turned away in disgust.

"That is bad," said Susa, "I will ask you again. Did the Taotaomo'na give you permission to take from their land?"

"No. You know they didn't."

"Then perhaps you have to ask for their forgiveness."

"Please forgive me."

Mariana applied the palai to the mass of ruptured flesh. Corporal Suzuki was in agony, as well as a state of panic. Takeshi and Hiroshi passed small smiles between them as they looked on at his discomfort, but the spirits were thick in the air. It kept them on guard against an attack, even though they were sure they were safe.

Mariana wrapped a bandage around the wound once again. She stepped out of the circle, still conversing with the invisible horde of ga'lågu. She turned back to face Corporal Suzuki.

"Down on your knees," said Susa.

"What?"

"The ga'lågu demand it. They must know you are sincere. Down on your knees and ask for their forgiveness. Until they grant it, your wound will never heal."

"I had to kneel, Gocho Suzuki-san," said Hiroshi, "It is part of the healing."

Corporal Suzuki scowled as he dropped to his knees, clearly ashamed at his loss of authority. "Please, forgive me."

A silence followed, a gust of wind blew past all of them, and the tense atmosphere evaporated with the breeze.

"It is over," said Susa.

Corporal Suzuki stood up and touched at the bandages.

"Some of the pain has gone already."

"Your wound will take longer to heal than Hasegawa-san, but it will heal,"

He smiled for a moment, but then he marched up to Takeshi and Hiroshi. His threatening ways had also recovered.

"No word to anyone about what you have seen today. Do you understand?"

"Yes, Gocho Suzuki-san," they both replied.

"We go back to camp now. We will organize a patrol to collect more medicine. Get the women on the truck."

Takeshi and Hiroshi helped Susa and Mariana get back on board. Corporal Suzuki returned to the cabin, and the engine started up.

"You didn't say you knelt before them," said Takeshi.

"I didn't," smiled Hiroshi.

"Your corporal didn't need to kneel either," said Susa, "that was just for my entertainment."

They all shared the joke as they headed back to camp.

***

The bombardment of the island had reached a new level of intensity. More ships, planes, and guns pointed on the island than ever before. To the Americans, Guam represented an important piece of land that would bring the cities of Japan within range of its largest bombers.

The Japanese defenders knew they were facing overwhelming odds. Most were conceding defeat and considering their chosen route to heaven. To take even one American with them was the best they could hope for.

The Taicho was already engaged on a new front—a plan to use the *world beyond* in the battle for the island. As he surveyed the troops assembling to follow Takeshi and Elena into the jungle, he contemplated for the first time in months that there seemed a chance to achieve the impossible. While General Takashima pursued the normal rules of war, the Taicho of Manenggon was following a different road. If his plan was successful, then this could turn not only the fate of the island, but the fate of the war itself.

With the hours moving on into evening since Corporal Suzuki's healing, he had seen once again that the medicine worked. The Taotaomo'na didn't appear to take sides, even after the atrocities committed by his own people. He had ordered the death squads to cease for the moment.

He recognized they were *atrocities*. He could just never give voice to the thought. He and his countrymen lived under a culture of shame and intolerance for individual expression. He and everyone else were part of the machine, the war machine designed to advance the power of an Emperor.

His sense of honor was so entrenched that his common sense could no longer fight it. He was betting everything on making peace with the Taotaomo'na. He would oversee a refreshed army. The implications were huge. He wondered if the CHamoru medicine could work far and wide. He even toyed with the idea that Guam could work as a base to restore the strength of injured and disease-ridden Japanese troops. That kind of effort could be transformative across Japan's entire theater of war—injured troops returned to service, almost overnight.

He observed Corporal Suzuki already using his right arm in directing troops and giving instructions. Takeshi and Hiroshi stood beside a group of CHamoru healers, female suruhana, and male suruhanu, about a dozen that had volunteered, to head for the latte stones. Their intent was to perform a ceremony. To call the Taotaomo'na to Manenggon, to ask permission to gather the plants that were required.

The Taicho strode over to Takeshi with his bodyguard of Kempeitai in close pursuit.

"Is everything ready, Takeshi-san?"

"Yes, Taicho-san. We are ready to go."

"You are in charge. Gocho Suzuki-san is the senior officer on your duty, but I have instructed him to remain *cooperative* at all times, unless he wants to end his evening on a reduced rank."

"I understand, Taicho-san"

"Do your best Takeshi-san, though we do not have time for failure. Perhaps when we have enough medicine, may my nightmares also end."

"Can you still see them, Taicho-san?"

"More. The number keeps growing. They are all around us now. I would have come with you to these latte stones, but I fear my presence may cause them to reject our plea."

"Excuse me, Taicho-san. Can you confirm if we are successful, may I remain in Manenggon afterward?"

"It is troublesome to keep changing orders. Your re-assignment will remain in place until I can confirm that we are sending enough to Agat to replace you. Please remind your CHamoru friends that this is an issue that is important to you. I would like them to know that my orders will show the results of their efforts. All of us will know our fate based on your mission tonight."

The Taicho directed his last comment at Elena. Her association with Takeshi had marked her out, and this was his way of making the point. If Takeshi was going to the front, then her own life would become a matter of choice for the Taicho.

He turned away and left Takeshi and Elena to think about what lay ahead.

Takeshi whispered. "If we become lost or separated, if something goes wrong, then head to our secret cove. I'll head there too. If the ancestors are with us, may they let us meet there."

"Everyone is ready to try their best for us, Takeshi," replied Elena, "So many here have lost so much, but I think they see some sort of hope if we survive. They do not care for the Japanese and they would die before helping the enemy that has taken so much away, but they want to help us. No one believes that all of our people will end here. The Taotaomo'na are ready for battle. This visit to the latte stones should reveal their intentions. The people will be ready with them."

Corporal Suzuki shouted one last command to tell everyone to move out, and the party began to walk before the coast. Whatever happened next would dictate the fortunes of all in the fast-approaching storm.

Chapter 16
Guardians of the Latte Stones

Takeshi and Elena led the participants of a temporary truce between the CHamoru and the Japanese through the jungle. They had plenty of people with them who knew how to ask permission for their journey, but Mariana was the natural choice to perform the task on behalf of all.

The remaining islanders followed on, and then Corporal Suzuki and Hiroshi led the other guards. They carried kit bags to store anything they collected. The Taicho was looking for a large harvest of the medicinal plants he needed.

It provided an air of tension. The healers knew this was likely to fail, but it was part of a greater plan to save those who were dwelling in the camp. All had agreed to work together for that purpose.

For many of the Japanese soldiers, this was a situation that made them unsure. They were being sent into a place inhabited by the demons that had attacked so many of their comrades. They were being led there by people who they thought of as witches. At the head of the line was Yoshida Takeshi-san, considered by many to be already in league with evil. It didn't provide them with the reassurance they needed.

"How do you feel now, Hasegawa-san?" said Corporal Suzuki.

"I feel as if nothing ever happened to me. My leg is back to normal."

"Do you believe it was the medicine or the healer?"

"I think it's both. You need someone who knows how to deliver the healing."

"That's my point. If we know the medicine to gather, would it still work with one of our doctors handing it out?"

"Wouldn't they have to learn the CHamoru ways?"

"Maybe, but they have learned to become doctors already. Is it just the language and the phrases they would have to learn?"

"I think it's more to do with the Japanese doctor not having CHamoru ancestors. They inherit the healing power. It connects through their history."

"I'm still skeptical. They are trying to survive. They will tell anything to the Taicho to stop him carrying out the extermination."

"Do you not think we would be better to allow them to live? If we hold the island, they could be useful?"

Corporal Suzuki chuckled. "If we allow them to live, we will not hold the island. The Americans will take any information they can get and turn it against us. No, they are still all going to die. Once they have provided us with the medicine, we can force the suruhana to help by showing the consequences of them not working for us."

"What do you mean?"

"Come on, Hasegawa-san. These healers all have children, or aging mothers and fathers. Do you think they will want to see them tied to a tree and beheaded? The death squads will resume their work in two days' time. How many they kill depends on how successful we are tonight."

"Does Takeshi know this?"

"Takeshi trusts everyone too much. He is too young to understand. He's weird, Hiroshi. Stick with your brothers from Shikoku. None of us know why you even talk to him."

"For one thing, he's the reason that I'm walking beside you, and then he's the reason that you can even think of going into battle with a weapon."

"I owe him one favor maybe, but that's it. When we are even, my conscience will be clear."

Up ahead, the conversation was taking a different turn. The healers were debating their role in the night's events, contemplating how they should handle the ceremony and discussing the right form of help to ask for.

"Many want to ask the Taotaomo'na for help to destroy them, not help to heal them," said Elena, "They are all certain that the time is coming. All of them are experiencing the power growing around the camp, like a volcano building pressure below the ground before it erupts. They are talking about seeing all the different kinds of Taotaomo'na, but mainly those that will cause harm."

"What are the different kinds?" asked Takeshi.

"You have already seen *tai mata'*, they are the ones without faces, but then there are *tai ulu'*, they have no heads. Yet they can still chase you. Some of the healers have seen *Duhendes*, these are small, they can run through the undergrowth without being seen. The *Ga'lågu* that attacked Suzuki are vicious animals. When they arrive, they are not here to help you."

Takeshi felt comfortable walking with Elena and the healers, but with the dark jungle closing in around him, it felt like he was wandering into a trap that he couldn't get out of. Even the CHamoru people were nervous; they couldn't just assume that these Taotaomo'na would just leave them alone.

"Twice I saw an old woman. First in the jungle the night they attacked Corporal Suzuki, and then after she appeared in a dream, or a nightmare."

"Do you wonder why the Taotaomo'na have chosen you?" asked Elena.

"I don't know. Events beyond my control brought me here. I might have been on the wrong convoy ship and died before even seeing this place, or seeing you."

Elena went silent, considering the thought. Susa, who was walking just behind, offered her thoughts.

"The Taotaomo'na didn't bring you here Takeshi, that was other gods, maybe the Japanese lucky gods, but when you came here, the Taotaomo'na must have approved of your arrival. They watch. They learn."

"They chose me?"

"They decided not to stop you. You have done the rest yourself. The soldiers back down the line are still talking about you; they don't trust you, but out here in the jungle and in the darkness, they fear you. Why would the Taotaomo'na hurt you when you are helping them?"

They arrived at the clearing. The latte stones sat in front of all arriving out of the trees. The people fanned out around one side of the circle. For the first time, they mixed. CHamoru and Japanese standing side by side. A breeze passed through the clearing. The stones felt as if they were creating an energy that filled the space. It wrapped around them. Mariana stepped into the center and spoke to Susa for translation.

"They are here. They want to know why there are so many of us in their place."

Takeshi stepped forward. "We are here to collect medicine for the people who are sick. We only ask to take what we need, but many are sick."

Mariana spoke again.

"Why are your people sick?" asked Susa.

Takeshi looked around himself before answering. All the Japanese soldiers, Corporal Suzuki, and Hiroshi, held their breath in anticipation of what may happen next.

"They disrespected the ancestors. Many times. Each man who is sick has upset the spirits of this island."

The place fell silent, and for minutes, Mariana nodded and acknowledged the message she was receiving.

"What is happening?" whispered Corporal Suzuki.

"They are considering your fate," said one of the CHamoru.

Mariana smiled and looked more relaxed. She spoke to Susa once more. The healers who were present began to gather around the latte stones, encircling the four pairs of capped pillars.

Corporal Suzuki ordered his men to form another thin circle around them, not out of any sense of worship, but an intention of being ready for trouble. The jungle behind seemed to move on its own. Even the most insensitive soldier amongst the Japanese couldn't fail to notice that they were being surrounded as well.

The lone voice of a suruhanu, a male healer, burst into song. The haunting melody brought a layer of reverence to the assembled crowd. Other voices began to join in harmony. The sound flowed out from around the latte stones and over the jungle. It reached out over the ocean and above the distant thunder of the bombs and shells that were even now raining down on the other side of the island. A rhythmic clapping began and provided the timing, helping to raise an energy.

Takeshi had read about the divine all his life. The Japanese government had rooted his education in respect for the divine authority, but in this moment he was experiencing divinity. He felt his energy joining with Elena's, with the other CHamoru, and with the Taotaomo'na themselves.

The song stopped, lending a great weight to the following silence. Mariana began leading a chant, and the others followed line by line, slapping the tops of their legs and clapping their hands to drum out a beat.

Another suruhana let out a high-pitched call, then another followed. The surrounding soldiers became lost in the moment. The power of the ceremony left none of them untouched by the energy it was creating.

The silence fell again, but this time a shrill bird call broke through the air. Takeshi noticed that many of the healers seemed startled with the noise, as if it was unexpected. The word *Itak* was passing around the circle. Susa seemed to glance at Elena with a deep sadness cast across her face.

The ceremony continued. Mariana spoke to the Taotaomo'na, then she would tell the CHamoru the messages she was receiving.

"What are they saying, Takeshi-san?" said Corporal Suzuki.

"Our ancestors are debating our request," said Susa, "they are many voices that wish to be heard."

"They take too long!" Suzuki complained.

Takeshi directed a sharp stare back at the corporal. The Taicho had assured him he had command.

Mariana began pointing to areas of the jungle all around her. She was handing out instructions of where to gather the medicine. Susa called Takeshi over and spoke to him. He, in turn, walked over to Corporal Suzuki to relay the command.

"We are to follow with our bags. Only the healers can pick the herbs that we need. The Taotaomo'na will only let us to collect the medicine for carrying. They will not give permission for us to do anything else. Get each man to follow a healer and collect what they harvest."

"Is that it?" asked the corporal.

"No, they have said that when we leave, then we Japanese should never return to this place. Anyone who does will have to face the wrath of the Taotaomo'na."

"The wrath of the Taotaomo'na or the wrath of the divine Emperor. I know my enemy, and you should, too."

Takeshi walked off to join Elena as Corporal Suzuki issued the orders to his men in his own harsh style.

Takeshi joined Elena and Susa who huddled together in a whispered conversation. They stopped talking as soon as Takeshi was close enough to hear.

"Is everything alright?"

"Yes," Elena smiled, "we have a lot to do; will you help me?"

"Yes, of course."

They walked off together. As she watched them leave, Susa felt a lump in her throat.

"The Itak delivers a blessing or a warning. Which is it to be?"

***

It was two hours later when the party returned to camp. Elena and the others could disappear back amongst the hive of imprisoned islanders. Takeshi and the soldiers continued to the gates, where three large trucks were sitting, engines running, and headlights on.

Takeshi heard the gruff tones of Kyota and his patrol ordering a large group of prisoners to board. Kindo stood translating the message, but most of them knew the basic Japanese commands that were shouted at them every day.

Takeshi and Hiroshi walked over to Kindo as the other soldiers laid down the gathered plants outside the infirmary building and dispersed.

"What's going on Kindo?" asked Takeshi.

"They are moving prisoners to work on defenses near Santa Rita and Fena Lake."

Takeshi scanned the crowd. Some were fit to work, but others were too young or too old.

"What kind of work do they expect some of them to do," replied Takeshi, "I don't trust this."

"What can they do?" asked Kindo, "They know that many do not return from these work details, but some do. If they refuse to go, then they still die. What is the best choice? And this time they have selected me to go with them."

"No, Kindo. I'll speak to the Taicho."

"And what then? They will choose someone else in my place. I couldn't live with that on my conscience. Do what you need to do, Takeshi. If that saves some, then that's all we can ask for. Goodbye to you and Hasegawa-san," he bowed, "I must board the transport now."

Kyota came over and gripped Kindo's shoulder, spinning him round in the truck's direction. "Get moving. We need you to tell them what to do."

"They're getting put to work?" asked Takeshi.

"More digging, lifting ammunition and grenades," confirmed Kyota, "We strap some to bull carts; it's amazing how much they can lift."

"And then they'll return?"

"They say they'd rather die than return to Manenggon. I can help them with that."

He turned away and climbed into a truck cabin before the convoy pulled out into the night. Takeshi turned back to see the Taicho examining the packs of medicinal plants that lay on the ground. He started to rush forward in a fury. Hiroshi struggled as much as he could to hold him back and do anything to stop him from ending up in the care of the Kempeitai.

"Takeshi, slow down, think," cried Hiroshi.

He drew Takeshi back not a moment too soon, but they were close enough for the Taicho to expect Takeshi's rage.

"You have done well, Takeshi-san. This quantity of medicine should treat many of the men."

"You said the death squads would stop. You promised."

The Taicho only returned a frozen stare, awaiting Takeshi's apologies for not showing respect. Takeshi inhaled a calming breath.

"I am sorry, Taicho-san. I am only concerned that we will have broken our promise, Taicho-san."

"I don't remember promising anything, but there are no death squads roaming the camp tonight. I don't believe they can hold me responsible for what happens on the entire island. I have allowed your lack of discipline, only because as Taicho, I realize that while making plans happen, I must work with the changing seasons, the winds, or the tides. You must work with the unexpected in the best way that you can. You have served me well. The one promise I made to you was that *your* death would be honorable. It is your choice to join your brothers against the Americans, or you can walk into the trees right now, with your rifle. Once you have fired your bullet, I will order men to recover your body with the greatest of respect. The decision is yours."

The Taicho walked off and returned to his office.

"Cigarette?" said Hiroshi.

They walked together to a quieter part of the compound. The burning tip of a cigarette, was the only sign of their presence in the darkness.

"We need to leave tomorrow night," said Takeshi.

"I agree, but how do we get enough people out?"

"I don't know. All I can think of is making one last trip to the latte stones, if we can get permission. The Taotaomo'na's message was that we shouldn't return."

"So why are you suggesting that we should?"

"It is only the Japanese that have been told not to return. So it's only the Japanese that will suffer harm if we go back through the jungle."

"I think I can see the flaw in this plan," said Hiroshi, "We are Japanese."

"We don't have another choice. I have to believe that they will spare us. If not, I'll be content that we saved the lives of at least some of the others."

Hiroshi reached for another cigarette of his own, while Takeshi still smoked the one they were sharing.

"I still don't want to die, Takeshi."

"If there's a way that we can avoid this, I will look for it, but if it's our only choice left, facing whatever lies in the jungle is our last hope."

Hiroshi ran through all the options in his mind. The idea of surrender was not among them.

"You are right. Perhaps the healers can save us one more time if the Taotaomo'na do not kill us outright."

"And if we die, then we die together—agreed?"

"Agreed."

***

Takeshi could see Elena from a distance standing at the banks of the Ylig River. She had wandered far from her shelter. Takeshi raced to reach her. There were fewer patrols at night now, but those that remained were only there to take what they could get for themselves; food, anything that would have some value, or a young woman like Elena.

"Elena, what are you doing this far away from the shelter? It's not good for you to be on your own."

"I had to get away for a moment. There is no place here to find somewhere to make peace with God. Do you understand?"

"Yes, I think so."

"We are religious people. There are old gods, yes, but the people of Guam converted many years ago to the Catholic faith that the Spanish brought with them. We share a firm belief in the teachings. It binds us together as much as fear of the Taotaomo'na. Sometimes I need that to carry on. To face each day. I pray for a good life, and a good husband," she smiled, "but I worry that I have made Him angry, that I have let Him down. I had to find a quiet place to let God know that I still have faith. That I intend to live a good life, if he can only lead me to it."

"If we can get through this, Elena, I will believe in any god that will help us."

"Imagine that all this hadn't happened. The war, the camp, you arriving on the right ship. Would we have met each other any other way? I don't think so, Takeshi. I wouldn't have had my heart filled with the joy that it knows when you are close. So was all this needed so that God could bring us together?"

Takeshi paused, just considering how to reply. He looked at the prisoners, trapped in the mire of Manenggon.

What did they do to God to deserve this?

"I don't think we would have met any other way. I would never have even known of the island. I may have ended up on a fishing boat within a few years, and maybe a storm would have blown my boat off course. Maybe you would have found me shipwrecked on the shore, and saved my life."

"I would have taken you to a suruhana," joked Elena.

"But we would both have been older. You would have had a husband, and I would have a wife waiting for me to come home. This *was* the only way we could be together. To be here now. Amongst all of this. So is it God's work?" he paused and looked into the water flowing downstream as it headed for Ylig Bay, "All I want to ask is that our time together doesn't end. That would be the last cruelty in life, if we were to be separated." Takeshi lowered his voice to the lowest of whispers, "We have to go tonight. I can't say anything here. Let's head for the shelter."

They walked back through the small spaces that compressed family groups together. Small fires burned to attempt the cooking of some food. Even that brought a risk of punishment if the guards thought that you were trying to signal to an American aircraft. The alternative was starvation or malnutrition. The people made life or death decisions at every turn of their existence in the camp.

The rain began to fall again as they reached Elena's shelter. Susa sat at the edge, next to Elena's mother.

"Are you alright Elena?" said Susa, as they shook themselves dry.

"Yes, thank you, Susa. I feel better now."

"You feel better because Takeshi is with you."

"Yes, yes, I do."

Elena squeezed Takeshi's hand with hers and they sat down on the wet ground together.

"We have to get the cooperation of the healers for just one more day, Susa," said Takeshi.

"It will be difficult to convince them all," she replied.

"The Taicho is not delaying his plans. He is still carrying out orders to exterminate the CHamoru. He's just not doing it in Manenggon. They are now shipping prisoners out. If we are to save anyone, we must go back to the latte stones later tonight."

"You heard what the Taotaomo'na said, Takeshi. I have no problem leading others to their death, but I also can't guarantee that you will survive."

"There is no choice. We must go through with the healing at the infirmary later. I know the Taicho will only give us one more day. If the men in the infirmary don't recover, the death squads will return with a vengeance. We have to save the island's healers at least. Then maybe after this madness stops, they will be able to help Guam recover."

Susa spoke in CHamoru with Elena and her mother. The looks of concern for Takeshi passed between all of them. They left Elena with the final decision. She gripped Takeshi's hands in hers.

"From what we said at the river, I have to believe that this is our path to follow together. If God chooses death, then I know he will not separate us forever. We agree with you. This is the only way. We must all show that we have faith. Susa will organize everyone for the rest of the plan. We will convince the Taicho that one more trip to the latte stones will give him everything he needs."

"Thank you, Elena, Maria, Susa. Thank you all. I know we can do this."

Takeshi breathed an enormous sigh of relief. "I hope you don't mind. I think I need a cigarette. I'll step outside for a moment."

"I can make us tea. I'll do that now," said Elena.

"Would you mind if I shared the cigarette with you?" asked Susa, "It's been a while since I had a smoke."

"No, of course not," said Takeshi, smiling, "please join me."

They walked outside, hugging a tree close for some shelter from the rain. Takeshi lit the cigarette and passed it to Susa. She drew in a deep inhale of smoke before letting it out into the sky above her.

"Earlier at the latte stones, we heard the call of the Itak," said Susa.

"Yes, I heard the other healers repeat the word," Takeshi replied.

"It is a very special bird. Magical. To the CHamoru it brings messages of life and death when you hear its call."

"Death?"

"Sometimes," she passed the cigarette back, "but also life. We say that the call of the Itak announces that a young unmarried woman is with child."

The silence that followed was enough to convey the rest of the message, Takeshi froze, the cigarette held from his lips as his mouth dropped open in shock.

"Elena is..."

"Finish your cigarette. Go back to the shelter and say nothing. Just hold her close. Hold your family close and pray that our plan goes well."

Chapter 17
Invasion

"Hey, Takeshi."

A whisper sounded in Takeshi's ear.

"Hey, Takeshi-san."

The second whisper cut through Takeshi's semi-conscious state, and he opened his eyes. Kyota's grinning face was staring back. Three other soldiers surrounded him, standing outside the shelter and laughing hard at Takeshi's predicament. He jumped to his feet in surprise, waking Elena and causing her to scream in fright.

"Oh, you are in trouble now." said Kyota with glee, "Did you sleep in, Takeshi? It looks like you were in a comfortable bed."

Takeshi made a lunge at Kyota, but the large soldier sidestepped the attack and the three others grabbed hold.

Elena tried to pull him back, but Kyota took hold of her hair and punched her on the jaw, sending her sprawling into the middle of the shelter. She went to fight back, but the other CHamoru held on to her.

"Well, it seems that you went absent without leave this morning. The Taicho is not happy, and he has sent me to bring you back."

"I haven't been absent. I was here to plan for the healing. I must have fallen asleep."

"Tell it to the judge, Takeshi. I don't care what happens to you. All I know is you should have been on transport back to Agat this morning, and you weren't there."

"What transport?"

"A dozen men transferring to Agat, except they only left with eleven. By the way, Hasegawa-san says to tell you he'll keep your space for you in the rifle pit."

"Hiroshi?"

"The Taicho decided to send your friend with you. He said it would be good for morale. He might not be so friendly now that you let him down. Take him!"

Kyota marched his way through the crowd, striking and shoving anyone who got in his way, carving a path through the crowd for his men.

Takeshi's mind was racing. He felt terrible as the sun shone down on him. He could feel every piece of energy draining away. He had no more answers. Torn away from Elena's arms, he was being pushed so fast he had no time to take a step. His captors delivered the jostling in combination with punches to the back and ribs. Takeshi had fallen out of the Taicho's protection.

"Wait!" said Kyota.

He stopped everyone and walked back to Takeshi. "I'm not missing out on the fun," he launched two quick punches at Takeshi's head, pulled him down and rammed his knee into Takeshi's face. As Takeshi lay outstretched in the mud, Kyota delivered two more heavy kicks into his ribs. He pulled his head back to see that blood was pouring from his nose."

"Pick him up," he ordered.

The Kempeitai were already waiting to relieve Kyota of his charge at the gates. The men that had marched him over handed him into the next line of abuse. The Kempeitai were experts at screaming at their own men. An officer shouted into Takeshi's face from less than an inch away. His rage filled eyes, his foul breath, and the spit flowing from his words was a well-practiced assault on the senses.

"Leave him."

They obeyed the command from the Taicho, pushing Takeshi to his knees before the military police stepped back. The Taicho drew his Katana and used the tip of the sword to raise Takeshi's head—for their eyes to meet.

"Get the girl," he commanded, "Tell her to bring the healers here now. Tell her Takeshi says it's a matter of life and death."

A flurry of activity followed his order as the Kempeitai organized soldiers to retrieve *Takeshi's sister*. Their laughter echoed in Takeshi's head. It wasn't just the pain of his beating fueling his rage. It was the years of cruelty; beaten at home, beaten at school, beaten by the army, and all to ask for his ultimate sacrifice, to give his life to a man—not a god. Takeshi could feel the ground and the air around him—an inexplicable tension in the camp. In that moment he realized that the Taicho could sense it as well.

He can see them.

The Taicho dropped his sword. The square had filled with his guards gathering to witness an expected execution. The air crackled with anticipation as the Taicho turned to address his men.

"During the night the American marines attacked at Agana and Agat. Two separate divisions are being held back by our heroic Japanese soldiers. From what I have been told, the battle is fierce, but we have been able to halt an advance. We have our orders to carry out. We have our own enemy to crush at Manenggon, and so we will resume our plan to reduce the prisoners in camp. Organize and arm yourselves. Time is short and we may all receive the call to the front. We must be efficient in our duty to the Emperor and ready to act on his command."

The Taicho returned his gaze to Takeshi, "What do I need more, Takeshi-san? A trophy of your head, or an army to command? What would the great samurai of history decide? Your death awaits you in so many places, but I find myself reluctant to help you get there. Glorious war is upon us. The chance for us all to prove ourselves. You? You have still to prove that you share that desire. When the healers arrive, you will make sure that they do their work. I need men more than I need your head; be thankful for that," the Taicho ordered his Kempeitai, "Take him to the guardhouse until the healers arrive."

They hoisted Takeshi to his feet. The camp rang out with commands. Troops prepared to head out, arming themselves for a purge of the defenseless CHamoru. Still half-dazed from the beating, his vision blurred, he gasped for breath as they hurried him through the door and flung him into a detention cell. It was an empty unfurnished space lined with iron bars only ever intended as a temporary holding space for those who had defied authority to await their punishment.

From inside the cell, Takeshi observed three officers discussing the invasion. Orders were coming thick and fast. They turned their backs to him as they grouped around a table. Calls were coming through for more CHamoru to be dispersed to the various supply points. The slave labor was required to shift ammunition to artillery emplacements and infantry sections preparing to counter-attack the American marines.

Takeshi listened to them discuss more transport heading to the heights above Agana, and others to be dispatched to the positions curving around Agat. He heard them talk about his regiment, the 38th Infantry. They were already in close fighting, with reports of bayonet attacks on American positions. Hills were being taken and re-taken.

The emergency reduced Takeshi's importance to an annoying inconvenience. He sat back against the wall, his mind finally beginning to make sense of it all. He lifted his gaze from his feet to see the old woman standing in front of him; it was the same one from the jungle and his dream. He looked to the Kempeitai officers. They were all engrossed with the matters of war and didn't appear to notice or see anyone sharing his cell.

He turned back and the old woman was still there. Her eyes were of a solid black, yet life stared out of them.

"*Lamo'na*," was all she said.

She raised her hand and pointed to the guards, then she spoke again, and the words traveled around the room, a ghostly disconnected voice that was issuing its own command. The old woman vanished.

Takeshi blinked and rubbed his eyes. Then outside his cell, an argument began. Two of the Kempeitai were challenging one another about what to do. Tempers were fraying and insults began being traded. Then fists were being thrown; the room exploded in a struggle between the soldiers. A scream of pain erupted from a man at the center of the fight. The others parted around him—he emerged with a bayonet stuck through his neck, blood pouring from the wound. The man fell with his head battering off the iron bars of Takeshi's cage. He lay dead with his eyes staring back at his killer.

"Takeshi caused this," said a blood covered officer, drawing his pistol.

"Don't shoot him," said the remaining man, "The Taicho wants him alive. I'll get help."

The door opened and slammed shut, followed by calls for help from outside the building. Meanwhile, the officer with the pistol bent down beside Takeshi, tapping the gun barrel on the iron bars of the cage.

"You think your demons can help you now?" he asked.

Takeshi remained silent, his eyes following the gun as the soldier raised it to point at Takeshi's head. A last sinister smile expressed a sneering resentment before the officer turned the gun toward himself, placed it his mouth, and pulled the trigger.

The fatal shot announced the arrival of more guards and the Taicho. They trained machine guns on Takeshi, even though he was still languishing as a captive in the cell.

Another guard followed him into the room. "Taicho-san, the healers have arrived to cure the men."

The Taicho viewed the gory scene. "Tie him up and bring him outside to inspire his friends. Remove the bodies and clear this place up."

***

By the time Takeshi emerged outside the guardhouse, the main square of the compound was a mass of activity. Troops prepared to move out to the shelters, armed with grenades and machine guns. Trucks backed up to be loaded with the CHamoru selected for disposal after a last period of work. Crowds were being marched toward the transport under screamed orders and occasional rifle fire into the air.

In the middle of it all, Takeshi spotted Elena, Susa, and Mariana, among the other healers. Corporal Suzuki stood with men from Takeshi's section. They seemed happy to be assigned the role of harassing *Takeshi's witches*, as they referred to them.

The Taicho marched forward, keen to stare into the eyes of his enemy. They dragged Takeshi beside him and once again brought him to his knees in front of everyone.

Takeshi and Elena looked at one another, both trying to reassure, even at this desperate time—a connection not lost on the Taicho.

"Takeshi-san, tell your people that time is running out. They must work if they hope to survive. Tell them!"

"Do what he says," said Takeshi, "You must help him. Please. If nothing else, try to save yourself."

Susa strode to the front. "How can we help like this? While the sound of your grenades go off around us? You tell us we will survive, but what of the others who have helped you? How many return? Do you think we are blind?"

"No. I think you are my prisoners. I can treat you how I want. Your life is of little value to the Emperor. The one chance you may have is to work in his service and hope that I find leniency. Or I can have you all shot now. What is it to be?"

"Please, Susa. Please do what he says."

"Release Takeshi to us," demanded Elena, "He knows how to help us."

The Taicho smiled in satisfaction. He realized just how to motivate the healers and keep Takeshi in check.

"Corporal Suzuki, find out where the next work convoy is heading."

"Yes, Taicho-san."

The corporal ran off to talk with the truck drivers.

"Your *sister* wants to be near you, even now. How touching."

He waited in silence for Corporal Suzuki to return.

"Where is it heading, Gocho Suzuki-san?"

"The trucks are bound for the caves at Fena, Taicho-san."

"Fena? Good. Take *Takeshi's sister;* put her on a truck, now!"

"No! Elena!"

A rifle butt smashed into Takeshi's back, forcing him face down onto the ground. A boot held his face pressed down in the dirt as he listened to her screams and calls of his name. He heard the engines of the trucks roar into action, and Elena's voice disappearing into the distance. Tears flooded from his eyes as they dragged him back up to face the Taicho once more.

"So now you know what you must do. The healers must begin their work. Once they have completed their duties, you will also go to Fena, to be with her. I hope your people do not take long over the decision. Her life is now beyond my control."

"Please, Susa," pleaded Takeshi, "You know I have to be close to her. You know."

Susa turned and spoke to the healers. The Taicho sniggered at his own wisdom. He had won control of the situation.

"Very well," replied Susa, "we will do what we can. Though you appreciate, Taicho-san, that the Taotaomo'na will not help you now."

"That is a matter for them. I expect you, the CHamoru, to do all you can. If I see by the morning that my men can hold a rifle or wield a sword, then I will decide what happens next. Fail to help and you can count this day as your last. And of course, our brave soldier Takeshi will never make it to his last resting place."

"Let us go to work," Susa said to the other healers.

***

They kept Takeshi back from the others, allowed to view from a distance to prove to the CHamoru that he was still alive. The scene played out in front of him against a background of even more shelling. The battleships of the US fleet had turned their attention to the land beyond their advancing troops, showering the hills with cannon fire to subdue the Japanese who were trying to drive the land forces back into the sea.

Planes joined the assault on the flanks where machine gun fire stood out from the engine noise. Anti-air artillery launched sporadic attacks in return. Takeshi could tell that the war for the Japanese was over on this island. He knew he wasn't the only one. As a rifle remained trained on him from behind his back, he could even sense that the soldier holding it was preparing for his own death.

They had prepared all their lives to die in war. The consequences for failure to complete this goal were severe. Takeshi had lost Yuki, his mother, and his father. There was nothing left for him to return to, but for many others, the threat was implicit. To suffer the ultimate shame of capture or surrender would ruin the lives of your family back home.

How did we even agree to this?

The doctors had encouraged the patients out of the infirmary. Many weren't keen to be treated, but since the Taicho had ordered it, there was no choice. Once again they faced the dilemma—regardless of their own thoughts—an order was an order. You did as you were told at all times, including charging into armored fire with a bayonet as your weapon.

Mariana and the other healers worked as fast as they could. Some prepared the medicine, while others applied it. Communication with the Taotaomo'na became a simple half-hearted ask for permission. There was no point in believing it would happen. They also ignored questions and answers. All of them had done something, from walking onto land they had no right to walk on, to other more serious crimes.

While they worked, the convoys of trucks returned to pick up more workers. Hundreds, if not thousands, were being removed to other locations. It was an industrial evacuation. Others who couldn't make the journey risked being shot, beheaded, or blown-up in the pits. The sound of sickening screams echoed across the camp from all around the Ylig River.

Takeshi noticed Kyota coming back to the camp several times. He looked happier and more joyful as the day wore on. Each trip to deliver more executions saw him and his men returning with anything they could loot from the now-empty shelters. His men were full of praise for every gift he returned with. He was a hero.

Takeshi's only comfort was that it wasn't only Kyota's men that surrounded him. The Taotaomo'na also followed them. The dark figures that had first terrified Takeshi were saviors now. He could see them just like the CHamoru healers could. He could see the healers looking between one another and quietly discussing their presence.

"*Lamo'na*," was the word playing out in his mind. Without translation, he suddenly knew what it meant. The sun was moving over in front of him as he looked west, but it was beginning to descend.

Tonight. That's what she was saying.

The hours had worn by. Takeshi's only objective was getting to Elena. He had to do everything and say everything he needed to convince the Taicho. He prayed, but not to the Shinto gods; instead, he asked the Taotaomo'na. He asked for their permission and their help to reach her in time.

The Taicho appeared from his office. His bodyguard had grown to around eight soldiers, and he chose not to notice Takeshi for the moment; instead, he walked over to Susa as the very last patients were receiving their medicine.

"How long until I see improvement?" he asked.

"It will be overnight. Not all of them. There were different conditions, and uncommon injuries. That means different Taotaomo'na were involved. Some of them didn't even hold the medicine in their stomachs, but the ones who are successful will be ready to join your charge by the morning."

"Some, not all, will have to do. The rest is up to General Takashima once I provide him with the extra men. Corporal Suzuki!"

Takeshi watched from a distance as Susa and the other healers walked back toward the camp gates. The guards left them to stand beside a waiting transport truck, with more islanders who were waiting to leave.

Susa broke from the group and strode over to Takeshi, ignoring the shouting of the guards to get back in line.

"We will meet again somewhere, Takeshi," she called out.

"*Lamo'na*," Takeshi shouted back.

"*Lamo'na*?"

Takeshi nodded. As the Japanese guard slapped and kicked Susa back into line, she knew what his message meant. Takeshi could see the word being passed between the islanders. Some crossed themselves on hearing it. The sun had now set.

A scout vehicle drew up in front of Takeshi. Corporal Suzuki was behind the wheel. He stopped and got out to pick up his passenger.

"Keep him tied up; put him in the passenger seat."

The other guards did their best to handle him as roughly as possible, dragging him up and throwing him into the seat. He was alone. No friends around him. The Taicho didn't even acknowledge that he was being taken away. He had fulfilled his purpose and was dead already to everyone in the camp. Only Corporal Suzuki was pleased because he was driving him to his fate.

Takeshi had heard how the caves had been used to massacre the CHamoru before. It didn't matter now; all that mattered is that he made it to Elena before the end. As Corporal Suzuki jumped into the driving seat, Takeshi had only one thing to say.

"Get me there."

"Takeshi, I will drive you to hell at full speed."

Corporal Suzuki pressed hard on the accelerator and the scout car drove out of the gates and down to the main road.

Susa watched it go and said her own quiet prayer for Takeshi and Elena.

The Taicho walked over again, having satisfied himself that they had carried out the healing on as many men as possible. He ordered that some CHamoru were to be removed from the truck, and the healers were to replace them.

"You want to kill us now?" said Susa.

"You will go to the front. We will pack what's left of the medicine. If the Taotaomo'na really want to protect the CHamoru, then you will survive. Put them on the transport."

Kyota made his way to the side of the truck, mainly to scream at the healers being bundled in. He pushed at them and rushed them, pulling other bystanders out of the way. He was reveling in his own unrestricted cruelty. The crowd screamed at him. Most of the healers were older and fell down under the punches and kicks. Mariana tried to climb on board, but not quickly enough. She incurred Kyota's wrath. He pulled her back from the edge of the vehicle and threw her on to the ground. Within seconds, he had driven his bayonet into her chest three times just as the sun went below the distant horizon.

***

The headlights cut through the darkness on the road, but the clouds overhead reflected the fire that was burning along the west coast of Guam. The sounds of gunfire seemed closer than Takeshi could ever have imagined. The scout car bumped and rolled over every part of the uneven road surface.

He could see what looked like flashing torches in the distance. Troops were moving into positions. Takeshi knew that the 75mm guns that lined the hillside would soon begin firing on the American tanks that assisted the infantry's move forward.

"How long?" shouted Takeshi as he struggled to keep his balance.

"Almost there. Don't worry. Maybe they haven't killed her yet."

Takeshi closed his eyes. He didn't know what to expect. They might execute him. He doubted that they would give him a weapon. He had a bad enough reputation that the other troops would treat him just like a CHamoru, but worse, because by now he was a traitor.

The car came to a rapid halt. As he opened his eyes, he expected to be surrounded by guards, but they were alone and in total darkness. Corporal Suzuki had parked the scout car next to the edge of the jungle. Without saying another word, he jumped out of the car and walked around to the passenger seat. He hauled Takeshi out, throwing him onto the dirt, and flashed the blade of a combat knife in front of his face.

"What are you doing?" Takeshi shouted.

"I'm returning the favor."

Corporal Suzuki slit through the restraints that were binding Takeshi's hands.

"Now I have repaid the debt. The next time I see you, I can kill you with a clear conscience."

"What?"

"Go Takeshi, into the jungle. Excuse me if I don't ask permission."

"I need to get to Elena."

"She will be dead, Takeshi. You go where you want. I'm going to do my duty, like a true Japanese. The sake is free tonight for anyone who's going to charge the enemy in the morning. I will toast your health. *Kampai,* and Tennōheika banzai.*"

He laughed as he returned to the car, driving off at high-speed into the darkness. Takeshi was shocked at the corporal setting him free. His only thought was that the Taotaomo'na must be helping him to reach Elena. There was no time to waste as he rushed out of sight of the road and into the cover of the jungle.

Even though the branches closed around him and the thorns scratched at his skin, he knew where he was going. He could hear the sounds of clubs hitting off wood and rock. An army running with him on either side toward the caves in a race to rescue Elena.

Chapter 18
Lamo'na

Inside Takeshi's old barracks at Manenggon, his former comrades were in a brighter frame of mind. The warehouse that had contained the supplies of sake for Guam and many other islands was now a source of courage for the remaining men set to defend against the invaders.

They destroyed the vacant beds that Takeshi and Hiroshi had slept in as part of the party celebrations. Everyone was glad that they were both gone. The laughter dulled the sound of distant explosions. It raised the morale of the men. Another two or three days and Manenggon would be clear of the CHamoru.

The men even swapped stories of how they killed some of the prisoners that day; tempted by food to stand in booby-trapped buildings; beheadings, where whole families watched their closest relatives being killed; then, of course, the pits used for efficient, mass slaughter.

Corporal Suzuki entered to a cheer. One of the men handed a bottle of sake to him as he arrived.

"Gocho Suzuki-san," said one of the men, "are we rid of Takeshi now?"

"You will not see him again."

The corporal flashed the hilt of his combat knife. The men cheered.

"I bet he cried as you twisted the blade."

"He would have been crying for his sister."

"She will cry because she has to see him again."

"No, Takeshi belongs with the demons, and which sister do you mean?"

The laughter erupted amongst the men, so loud that they didn't hear the first sound of a club knocking against the wall of the building. They didn't notice the timber frames shake on the second knock.

The drink continued to flow and the singing began. They bellowed patriotic war songs to the rafters, covering the scuttling of feet and the scraping of claws on the roof. As the cheering and clapping flowed inside, the banging of the walls increased around the outside of the building.

The song slowly began to fade away as each soldier realized that they were not alone and might even be under attack. Expecting the American marines, they raced for their guns just as the doors flung themselves open. Silence fell.

The men gathered behind Corporal Suzuki, pushing him to the front. They gathered behind with their rifles pointing into the dim light.

"It's nothing," said Corporal Suzuki.

The others weren't so sure. They all continued to edge forward, taking small steps closer. All was quiet.

"Look, there's nothing there," said Corporal Suzuki, "You're all drunk."

He walked forward on his own and looked out to the compound.

"See, there's nothing."

He turned back to face his men. As he did so, a tall, dark figure rose behind him. Towering and muscular, the spirit had no face. Yet it screamed with a force that filled the room with dread. The drunken soldiers reacted the only way they knew how. A volley of rifle bullets punched through Corporal Suzuki's chest, tearing his body apart.

Then a rush of air filled the room with the first onslaught. The Taotaomo'na flowed in on a cloud of dark, swirling mist. They clawed, scratched, and bit through bones. The room filled with blood and the screams of every soldier. It was an all-consuming powerful force that tore the victims apart until nothing remained—a brutal and violent end that vaporized its victims in a matter of seconds.

Corporal Suzuki was still breathing as he lay in the room's silence. His hearing was the only sense that remained. He could make out the scratches of dog claws on the floor around him and then he felt the bites—endless small tears at his flesh. The Ga'lågu would not allow him to die. Each snap from their teeth kept him alive until they decided they had done enough. As the corporal followed his men into another world, there was no sensation left but lasting pain.

After the carnage, the barracks door slammed shut, with not a single survivor. Painted red and destroyed, it was only the beginning of the Taotaomo'na's revenge.

Outside, a mist was growing in the main square of the compound. It helped to hide the lack of that night's guard. The men posted at the gate had been the first to fall. A hundred slingshots had cracked their skulls into tiny pieces, before the swirling mist sucked them out of the world they once knew.

The murky haze stretched back to where the prisoners gripped each other in fear. The Taotaomo'na were here to fight for them; they were sure of that, but for many years the CHamoru had also learned to fear them. As the mist swirled, all the figures of legend appeared; human-like, animals, and creatures that slithered along the ground with serpent-like bodies. An army moved through the trees with speed, as the branches rustled above them.

All headed in one direction, assembling for their turn to take their anger out on the men that had trespassed, murdered, raped, and stolen from the peaceful descendants of an ancient race.

***

The doctors in the infirmary were ending their shifts for the night. They had gathered in a small room to the rear of the building that housed the patients. They had worked on settling everyone down after their day of treatment. Many had still been worried about what they had done to them. The doctors had committed to handing out the last supplies of sedation they had. They knew that if the men recovered, further sedation would not be required.

Once again, they indulged in sake. The room was calmer than the barracks. The doctors sipped on their drinks and discussed why the medicine might work. Some senior medical officers were high-ranking enough to be equipped with Katana. They admired the swords that each other had. They knew that they would be called on to use them before long. They also discussed the popular idea that the banzai charges had worked in Manchukuo. They felt there was no reason for them to fail this time.

A cup fell on to the floor in the ward next door. It rolled across the room and came to a stop in the open doorway. They noticed it, but carried on with their conversation. A few minutes later, another object fell, then another.

"Someone see what's going on," said the senior doctor.

One of the others attempted to get on his feet and take a last drink from his cup. He strode to the doorway, and to his surprise, he found six of the men wandering around as if they were sleepwalking.

"Quick, come here," he shouted, "Some of the men are out of their beds. I think they're still asleep."

The other medical staff came to look for themselves. As they watched, another man rose, and another.

"We should get them back to bed. It must be an effect of the medicine."

They moved in as a group to steer the men back to their bunks.

"Their eyes are open. I don't think they're asleep."

"Maybe it's the sedatives, reacting with the medicine," suggested another doctor.

"They are smiling as well. Maybe they're having pleasant dreams."

All the doctors laughed, and they coaxed the men back to bed. As soon as they completed the task, they turned to see more men standing, with eyes wide open and smiling faces.

"Oh, we're going to be here all night."

The original group of men started to stand up again.

"What's going on here? We need to get some of the men in here to help."

"But we can't get out," said another.

Almost twenty of the patients stood between the medical staff and the door, with more rising all the time. Caught in a trap, they clung together as one of the patients opened his mouth and released a horrifying shriek. The other patients then joined him in a disturbing, rage-filled chorus.

"Draw your weapons!" commanded the senior doctor.

Swords slashed and pistols fired, but they seemed to have little effect as the patients charged toward them. They surrounded their victims, slashing skin with their fingernails, and consuming flesh in a frenzied attack.

The doctors did not die quickly. They lived long enough to see clouds fill the room. As they suffered from the unrelenting assault, faces extended out of the mist, snapping and devouring them, clearing away any remnant of their existence. The patients then fell upon one another. Some awakened from their trance-like state just long enough to feel the impact of sudden violent forces twisting and crushing their bodies.

In the infirmary, the killing had been slower. The shouts of the victims had lasted long enough to bring the other camp guards outside into the square. Panic gripped the men as dark shapes surrounded them, speeding in a vortex. With each pass, a blade, a claw, or a fang would draw blood, slashing at arms, backs, and legs. In the chaos, rifle and machine-gun fire added to the mayhem. A hail of bullets brought down many, but the Taotaomo'na seemed to have the power to prolong their suffering, allowing them to witness their own descent into darkness. The last cries for mercy met with no response.

The Taicho sat inside his office in icy fear. As the calls of his men reached a violent crescendo, he looked around himself at the dark faceless figures that surrounded him. They crowded close. The power that they generated overwhelmed him. Tears ran from his eyes as he shook in terror. They had made him sit and listen to the fate of his guards. They had terrified him so much that he couldn't even move his arm to reach for his sword.

"I am sorry."

Those were the only words he could say. He said them again and again.

The noise from outside grew even louder, creating a scene in his imagination of the brutality taking place. The office he sat in shuddered and rocked with the force of his soldiers being slammed against it. The splitting of bones cracked through the air along with the shrieks of those dying and disintegrating as each part of them became part of the dark foggy cloud that surrounded the camp.

"Wh-, who are you?"

They never answered the Taicho's question. He felt as if the foot soldiers were surrounding him. His meeting with the leader was yet to come. The figures leaned in even closer, grazing his skin. They seemed to be made of the thorns that stuck and scratched at you as you passed through the jungle.

The chaos from outside faded away. Then another wave of sound started to emerge. The screams of women echoed all around the building, children crying, and men shouting threats — calling for the Taicho's head.

The Taicho still couldn't move. The desk that marked his authority slid away and smashed with force into the wall, sending splinters flying around the room. Without him playing any part in his own movement, he could feel himself standing up, and his chair sliding back from under him. The dark figures lined up on either side of him. There was only one direction he could go as the door of the office swung open, and another silence fell.

He took slow steps forward. His feet felt like lead weights, just able to move. He couldn't stop quivering and shaking.

"What lies outside of here? What waits for me?"

With each step he made, the space behind him closed. The faceless spirits seemed to hiss like snakes. He could feel their hunger. He knew they wanted to strike. The constant threat drained him further. His mind turned to everything he was about to lose. A picture of his wife and daughters formed in his mind and tears streamed from his face. He recalled the happy memories of family, of love, and of caring for one another. Each thought cut into his soul. Now he had arrived at his end.

He stood in the doorway, looking out. The square outside his office ran with streams of red liquid. Shattered bones and flesh remained, but no single, identifiable human form. Nothing that he could recognize. The black clouds swirled again, and when they dispersed once more, the ground was clear and empty. All that remained was a single chair, and a razor-sharp Katana, lying across an executioner's block.

The Taicho felt clawed hands push into his back, they lightly tore his skin. He stumbled forward, toward the chair. As he did, figures began to appear by his side. At first, only a few, but then they grew in number, starting to press against him. He could see they were CHamoru. The islanders that his people had murdered. They reached out at him with grasping hands, pulling and pushing at him, faces twisted in anger. The rage surrounded him. He felt like he was drowning in a sea of people, sucking the last of the air from around him. He stumbled and tried to crawl forward. Hundreds of hands reached on top of him, dragging him against the hard ground, pulling at his limbs until he felt the ghosts were going to rip him apart.

Once again, when he felt he could take no more, the sea of bodies dispersed into the clouds. A lacerating touch pulled him back to his feet. He looked down at himself. His uniform was shredded and lines of blood dripped on to the ground around him. The single chair slid in below him and unseen hands pressed on his shoulders to force him to sit.

The blade of the Katana glinted with a strange light. A figure began to form in front of him. An old woman. The Taicho knew that his judgement was approaching.

Her body never formed completely; she remained half-composed of the dark mist. She floated and flowed around him. He could feel her breath as her head moved close to his.

"Please, spirits," said the Taicho, "if this is my end, I ask for the mercy of a single cut to take my life."

The old woman laughed and snarled at him. Once again, he saw images of CHamoru islanders being tortured, whipped, and beaten. Their wailing filling his head with noise.

"Stop it! Make it stop!"

All fell silent once again. Then the sound of planes appeared overhead. Close and low. The Taicho could hear the bombs increase in pitch as they fell toward the compound, blowing the buildings into pieces. A circle of fire erupted around him. More screams of the dead and dying—haunting memories of those who had perished in flames. The Taicho was being forced to watch every part of his personal empire being razed to the ground.

***

The smell of burning twitched at Kyota's nose. He lay in a wet ditch, in a drunken stupor, swatting at insects that gathered around him. He was so used to the sounds of bombardment that the explosions had no actual effect on him, but the smell was close. He struggled to open his eyes, but as he did, he saw the sky glowing orange and red as the clouds reflected the destruction.

Still trying to process the image in his mind, he pulled himself up before brushing the worst of the dirt from his uniform. A half bottle of sake lay embedded in the mud. He smiled and lifted it. Wiping it clean with his hand, he raised it to drink. As he did, the image in his mind came into focus. The compound was an inferno.

He stumbled to his feet and raced toward the destruction. He called out for help, but no one answered. His pace quickened. Kyota didn't care about much, but all he had built up was on fire; the wealth he had stolen from the dead. All of it was burning in front of him. The gates he passed through were already a halo of flame. A shocking sight met his eyes.

In amongst the circle of fire, the Taicho sat alone on a chair talking at nothing and into nowhere. His voice rambled on, all the time calling out *I'm sorry*.

Kyota staggered toward him. He didn't notice the black mist that was now twisted together with smoke from the fire.

"Taicho-san! Taicho-san!" he called, but the Taicho didn't react.

The commanding officer was speaking, but his words were almost indiscernible. He seemed to recount his life, for the benefit of who? Kyota couldn't see.

"Taicho-san! The camp is burning, can't you see? The camp is burning, where are the men?"

The Taicho stopped. He stared back at Kyota with the look of a possessed man.

"Ah, Kyota-san," said the Taicho, "now we are *all* here for our final reckoning."

"What, eh, Taicho-san?"

"Kyota-san, we are here together to die."

"Yes, we are here to die. That is the Japanese way. No surrender."

The Taicho seemed amused. "Who first told you to die for the Emperor?"

"What? School, I must have been at school."

"A child?"

"Yes."

"Is that not wrong, Kyota? Telling a child they must die for the whims of men they will never meet?"

"What are you saying, Taicho-san?"

"The Emperor is not a god."

"This is treason, Taicho-san. Have you gone mad?"

"No. Those who rule have gone mad with power. They cannot see what they have done. The lives they have taken. The pain that they have caused. They have turned the entire world against us, and for what? It is not only those we have attacked who have suffered. Our own families have lost, sacrificed their sons for the vanity of people who believe we will recover a lost golden age. War is no longer a glorious fight to the death between two feuding samurai. It harms everyone it touches. It destroys the innocent who cannot fight back, and it tries to erase history. War destroys not only the living. It destroys the ancestors as well. Their knowledge, their teaching, their souls. The victor erases all. Wiped out and forgotten. All so that we can believe in new gods that serve only themselves."

"I cannot listen to this. You have gone mad. Where are our men?"

"Dead. All dead."

Kyota picked up the glinting Katana, reflecting the orange glow of the flames around them.

"Then we should choose our moment to die and meet them in heaven."

"There is no heaven for us!" said the Taicho, "For us there's only darkness, an eternity spent in pain and regret. They lied to us Kyota. They lied to us all. Just because men think they are gods. They cannot lead us to that golden life. They can only treat us like children who give unquestioning faith to the parents who raise them. Children who promise to die from their first days at school. Kyota, your future and my future lies only in hell."

In one move, Kyota leaped towards the Taicho, slammed him down on the executioner's block and brought the Katana down on his neck. The head severed and rolled out over the ground.

A rush of dark mist swirled at his feet, and the rest of the Taicho's body was devoured before his eyes, breaking down into its parts before disappearing. When the mist pulled back, the fire still burned, but the main square was empty. Only a circle of dark, faceless creatures remained around Kyota.

He raised the Katana and charged at the human-like forms. They pulled away to the side as he pushed his way through, allowing him a gap to run. He moved as fast as his legs could carry him. Rushes of air to his side buffeted and jostled him. As he reached the still burning gates, the flames blasted in toward him, searing his skin with fire.

Using wild swings of the Katana he scythed his way through the burning timber. He ran through mud and slime. Slipping and tumbling, he picked himself up, each time covered in red stains of wet soil mixed with blood,

A thick mist burst up from the river, shrouding his view— a fog to slow him down and leave him at the mercy of claws and teeth. His skin burned with raw sores appearing on his arms. Faces lunged out of the dense blanket of cover, and then hands grasped his legs and ankles from below, arms stretching out as if from graves below.

He realized he was running between the lines of pits that he had ordered the CHamoru to dig. The people he had slain and stolen from were returning out of the earth he had buried them in. He thrashed around with the sword, hacking at the visions of the spirits assaulting him. No matter how many times he swung at the corpses, they kept coming. The lines of pits were never-ending; a full cemetery of murdered victims with Kyota being the sole reason for their end.

He slipped for one last time and felt the muddy surface disappear from beneath himself as he tumbled into an empty pit. His pelvis cracked on impact, and a shooting pain went through him, causing him to cry out as the shock coursed through his body.

The surrounding mist suddenly evaporated. He looked around himself. The mounds of earthen walls around him were too high to reach on top of, and besides he knew he had broken his leg.

He gritted his teeth with the pain and laid stretched out on his back.

"Maybe the Americans will find me. They are soft. They will heal my leg and send me back home. I just need to keep breathing for a little while longer," he laughed, "Yes, the Americans will help me. Good old Uncle Sam."

Suddenly he heard a melody from around him. The CHamoru in the camp were joining into song. A song about Uncle Sam. He had heard it before as he toured the camp looking for victims and property to steal.

He sniggered to himself and began to join in.

Then a figure appeared, standing over him at the side of the pit. To Kyota, she was nothing to worry about—an old woman. But as he stared closer, he could see that her eyes were solid black. He suddenly panicked and started to struggle up from the ground.

"Get away, woman. I'll kill you if I get out of here. Get away."

The woman smiled and stepped back out of view. Then from over the side, a grenade fell into the pit beside him, then another, then another.

Kyota scrambled to reach them. He had five last seconds to realize his time was up.

A series of explosions rocked the ground and incinerated Kyota in an instant. The smoke from the grenades sucked back down and through the earth, taking every part of Kyota with it.

The dark figures retreated, and the mist cleared away. The Taotaomo'na had reduced the compound to smoldering rubble, and not a single Japanese soldier remained.

Slowly the CHamoru who had survived the last few weeks realized they were no longer prisoners. The Taotaomo'na had freed them. The ancestors had exacted their revenge. In the aftermath, the people gradually left their shelters and hugged and held one another in relief, praying that the entire island would soon be free.

Chapter 19
Fena Caves

As Takeshi rushed through the jungle, the battle raged. The US battleships were pounding the hillsides with shells. Explosions were erupting in every direction. It was *covering* fire. They didn't intend it to hit a specific target. It served only to disrupt chances for an organized counter-attack.

High-powered searchlights did their best to illuminate Japanese artillery units. Tracer fire also lit up the search for targets. Machine guns, rifles, and blasts from tanks joined in volleys launched from either side. The lines of attack and defense were moving back and forth.

From his elevated position, Takeshi could see the source of the onslaught. The ocean was full of ships and amphibious landing craft, all pushing forward in between the flashes and the smoke.

The coastline to the jungle was burning. Fires raged from the valleys to the peaks. Takeshi knew this place well. His original post wasn't far away. He had patrolled in this area many times before, but in the shelling, he had to run and take cover.

The light from the falling munitions gave brief glimpses of the army that was advancing with him. The Taotaomo'na were by his side. They hadn't left him to his fate. They were following him to the end.

Takeshi was guiding them to the next target. Wherever he went, they went. The bombs and the gunfire couldn't harm them as they all pressed ahead, together.

There was only one thing on Takeshi's mind—saving Elena at all costs. He hoped and prayed that the Taotaomo'na shared his desire to rescue her. He would need all the help he could get.

A torch flashed ahead of them—a Japanese patrol, out looking for a way through the American lines. Takeshi came to a halt. The Taotaomo'na stopped with him. He felt their power around him, brief flashes of shadows blending with the surrounding trees. He knew the soldiers nearby were no match, but he was near the caves. He would still have to be careful to avoid attracting the attention of the full unit that were protecting essential ammunition supplies.

He kept low and moved to an elevated position, a slope just above where the men were passing. There were only two, armed with rifles, bayonets fixed, and carrying grenades. The flashes from the shelling illuminated the jungle as if it was in the middle of a great thunderstorm. Each explosion revealed more detail.

Hiroshi!

Takeshi knew he had to act fast. Elena was near, but with Hiroshi, he would have a better chance of saving her. It forced him to take a risk. He bounced and slid down the uneven rocks, landing on the trail behind them. The crash of branches caused Hiroshi and the other man to wheel back to face Takeshi.

A rifle pointed at Takeshi's head, but his appearance in a Japanese uniform caused a slight delay for the soldier taking aim, just long enough for Hiroshi to place a bullet in the back of the other man's head.

"Takeshi! How did you get here?"

"I no longer know. The Taotaomo'na in this jungle, they're running with me. It is tonight, they are rising tonight, and the Taicho has sent Elena here."

"Trucks were coming just as they sent me on patrol. I didn't see who they brought off. The guards are well-armed. I don't know how we'll get through them.

"Look."

Hiroshi cast his eyes around. The jungle was full of Taotaomo'na. The tall figures were standing, waiting, and watching over Takeshi.

"They're giving us a chance for escape. They're protecting us. We can get to Elena."

Hiroshi picked up the dead soldier's rifle and threw it to Takeshi.

"If she's there, we need to be fast,"

They began running toward the caves. Dodging the never ending sea-assault was tempering their speed. Takeshi knew he had to reach his target at all costs. He sped through the trees, just like the Taotaomo'na.

The jungle edge ran alongside the road, allowing them to stay undercover and study the scene. The trucks used for transporting the human cargo were departing again. There was no sign of Elena, but they could see other CHamoru being led away in the direction of the caves.

She has to be in there.

Large rocky outcrops covered the entrance to the caves. The natural defenses were the main reason they were being used for the storage of important supplies.

They edged further until they could see the troops that were manning the entrance. Takeshi could feel a rage growing around him. The Taotaomo'na that ran with him were making ready to attack, and he could see why. They were among a group of dead CHamoru men, tied to the trees and left to rot, with their heads already removed. He felt the danger of the moment. The Taotaomo'na were here for their own war, and it would begin on their terms. He sensed that he had to make his intentions clear.

He stopped one last time as another barrage of shells rained down into the jungle.

"I ask permission. I ask permission to enter the caves and reach Elena. Help me and help Hiroshi, so that we may all survive this night. I ask permission for all of us."

The figures stared back in silence. Then they seemed to swap glances between one another.

"What's happening?" said Hiroshi.

"They are considering my request."

"How will we know what they decide?"

"I don't know. I don't feel that they are angry with us."

The seconds felt like long minutes, then the breeze of air blew past them. The Taotaomo'na had gone, but Takeshi was sure that they hadn't gone far. Hiroshi looked confused.

"I don't understand, Takeshi."

"I think I do. If they grant permission, then it's a silent acknowledgement. We just need to complete the task that we asked for, nothing more, nothing less. They will help. I trust them."

The friends continued edging nearer. They were close enough to see that many of the soldiers were drunk.

"I spoke to some of them today," said Hiroshi, "They've given up already. They're just trying to drink themselves to death before the Americans start to climb the hills."

"What's happening in the caves?"

"You don't want to know. The women may survive a last few hours as long as they comply."

Takeshi felt sick. He looked over at a heavy machine-gun nest that was covering the road. They couldn't break cover near it or their rescue attempt would be short-lived. Defensive positions spread other troops out across the hillside, not all in one place. As soon as an attack was underway, they would rush toward the source of the trouble. Someone could trap Takeshi and Hiroshi within the narrow cave entrances, and then hold them back.

"We can't rush this, Takeshi. Can we rely on the Taotaomo'na? Will they attack tonight?"

"I'm sure of it. I was told."

Just then, an explosion to the east lit up the sky.

"That's Manenggon," said Takeshi, "I'm sure of it."

A howl rang out from the jungle and the fast moving shadows charged toward the hillside. Moving like the wind, they emerged from the trees and arrived at speed. The first soldiers fell in an instant. They were drunk and unprepared. Wrapped in a torrent of thorns that wore them down to nothing and removed every physical trace.

The first wave was over at such a pace that the other soldiers didn't know how to react. Takeshi and Hiroshi moved nearer their target. They could see officers looking at the place where the men had been standing, and then pointing to the sky, almost as if the Americans had fired a new secret weapon. They blew whistles to put every soldier on alert. Men raced to strengthen the unit. A cluster of troops positioned themselves at the entrance to the caves. More soldiers were arriving from positions further back, sent forward to bolster support.

"How are we going to get in?" asked Hiroshi.

"We just need to get close. I have to believe the Taotaomo'na have heard us and will help us."

More screams followed from different points along the road. The attacks were fast and furious. The soldiers fired shots, but with no effect. They were more likely to hit one another as they aimed into glimpses of what may have been an enemy.

At that moment, a truck full of soldiers arrived at the road beside Takeshi. The men jumped out and started racing toward the caves.

"We have to go now," said Takeshi, pulling Hiroshi with him as they joined the back of the troop.

No one noticed, or if they did, they didn't care. The caves were under attack. They needed as many reinforcements as possible. Where they had appeared from simply didn't matter.

As they ran towards the cave entrances, the rush of air that surrounded them signaled another massacre. The Taotaomo'na cut the new arrivals down before they even reached their destination, only leaving Takeshi and Hiroshi standing. Where there had been twelve men ahead of them, now there was nothing left. Further screams from the machine-gun nest confirmed the removal of the gunners.

The officers that were left started calling a retreat, ordering the surviving soldiers to get into the caves along with the CHamoru. The panic caught Takeshi and Hiroshi up in a crush as everyone tried to take cover. The opening to the cave was tight and narrow. With the CHamoru already packed in, it was almost impossible to move. The captain in command pushed some of the CHamoru to the front—a human shield to protect his men from further attack.

Takeshi pressed himself against the cave wall. He searched the crowd until he saw Elena looking back. The other CHamoru knew Takeshi from Manenggon. They knew he had wanted to help them and now they could help him. They parted and created a passage to allow him to reach her.

Hiroshi was nearer the entrance. He could see that they had found one another. He gave nothing away, but he was happy that the Taotaomo'na had permitted them to be together again.

Soldiers that were near the mouth of the cave kept firing through the gaps, but rifles were just using up bullets. Rumbles, bangs, and howls—mixed in with the terror of the soldiers who hadn't made it to safety—confirmed that a battle was still raging outside in the hills.

The cannon shells and bombs were dropping at close range. Something had caused the barrage to be pointed in their direction. The ground shook around them and loose rock crumbled down around the cave walls.

Takeshi and Elena swapped glances. It felt like the world was ending. Japanese or CHamoru, all felt the same fear, the same emotion and terror. For the next few hours, it brought them together in fear for all of their lives; jailer and prisoner shared the tight confines of the cave and its protection.

All were giving in to tiredness. People found places to sit shoulder to shoulder. The captain insisted on keeping a silence in the cave. Takeshi and Elena were struggling to give each other a message of hope. In the crowd, all they could do was hold hands on the cave floor. A small point of contact that the other soldiers couldn't spot.

As they all sat through the remaining part of the night, eyes tracked round the room. People looked around themselves and at one another. It had been becoming clearer to the captain that the young soldier at the very rear of the cave seemed to be too relaxed in the company of the young

CHamoru woman. Not that he blamed him, but it didn't look normal.

Hiroshi watched him, watching them. He held his rifle close, as suspicion seemed to grow on the face of the officer. Takeshi had fallen asleep, and so had Elena. Their heads had moved to rest against one another. The commander spoke in whispers to one of his men. They laughed. Hiroshi realized that the other soldiers based here were from the 38th Infantry. Takeshi had been part of a mountain artillery unit, but they had all arrived together on the island. It was possible that the other soldiers recognized him.

More time ticked by until the sun began rising into the sky. The captain gave his approval for the first of his men to leave the cave. They edged outside through the large protective rocks. The Taotaomo'na and American bombs had destroyed the immediate area, but there were no bodies to pick up or bury. The victims had vanished. The enemy who attacked were nowhere to be seen. Another whistle blew to signal the all-clear.

The commander ordered his men out of the cave and told the CHamoru to remain. He insisted that the Americans were moving closer and he was only thinking of their own safety.

Hiroshi took his turn in line to leave the cave. He lit a cigarette as soon as he was outside, waiting for Takeshi to join him. Then a commotion started.

He turned to see Takeshi being stripped of his rifle and army jacket, two soldiers were pinning him to the side of the cave entrance.

"Yoshida Takeshi-san, 38th Mountain Artillery?" asked the officer.

"Yes, *Rikugun-Chui-san.*"

"I was told you were coming, but then you didn't arrive."

"The scout car didn't make it here, *Rikugun-Chui-san,* I had to walk."

"That is very noble of you. Do you hear that, men?"

The other men laughed at him, just like at the camp. There was no point in fighting back.

"You know the Taicho at Manenggon was very keen that I brought you to the front line. He mentioned how you were affecting morale at the camp. The other men thought you were bad luck."

"I'm sorry, *Rikugun-Chui-san.* I don't know why they thought that."

"Then can you explain last night? You appeared during a secret attack by the Americans?"

"I don't think it was Americans, *Rikugun-Chui-san.*"

"Then can you tell me who it was."

"No, *Rikugun-Chui-san,* I can't."

"And can you also explain why American airplanes destroyed Manenggon last night. I presume, after you left?"

"I can't explain what happened in Manenggon, either, *Rikugun-Chui-san.*"

"Well, in that case, you will stay in the cave with my other prisoners. Get back inside," the captain turned to his men, "If he sets one foot outside, kill him."

Hiroshi stubbed out his cigarette and walked away, so as not to attract attention. He would need to come up with another plan.

Takeshi returned to the cave. He ached to hold Elena in his arms, but that could get her shot. He just returned to where he had been sitting. He at least had a good view of the cave entrance. He would know when he could speak with Elena.

***

Hiroshi idled over to some of the other men. It was still early morning, but there was sake to be drunk and there was no food, so it was the next best thing.

"Hasegawa-san, you came over from Manenggon. Who is that guy, Yoshida?"

"I thought you would know. He's from the 38th. That's your lot."

"I think I've seen him," said the man, "I don't remember him much."

"I do," said another, "they say he brings bad luck. The Americans torpedoed the ship we were on, the Aki Maru; it had to crawl here at half speed after that."

"And so, he would be a survivor from one of the units that were hit by the dive bombers?"

"Bad luck, or a spy?" said the second man.

Hiroshi didn't contribute any more, but it was easy to see why they might be jumping to a wrong conclusion. The facts seemed to add up.

"What will happen to him?" Hiroshi asked.

"The worst punishment if they think he's a spy. It doesn't matter, he's a dead man in that cave. He'll get what's coming later. The same as the others."

"They're... we're going to kill them?"

"They're no more use to us. We're moving out today to join with the rest of the infantry, and we can't take them with us," he paused, "Have you never done this, Hasegawa-san?"

"Kill them in the caves? No, I haven't done it."

"It's easy!" the man assured him. Toss some hand grenades in and stand back, spray a few bullets on the ones that are still crawling, and then a little walk around with a bayonet. Some will hide under the dead. They're animals, eh?"

"Can I use a machine gun?"

"Yes, of course," the other man laughed.

***

"I haven't given up hope," whispered Takeshi, "Hiroshi will think of something. Why did the Taotaomo'na not finish the battle?"

"The commander seemed to know that they wouldn't harm the CHamoru," Elena replied.

Takeshi paused. "Elena, I want you to promise me something."

"What?"

"If the worst happens. If they try to kill us. I will do my best to protect you. I will cover you. Then lie still. They will go, and you can leave this place. Get out and hide."

"I will not let you die, Takeshi, I will not let that happen. Everyone in here is praying for help. It came last night, why not tonight?"

"Elena, just promise me."

"No, Takeshi. Quiet. Be still. We will get out together. We will leave this place together. Don't even think about anything else."

The afternoon wore on. One guard was rotating every hour to man the cave entrance. As the sun was beginning to set again, Takeshi was glad to see that it was Hiroshi on duty. His friend waved him over as he kept an eye out for anyone who might catch them talking. Takeshi stood just out of sight of the entrance.

"What's happening Hiroshi?"

"The worst situation. The captain is moving down nearer to Agat. He will leave four of us to blow this place and take the last transport to follow him."

Takeshi nodded at the news. It was no surprise to him. He knew only too well the fate of Japanese prisoners who had outgrown their use.

"I will do what I can, my friend. Be ready. When we come, there will be two with grenades. I will be the gunner. A man with a rifle and bayonet will stand behind me. I think I will die regardless of how this plays out," he smiled, "When they throw in the grenades, try to throw at least one back and take cover."

"That's our best chance?" asked Takeshi.

"That's our only chance. If I try outside, it's too open. I'll get picked off. Then I die and the survivors will come to kill you. If we can break you out, then we might have a chance, the two of us. Try to get the others to the back of the cave. If they crowd together, no one will get in your way."

Takeshi took a deep breath. "When?"

"I think when I finish this guard duty. We head straight from here. They've gathered troops for two banzai charges. I'm in the southern charge. As much sake as I can swallow for two days, then we go," Hiroshi smiled as he often did in dark moments, "I don't want to die, Takeshi, but the Emperor keeps coming up with ways to kill me," he paused again, "You are my best hope."

"I'll be ready, my friend. As long as we have a plan."

Takeshi returned to Elena. It was safe for them to hug with Hiroshi on duty. They held each other in a tight embrace, then stood to gaze in each other's eyes. The tears fell for both—no words needed to be spoken. Hiroshi's warning was in Japanese, but even the other CHamoru could understand what was being said.

"You must let me try to help Hiroshi, Elena. It's the only way to save at least some."

Elena nodded her head and hugged Takeshi once more. They shared a kiss, both praying it wouldn't be their last.

Takeshi had never felt so nervous. He thought back to his training camp. Accidents happened with grenades; you could escape with an injury. He explained to the others about how to reduce the risks. He gasped long deep breaths, as he prepared to steady himself. He tried to decide if it was better to position himself at the front of the crowd or hide to the side. Would they roll the grenade on the cave floor? The cave dipped down. It might be hard to catch. It frustrated him that his war had come to this moment.

Elena and the others sat as far back as they could. They had argued over who should sit behind who. Which of them would be likely to catch the blast, who would be best to survive. It had come down to a vote in the end, and Elena was to be protected at all costs.

A call came for Hiroshi from the outside of the cave. He gave a last wave to Takeshi and walked away.

Takeshi could tell from the other soldier's voices they were drunk. It gave him hope that they might be easier to overpower.

The group held on to one another as they heard the men heading towards them. Some of the islanders sobbed as they prepared to shield one another from the blast.

The four guards, including Hiroshi, arrived at the entrance. Takeshi panicked; Hiroshi was too close. He would injure him in the explosion. Hiroshi only had a second to grant Takeshi *his* permission.

The first guard sniggered as he tossed two grenades into the middle of the group. He stepped back to take cover, and Takeshi flung himself forward. He could only choose one. He grabbed it with only a second on the fuse to throw it back. He cast it through the entrance, and it exploded. The second grenade detonated inside the cave. Takeshi felt the searing heat burning at his skin. The explosion deafened him, but he could hear the machine-gun fire. Bullets ricocheted off the narrow entrance. He knew that Hiroshi was playing his part until a rifle shot brought a halt to the shooting.

Takeshi struggled to turn his body over. He could see that Elena was still alive, but hurt. She started to pull herself out when Takeshi heard more noise. Someone was moving, just out of sight.

"Stay where you are, Elena. I'm not hurt."

They turned together to see the rifleman standing at the door. He was bleeding heavily, and looked like he was about to use his bayonet. Instead, he dropped to his knees and laid the rifle beside him. Elena was still trying to work herself free. Takeshi could see she was going to get the rifle.

"The war is over for us, friend," said Takeshi to the soldier. "The Americans are here. We can't go on killing one another."

"You can't Yoshida-san, but I am loyal to the Emperor."

The soldier produced the last grenade that every Japanese soldier carried. He pulled the cord, smashed the fuse against his helmet, and held the grenade to his chest.

Elena made a dive for him.

"No, Elena, no!"

"Tennoheika banzai!" shouted the soldier.

Another blast burst inside the small cave. Takeshi heard no more. The cave seemed to spin and revolve around him, then his eyes closed and he blacked out.

Chapter 20
The Final Patrol

✦

Takeshi's eyes opened again. He faced the cave wall and all the memories of the last few hours came rushing back.

"Elena?"

There was no reply. He was terrified to turn round, but he had to know. He pushed himself up and twisted to look into the center of the cave. Elena lay face down. His mind played hopeful tricks on him as he wondered if she was still breathing. He reached out, hoping for the smallest response, but he knew right away that she was dead.

The grenade had gone off as she lunged forward. She and the soldier that committed suicide had absorbed the blast between them. He scrambled to lift her body, angry that the man responsible for her death was even near her.

Her injuries told him that her death would have happened fast. That was the only comfort that he could find—the only thought that calmed him.

Why?

His own burns were raw and painful as he pulled her close. Her bloodied body marked him and he broke down and wept. The anguish took over every part of his being. He yelled out at the top of his voice, a painful call that echoed all around the walls. In that grief-stricken moment, he didn't care if another soldier appeared. He wanted to die. He wanted to be with Elena. Nothing else mattered.

No one came. His tears stopped rolling down his cheeks. His only urge was to care for her. He wanted to tend to her and keep her safe—even now, as he lay her body down on the cave floor. He prayed over her and wept even more when his words struggled against his breath. He tried to arrange her body to lie with dignity. He took off his army shirt and covered her before praying again and asking the gods to help her on her journey to heaven.

"Takeshi?"

The voice startled him. He turned around to see one of the other islanders, still alive, but barely breathing. A woman was sitting up. She had cuts from shrapnel. He rushed to help her, pulling other bodies that crushed against her, doing his best to raise her up. She choked and coughed on her own blood.

"I will fetch you some water," said Takeshi.

He stood up and felt a pressure on his head. He waited to balance himself before stepping out amongst the dead and the *dying*. Hiroshi caught his attention. His friend lay against the wall, clutching his stomach. He had lost blood, but he was still alive.

"Hiroshi, hang on, I'm here. I'll help you."

"Takeshi? Elena?"

Hiroshi looked at Takeshi. His face said everything.

"I'm sorry, Takeshi. I'm so sorry, my friend."

Takeshi wanted to be with her more than anything. The pain of losing her, and not being next to her at the end, filled him with sorrow like he had never felt before. He closed his eyes and hoped that she would just be there when he opened them again, but he knew that not even the spirits of the island could bring her back to him now.

He took a deep breath and looked at Hiroshi, "Elena would do her best for everyone right now. Yuki would be the same. I don't want to lose anyone else today."

Takeshi stumbled out into a cloud-filled day. The sound of battle was louder than ever. Tanks and small arms fire dominated while airborne fighters and dive bombers delivered their payload. There were no soldiers to face. All had gone to prepare for the charge, but they had stocked Fena with supplies. Other caves held bandages and some food. There was basic kit and equipment, including canteens to fill with water. His mind was racing. His army training had paid little attention to the treatment of wounds. You were just expected to die.

Takeshi hadn't sustained so much damage, just burns and cuts to his body—nothing deep or life threatening. As he began to focus on saving lives, his thought for his own discomfort disappeared. He had to help the others. If he couldn't save Elena, he would try to save everyone else that he could.

He arrived back by Hiroshi and worked fast to apply pressure to the bullet wound. His friend yelled out in pain.

"I'm sorry, Hiroshi. I have to stop the bleeding."

"Water!" came the choking voice of the other islander.

"I will get it," Takeshi shouted, "Can you hold this in place, Hiroshi?"

"Yes, yes, I think I can."

"I need to fetch water."

He picked up speed as he made his way around the rocks that surrounded the caves. The river wasn't far. Planes were flying low overhead. He had to make it to the jungle as fast as he could. He cursed himself that he had never learned to use the CHamoru words, but he stopped to ask permission to enter, and permission to take the water that he needed for the wounded. The Taotaomo'na were silent.

He pressed ahead toward the river. He passed through the woven foliage and arrived at the fresh, flowing water. He filled the canteens to the brim. As he gathered what he needed, he noticed a figure staring at him from a distance. The onlooker startled him. It looked like Yuki, standing, watching over him. He splashed his face and rubbed his eyes. When he looked again, the figure was gone. His head throbbed with pain. He cursed it for making him see things. He checked one last time before heading back to the wounded.

The journey back revealed a scene of devastation stretching down the hillsides to the beaches. It looked like hundreds of ships out at sea—an overwhelming force sent to obliterate the island.

Before long, he had returned to the cave. He passed the first canteen to Hiroshi. "Sip from this and take it. There is a woman inside who needs my help."

"There is more than one."

"What?"

Takeshi entered the cave. For a very brief moment he had hoped he was wrong and Elena had come round, but it was not to be. Her body still lay covered, but other injured CHamoru were starting to regain consciousness. The blasts had affected all in some way, but at least now he was counting six survivors in total.

He did what he could to make them comfortable, and as he ran back and forward, they started to help one another. Takeshi returned to check on Hiroshi.

"Cigarette?" said Hiroshi.

"I'll try to find some. There are rations here. You can have a whole packet."

"That might kill me," he joked.

"First you need to help me. I need to clean your wound and bandage you."

The procedure wasn't easy. Hiroshi screamed out in pain as Takeshi tried to pour water over the point where the bullet had entered. He only wanted to see it, but Hiroshi acted as if he was getting shot again. Takeshi bent his friend forward, but intense pain accompanied every inch of movement. He washed blood from Hiroshi's back. There was no exit wound.

"You've held on to that bullet."

"Tell me something I don't know," Hiroshi spoke through gritted teeth.

Takeshi wrapped the bandage around, trying his best to keep compressing the injury; some blood still leaked, but it had slowed.

"I can move you through beside the others."

"No, leave me here. Tend to them. I'm happy to stay where I am."

The time passed. Two of the injured had regained limited movement, enough to help and check on Hiroshi every now and again.

Takeshi took his chance for a brief rest, staying with Elena's body. Her hand lay uncovered, and he took it into his. He remembered how just a few hours ago they had been holding hands—the only way they were able let each other know the love they shared for one another.

He looked over at the soldier who still lay on the floor. Elena's murderer filled him with anger. His rage took over again. He used every ounce of strength to drag the body outside of the caves. He didn't care about this corpse. The soldier had robbed him of his life and his happiness. He was placing him outside hoping the Taotaomo'na would come along and devour him, like the other Japanese who had paid for their cruelty.

Hiroshi watched him drag the body along the cave floor. He understood Takeshi's reaction. The body was nothing to him. He felt no need to pay any respect. He dragged it outside of the cave. The rain had returned, and the mud lay thick around the roadside. He dragged the dead soldier until he could deposit the body into a ditch, face down.

As soon as he carried out his plan, he felt remorse. Here lay a person who Takeshi could have been. He might have been the one to sacrifice himself for the glory of the Emperor. It was a selfless act, and Takeshi knew he could never have it carried out.

"So are you better than me?" he asked. "You gave what I could never give. You showed strength, where I would have been weak, but I hate you and despise you. You fell for it. Like all the others. I didn't fall for it. I didn't kill the people that I loved."

The rain became heavier. Takeshi wasn't sure if he heard thunder above the guns. He sighed to himself and returned to the store. Finding a blanket, he carried it back out to throw over the dead soldier.

"That's the best I can do for you now."

Once again, he felt he was being watched. He looked up, and on the other side of the road that passed the caves he now saw Yuki and Elena standing together. His heart leaped, his mouth went dry. They smiled at him and turned to walk away. He had to get closer. It felt like he couldn't quite reach them, no matter how fast he walked or ran. He called out their names as he followed them into the jungle.

The ancestors of the island were suddenly surrounding him, watching him, following him. The vision of two figures in front merged and became a single blurred light that he followed through the heavy rain. He didn't know where he was going or even where he was. The darkness wrapped around him, both in the sky and in the formless shapes that traveled with him.

He had no fear as long as the light led him on. He trusted where he was being led.

"Yuki! Elena!" he called. The light stopped moving.

As he stepped nearer, the light separated into the two distinct figures once more. He could see a small lake beyond them and he could see a double row of latte stones. He could feel the power being drawn from the land, the water, and the sky. He could feel the CHamoru ancestors. The vision of Yuki and Elena dissolved into a mist. He knew what he should do.

***

Takeshi checked on the others. He left them with some rations and he found the tools he needed to dig a grave.

He worked hard all through the night. He didn't feel the need to rest. He hadn't eaten for days, but that was nothing new for a Japanese soldier. The smoke and the fire from the invasion continued to be reflected by the gathering clouds. He felt sure that even amid battle it wasn't his time to die yet. He felt the gods and the ancestors were going to allow him *his* choice of when to go.

Returning once more to the cave, he found that most were asleep. He wrapped Elena's body in a blanket and lifted her up into his arms. He made his way out past Hiroshi. He was awake, but said nothing. He dropped his gaze to show respect.

Takeshi didn't know where his strength was coming from as he carried Elena step by step through the jungle. Once again, he walked without stumbling or faltering. The darkest part of night was over as he returned to the grave that lay across from the latte stones. He laid the body down, and with a heavy heart, he covered Elena with the wet soil.

"I ask you, the Taotaomo'na, to welcome Elena to the afterlife; may you bring her comfort as she passes over. She will be happy to lie beside the latte stones. Each morning, she will gaze upon her beautiful island. Each night she will dance below the stars. This place will hold my love forever."

With the first rays of the rising sun creeping over the horizon, he broke down once more and the loss overtook him. He had accomplished what he set out to do, but his only reward was emptiness. A shadow had replaced the joy in his life. Yuki and Elena had passed on. His one last wish was to follow them.

He searched amongst the tools he had brought down to prepare the grave. Among them was a combat knife. Clean and new. Perfect for his intention.

The sun began to melt away the morning cloud. The sound of battle still raged on, but there was something serene in the air. Something that reminded him of home. He stood up and took the knife back into the jungle. He walked until he found some orchids. He asked permission of the Taotaomo'na to cut them for his sister. He knew this would be his last request to them. He took the flowers to the grave and placed them on top. He felt that he was now saying goodbye to everyone he had ever loved.

"This is for Yuki and Elena. Now I must say goodbye."

"Hands up, buddy. Nice and slow, *Te o agete*, Te o agete."

Takeshi raised his hands and looked to the sky. As the American marines surrounded him and tied his hands together, he wondered what he had done to enrage the gods so much.

"Who's in the grave?" asked one of the soldiers.

Takeshi couldn't answer. He only knew that by accepting surrender, he had failed the ideals of a nation and the will of the Emperor. His life was over, but not at an end.

***

As he gazed out from the back of a covered truck, Takeshi watched the survivors of the cave massacre being brought out by the American troops. A stretcher carried Hiroshi out. As the truck set off back to the beachhead, he watched the hills disappear behind him. He wondered how fate was about to twist the knife again.

A cage filled with captured Japanese was to be his temporary new home. The brutal army training took its toll in a place like this. Capture was worse than death. The men had lost their freedom, their dignity, and their honor. They never completed the contract. They never gave their life.

He had only just arrived at his destination, and they had fed him and delivered some basic care for his own injuries. They examined him for disease and general condition. He was the prisoner now.

Two soldiers marched him in front of an interrogation table; his value now was as a source of information, nothing more. As the questions flew at him thick and fast, the head injury he had suffered in the blast began to take its toll.

He heard himself say again, and again, "Ittohei Yoshida, Yoshida Takeshi, 38th Infantry, mountain artillery."

Somewhere in his mind, he knew he was being shouted at and threatened. He could see the hatred in yet another figure of authority. Nothing had changed.

The interrogator screwed up his face and began to resemble his Aunt Keiko, berating him for failing to do something. He saw the fist of his Uncle Taro being held in front of his face, to punish him for his wrongdoing or lack of respect. All the time he only spoke to say, "Ittohei Yoshida, Yoshida Takeshi, 38th Infantry, mountain artillery."

He was ill. Even the interrogator could see that. The world spun around him as they marched him back to the medics. Another examination, more words that he didn't understand. The tension was building inside him again. The resentment, the grief, the outright hatred for those who forced their doctrine on his life. He couldn't take anymore. The constant shouting, the bullying, the pressure.

"Na'para! Na'para!"

His voice took on a strange tone as he spoke the word.

"What's he saying?" said the interrogator.

"I think it's CHamoru he's speaking, sir," replied one of his guards.

Even though they didn't know what he was saying, the message seemed to get across to them. They gave him two pills to take and sent back to the cage for a constant ringside view of the American deployment.

***

He had spent the night on the ground. His captors handed out a basic breakfast. There was little of it, but it was a second meal in the space of a few hours. He ate with his fellow inmates, but nobody spoke. The shared sense of shame enforced the silence. Takeshi stared out of the cage, where he could look out to sea. The coastline was so different from when he had last been here. The palms were burned and dead; they had choked the sea with fuel from landing ships or vehicles that never made it to shore.

He could hear the gates open behind him.

"Takeshi-san."

He spun around when he recognized the voice. "Kindo?"

"Yes, Takeshi-san. I'm glad to see you made it."

"Kindo. I'm so happy to see a friendly face."

"I work for the Americans now. The rations are better. I can't complain," he paused, "They need to ask you questions, Takeshi. They wondered if you were CHamoru. I told them you weren't, but for a Japanese, you were alright," he smiled, "Trust me, I will help you with them."

Takeshi felt better when he was next escorted to the interrogation officer.

"Ittohei Yoshida, Yoshida Takeshi, 38th Infantry, mountain artillery."

"Yes, they know that part. They want to know about Manenggon. They want to know about the men who were there."

"I wasn't there on the night they bombed it. They had sent me to Fena, where you found me."

"How many troops were based there?" Kindo asked.

"A hundred, maybe more. There were always troops passing in and out."

"I told them that," said Kindo, "but they say they found no one. There were no bodies, just the CHamoru that were left. They just walked out the camp and followed the Marines back to Agat."

"Well, they destroyed the buildings in the bombing. Didn't they find bodies?"

"They found nothing."

"Then it was the Taotaomo'na."

"I don't think they're ready for that, Takeshi."

"The Taotao-what? What was that he said?" asked the interrogator.

"Tell him, Kindo."

"Eh, he's talking about the spirits. The ancestors of our island."

"Kindo, the Taotaomo'na take the bodies away. They leave no trace when they attack you. Tell him."

"I don't know, Takeshi."

"Tell him if he wants to know the truth."

Kindo translated as well as he could. He told them that Takeshi was unusual. He could work with the spirits of the island, the Taotaomo'na.

The interrogator laughed. "I gotta admit, that's a new one on me. Can we get these guys to man a platoon? They would make the cleanup better. Alright, I believe you. You've had a knock to the head. I'm finished here. Take him back to the cage."

"What's he saying Kindo?"

"He thinks you're going crazy. They'll leave you alone now, at least."

"But you have to tell him. Or they will lose their men. They will start to suffer from sickness. The Taotaomo'na don't care what uniform you wear. Warn him."

"Sorry, Takeshi. You know they won't listen. They call it superstition. One day they'll learn more about the CHamoru, our culture, our medicine, our way of life, but we'll have to give them time. Let them learn from their mistakes, eh?"

"Take him out," the interrogator ordered.

The march was quick. They didn't give Takeshi any more time to think.

"I'll check back on you," said Kindo as the gate of the cage closed between them.

Takeshi found a small corner to sit in. All he would kill for now was a cigarette.

He thought back to Japan, to a life that was full of bitter memories, all except for Yuki. Her wisdom and love had made him human. She had encouraged him to be himself and not just another obedient servant to the rules that were imposed from on high. She had kept the laughter in his life and gave him dreams to strive for. He had pretended to look after her, but he always knew she had looked after him.

Then there was Guam. The island that had become home. The Imperial Japanese Army had put him through hell, only for him to find a heaven instead. Elena had brought love into his life. She had shown strength and wisdom. She had been a rare spark of light amongst the darkness and had made him *superhuman*. Elena had taught him how to be a better person in the present, through honoring the spirits of the past.

The last year of his life had been a lifetime of its own. Now he felt that it was over. The days would stretch out before him. There would be plenty of time to consider what might have been. As the weeks and months went on, he would try to glimpse the apparitions that gave him some comfort whenever they appeared; a hazy shoreline, or through the clearings of a ranch, the fringes of the jungle, or the hills that stretched out from sea-to-sea.

Takeshi would look for signs of Yuki and Elena wherever he was—whatever he was doing.

When the war ended, they returned the captured men to Japan, but Takeshi's heart always remained in Guam.

For as long as he lived, he never returned to the island, to the place where he really wanted to be—beside the lake and by the latte stones.

From the Author

Dear Reader,

I am of mixed ethnicity but I feel that my CHamoru heritage is underrepresented in mainstream media. I use my stories to share the CHamoru culture with readers. I am honored that you have chosen to read this story.

During World War II, Guam and the Mariana Islands were American soil captured by Japanese forces. The CHamoru people on these islands were robbed, raped, tortured, and even killed in their own backyards during the Japanese occupation. I wanted this story to bring more awareness of what the CHamoru people endured during this war.

In this story, I took CHamoru legends of the supernatural and wove them into actual historical events. I hope you enjoyed the story and that it has piqued your interest in learning more about the CHamoru people.

If you enjoyed this story, I humbly ask that you post a review of "Guardians of the Latte Stones" wherever you buy books. Please also visit my site online at mkaleja.com where I have links to stories from actual survivors and more.

Thank you so much for reading!

Also by M. K. Aleja

"Highly entertaining." – *Kirkus Reviews*

"Highly atmospheric." – *Readers' Favorite*

"Gripping." – *Literary Titan*

Visit mkaleja.com for more information.

www.ingramcontent.com/pod-product-compliance
Lightning Source LLC
Chambersburg PA
CBHW021437310726
48971CB00005B/1395